WHERE WOLVES

FOLLOW

by

Gavin Woodcock

SPECIAL ACKNOWLEDGEMENTS:

An extra special thank you to my friend in Canada, Andrea, whose conversations about her homeland inspired much of the setting, and who encouraged me to keep working on this story through dark times.

I'd also like to thank Amy, my kind and helpful therapist who got me through the last leg of this book while teaching me to continue healing and growing.

First Print Edition – 2023
ISBN:
978-1-7394942-1-6

For 'A'

Fly free, brother

CONTENTS

PART 1
CHILDHOOD

1

WILD

The day was young, and it was getting cold. So cold that despite the bursting affection of the shimmering sun, an uneasy chill still hung around long after the night had subsided. A change was coming – as change always was – evident by the tingling omens of frost that floated through the morning air. The icy chill betrayed an otherwise warm-looking landscape that could not have seemed kinder or more serene, where a visual orchestra of jade and maple treetops sang far off into the distance and a crown of rocky slopes reached upwards into an unfettered sky of silken blue. The natural world was often rife with these contradictions; its quietest spots were often the most foreboding, its smallest residents were sometimes the deadliest, and the shining liveliness of spring could sometimes seem daunting and sorrowful to creatures best suited for winter. In the same manner, darkness – which often puts to mind the ideas of danger and unknowability – could be a respite of peace, silence, and comfort. Just look at hibernation, where critters hide away into dank nooks for a considerably long time for the sake of their safety.

Yes, the forest held many instances of these wild contradictions, where the light and colour exposed a hectic rat race of thumping hearts and ravenous eyes, while other animals felt quiet and safe in the cold dark. All of them, in their own way, danced the dance of survival and few were caught between one preference or the other. By effect of their species or upbringing, they had bound themselves to a basic natural preference – either ecstatic light or serene darkness – and stuck with it. They knew what animal they were and where they belonged. Squirrels gathered nuts and scurried up trees, beavers lazed in rivers and built dams, bears slept in cold caverns and gorged themselves on anything and everything, wolves hunted in packs as grim and fierce predators. Very few animals broke from the strengths of what they ought to be. Despite this, the wilderness was still vibrant and varied. Its corners were all distinct from each other – some soothing, some hostile, some mystical, some tepid – and stumbling upon any of these corners would tell a very different story. Looking down over the top of a forest can give the impression of a purgatorial stretch of tree after tree with no variety, but under the emerald cloak there will always be something happening; something changing. Nothing in the wild world can seem to sit still for very long.

Deep beneath the unending sea of foliage, where the sun's

brass beams fell softly through the cracks in the leaves, a village of trees sat solitary and undisturbed. The ground here was flat, and its crumbled dirt was freshly tossed by all the oafs that constantly barrelled their way through, bison and ram and the likes. It was messy and overgrown; its trees were lanky with withered chalky skin. Although they stood tall with plentiful leaves, the dusty-looking bark made their apparent strength seem like a surface-level façade. In truth, most of them had hollowed out on the inside and their roots had grown short from lack of nutrients. One of these trees, a feeble and elderly-looking pine tree, stood fittingly among the others. Like many of them, its large stem was full of aged notches and holes, the most prominent of which was a large triangular maw that sat at the foot of the trunk. The sun that bled through the foliage and glinted across the forest floor still failed to pierce into this black cavity. Its darkness seemed as thick as ink and infinite in depth, as if the tree had captured some silent stillness of the previous night's sky, midnight in both colour and time. Despite the pale illness of the tree bark, along with the gloom of its innards and the morbid stagnancy of its standing place, something colourful and bright and full of life was concealed inside; something that had found comfort and safety in the simple blackness but was waiting to spring out into the bright carnival of the open world.

Among all the noises and motions of the local forest, many belonged to the plenitude of bugs that crawled up twigs and buzzed through the air. One of them, a butterfly with wings as white as paper, fluttered past the dense opening in the tree. As is did, its movement caught the attention of a living being inside. Two glaring golden eyes as warm and intense as the early sunrise flashed open and caught the light as they peered out of their hovel, watching the little butterfly float past. The eyes seemed enraptured by its frolicking movement and the purity of its wings. Before the butterfly had a chance to pass safely beyond the borders of the tree, the eyes launched forward out of the hole. Their playful colour splashed against the butterfly's wings as the animal they belonged to leapt from out of its dark room towards the terrified critter and thrust two silvery paws down into the dirt, having missed the butterfly. The coat of the creature wasn't unlike that of the butterfly, shadeless and unspoilt but with a little more of a grey tint to their otherwise snowy fur, and rightly so; he was a young grey wolf.

As the panicked insect flapped higher into the air out of harm's way, the wide golden eyes of its hunter tracked it upwards until it went higher and higher out of his reach. The wolf's paws took a couple more futile swipes up at the bug, but it continued to fly effortlessly up with its graceful wings to where he couldn't catch it. Realising that his goal was too high to reach, his eyes tracked back down to the even flooring of the forest. He'd only wanted to play with it anyway – he was definitely hungry after a night's sleep, but there wasn't much nutrition to be gained from one little scrap like that.

The wolf looked around at the woods he'd emerged into. He looked from one way to the other like a child in a playground looking for someone to play with. Indeed, there were various animals around that caught his attention and he'd caught theirs as well, but none seemed interested in mingling with him. None were wolves. A school of deer, who galloped proudly forward in uniformity, sought to escape his unruly and scruffy disposition. A family of raccoons peered out from the high hole of another tree; nestled in the pleasance of their own kin, they were nervous about how big this one independent wolf was. One solitary porcupine waddled by the wolf. It was vastly different from him, small with protruding needles across its body and a piggish snout. It had no fear of him, seeming very content, and its relaxed friendly movement appeared almost to be a wish of wellness to the wolf in of itself. But because of their stark differences, it had no desire to mingle with him and was on its own journey somewhere else. A gang of foxes slithered through the bushes ahead of him. Ferocious and intimidating in their own way, it was rare for them to be out in the daytime as they usually conducted their mischief after sundown. They travelled as a group of four and smirked at the wolf for his apparent lack of cohorts, viewing him as an outsider. They weren't wrong. There was no wolf pack around, no kin that a wolf pup as healthy as this should belonged to. With all the other species keeping their distance from the four-legged child, he chose a direction and wandered off into the forest without any other wolves around.

He trod on between the gangly trees until he heard a soft sound rising in his peripheral senses. Something that would be indiscernible in the hectic mind of a deer, dampened by the sheltered habits of raccoons, and ignored by the graceless ignorance of foxes. But the wolf, with his exquisite hearing and his keen awareness of everything around him, heard it. Some kind of wistful billowy flapping, like of something soft hitting the wind. Between the gaps of the trees, a shadow glided through the air. The wolf's shimmering eyes were instantly intrigued as what appeared to be a pair of wings fluttered by. They belonged to something much larger and faster than a butterfly. Whether it was the creature's natural coat or simply the shade of the trees, it seemed to be drenched in simple blackness. It flew on alone much like himself, but unlike him it stayed unseen by all other animals as it weaved around in the distance, free yet directionless. The fleeting phantom disappeared in-between the garden of trunks and out of sight, causing the wolf to give chase in the hopes of identifying whatever it was.

Full of intrigue, the pup worked his way over roots and between tall cylinders of wood as little by little, he caught further glimpses of the oddity fluttering around in the distance. It seemed to hide in the shadows of the trees and then pop out into the streaks of light between them, much like how he too liked to hide away in the dark spots of the forest and then galivant out into the brightness for all to see. While he couldn't quite see the details on its surface, the swooping unrestrained nature of the thing was intoxicating to watch, as had been the butterfly – the way they could defy the friction of the earth and swirl around in any direction they wanted to or disavow the natural pull of gravity that restricted down-to-earth creatures like himself by flying as high and far as they wanted. As his focus stuck to the focal point of the creature, his other senses read the world around him, manoeuvring the obstacle course of the forest with natural awareness and aptitude. He could feel himself getting closer and closer to the flying thing, making out little distinctions of features here and there through glints and textures until without warning, he followed it to a place where all the trees dropped away. He'd wandered onto an open field covered in prickly saturated grass as flat and dry as the forest floor he'd come in from. But the sudden lack of trees wasn't the most surprising sight ahead of him, as although the flying shadow had seemingly disappeared, a new flightless creature stood far ahead. In the centre of the field with its head turned away, a lone elk grazed on the crisp grass. Much like the papery wings of the butterfly, the dulled meadow gave the impression of a large, stretched canvas ripe for painting with the bright passion of his golden eyes.

His stomach rumbled.

Alone and unaware against the flat land, it was an easy target for even one inexperienced wolf. That being said, he had a problem. The elk stood out in the open with no way for him to creep up silently; no trees to take advantage of, no high swaying reeds for him to use creatively as cover. There was no source of inspiration for him to play with in his tactile approach. With the elk turned away, he could almost certainly try to creep up without being seen, but with the crinkling grass giving his position away quickly and with no other distractions to lean on, it was very easy for his target to get away from him. If he had a wolf pack as most wolves did, they could combine their efforts – combine their creativity – and circle around to different points of the field so that no matter where the target ran too, they could corral it into the group's clutches. He was almost certainly going to make a move - as hungry as he was - but while he was alone, the odds were tilted against him.

The wolf was an instinctively calculative creature, weighing his chances of gaining a good meal, reading every inch of the elk's frame and how it compared to his own, organically recognising all the different possibilities of approach and which worked best. Maybe he could wait for the elk to move on into the woods before he made a move? But then, deer are experts at escaping through the trees. He could read this ground more easily and there was more free room to chase it around. All he had to do was put more effort into hunting the elk than his target had in staying ahead of him, something he was sure he could do, being so confident in his own tenacity. But he absolutely needed to get off on the right foot and close a gap that made it hard for the elk to simply run into the trees; stick close by and keep it locked where he wanted it to be by constantly nipping at its heels. The field was a sort of oval shape, with the wolf spying from a bush on its southeast line, frozen as a statue in case of startling the animal. The elk stood in the centre, facing the north-northeast direction with its head down grazing. It wasn't turned so far away that it would take very long to sense movement off to its side once the wolf started moving in. He could slink around the edge of the field, but every step was a risk of alerting the animal. His skill level was mixed. He was fantastic in an energetic chase, but lacked the decisiveness of making the first step, struggling to ever even know what the first step should be. To dive in, or to hold out and see if a better opportunity came around? What to do? Where to start? How was it going to end-

"CAW!"

An unexpected call echoed from the western treeline. It took both the elk and the wolf by surprise as they looked up to the source of the sound. Up on a shade-drenched branch and sitting solitary without a flock, a raven peered down at them eagerly. It held a familiarity to the wolf – it looked something like a shadow, with frantic wings much bigger than a butterfly's. Its coat was as dark as obsidian and as deep as the night sky. Its ebony eyes were bulging with energy and held a reflective shimmer of the high sun that gave them a curious juxtaposition - they were both dark and light at the same time. He had seen ravens before but usually in flocks whizzing by and never sat alone. Odd for such a creature to be alone. Almost as odd as it was for a wolf.

The elk's head had spun around to see the bird, who was now sitting still after its randomly interjection. Beyond that, the elk had kept its position. It was clear the raven had seen the wolf, but he wondered if the raven had also realised that he was trying to engage in a hunt as well as realised the predicament he was in. Perhaps by calling out, it had sought to give some assistance in distracting his target. Having stolen the elk's attention, the bird started bobbing about and dancing on its branch, continuing its noisiness with an incessant string of clownish squawks. The elk, becoming even more baffled by the unnatural movement, turned its whole body and stepped forward towards the bird on the branch. The wolf looked up at the raven with wide eyes and thankful relief for the fortunate opportunity.

The raven's introduction had provided, in this situation, the perfect counterpart to the wolf's tactics. The impulsive icebreaker had helped bypass the difficulty of knowing where to start and placed the elk in an advantageous position for him to now jump right in. His target had turned entirely away from him, facing the western direction towards the bird. Slowly and methodically, he pushed his paws deeper into the centre of the field. Each step pattered against the stiff grass with the risk of alerting the elk, but the persistent singing of the raven acted as a musical chime that kept his target where he needed it to be, giving the wolf some extra confidence that inspired his flourishing steps against the field's canvas. He knew, however, that this opportunity wouldn't last. The elk would get bored of the ineffectual show of the raven, or his steps would get too close to ignore, or something else would tip the scales out of his favour, just as the changing spontaneity of events had moved the elk from a less than agreeable spot into a much more fortunate one. Change came often, these spots of luck didn't last forever, and risks had to be taken to snatch up opportunities while they were around. Sure enough, as the wolf gained closer and closer on the elk's back, the raven's calling grew quieter, and its dancing calmed down as it noticed that he was moving into place. When the bird's cries had closed to a full silence, the only sound that was left to be heard was the crackling of rough grass under paws. The elk's ear twitched as it caught wind of the grim dirge. Its head spun around in an instant as its large frantic eyes caught sight of its ravenous assassin some ten feet away, and at once it fled off in fear of its life. The wolf's reaction time was just as fast, speeding off and keeping hold of the tight gap that he'd managed to make on his prey.

And just like that, the chase was on.

The wolf's legs were much shorter than the elk's and his frame was weedier, built more for stalking than galloping. But he had utilised the raven's calls effectively, sticking close enough to his target so that whenever it tried to turn and escape into the trees, he was there in its peripheral. It moved wherever he wanted it to move, adhering to the design of his will. This was the wolf's way. He was fully aware of his shortcomings; he could feel in his body how much shorter he was than he ought to be, being barely past the status of a pup. He knew that a faithful pack or infinite chances were not his greatest features, having to carefully choose his battles and make them work to his disadvantages. But he was patient, creative, and intelligent as well, as he had seized his limited opportunity from the raven's calls. He wasn't much - not for what a young wolf ought to be - but he was smart. He had that going for him.

As the two began the chase, their sprinting made enough racket to disturb an assorted flock of birds hidden in the trees. They scattered into the sky in a multitude of chaotic directions. In doing so, they shook every piece of foliage around them, causing a mighty and persistent shuffling throughout the forest.

The elk dashed ahead and began to take a wide left, which was a mistake. The wolf had a slight bearing on the left side, shortening the distance as it turned. He thought ahead - rather than run towards its backside, he dug his front paws into the dirt and bounded even sharper to the left, jumping at an angle towards its side. The elk compensated and pulled a sharp right, aligning it to a clearing in the trees that lay dead ahead. It committed itself to this clearing; an escape, it thought. But the wolf's ploy had taken its toll and the gap between them was closing even smaller against the elk's favour.

His burning eyes never shifted from the rump of the frightened elk where he would clamp on for the takedown. It was all talent and instinct now - the wolf barely felt the movement in his legs as they made long strokes against the field. His shimmering silver coat wafted aggressively from the speed, giving him the appearance of a swift ocean wave; a frothing white edge cultivated by a harsh wind that threatened to roll over anything caught in its path. As the wolf closed in, the elk never looked back. It focussed only on escape, believing more and more certainly that it would survive the encounter as the opening in the trees grew closer. It began to envelop the animal's entire peripheral view with a promise of survival that seemed to beckon to the poor beast, "Get in! Get in here now!"

Its focus on freedom was brutally imposed upon as a stinging sensation seized its backside, causing its leg to buckle. An unsubtle sense of discomfort took hold of its entire body, a feeling like large chunks of cold rock coursing through its nervous system at high speed. The wolf's teeth had stuck into its flesh and refused to let go until his prey stopped moving. His claws dug into the hide, opening deep jagged wounds that the elk's blood began to pour out of. The helpless beast battered down onto its side, throwing dirt and loosened grass into the air. In its panic it never stopped flailing about, trying to reorient itself onto its hooves. It succeeded, though the force it took to stand back up was tiring; it had already expelled so much energy and more was leaving its body as its blood gushed out.

The wolf had been knocked free by the impact, having fallen to the side of his target. This was only for a moment as he clambered back to his paws and rushed back over to the disoriented elk, determined to plunge his claws and teeth back in. He never calmed his ravenous assault as his prey poured what little energy it had left into a futile attempt at bucking around, hoping to shake him loose. Rather than target the neck and head, he knew he would have to let go and move upwards on the body for that. That would risk letting his target gather some possibly preserved burst of energy for a last minute strive for freedom. Plus, he too was putting all his power into hanging on, uncertain if he had another chase in him right now. The wolf opted for a slow guarantee over a risky execution, even if it would have more quickly ended the chase.

He played smart. He played selfish.

The elk slowed with each new second of the wolf's assault as its consciousness slipped away. Eventually, its front knees crashed down onto the dirt, all the while letting out helpless infantile pleas of pain. Its body began to waver as it dipped sideways to the floor, its life finally giving out as it toppled onto the right side, with the wolf still clamping down onto the left. He slowed his harsh tugging as his victim noticeably gave up and perished in the brawl, its eyes turned upwards into bloated milky-pink orbs and its tongue hanging out of its mouth.

The wolf resettled from the now-dead animal, giving it a few sniffs to make absolutely certain it had been killed. Victorious, he began to dig into his prize. Wherever the elk had sprinted, streaks of glistening crimson had splashed out against the off-cream grass in an expression of life, death, and adrenaline. In his vigorous movement, the wolf's claws had dug into the ground and caused deep impressions, where chaotic bursts of coffee-tinted soil had been unleashed from under the layer of flat dry grass. The wolf's tenacity had caused this, painting a previously dull plain with an exceptional mosaic of colour and passion.

The champion took his time to enjoy a hearty and well-earned meal. His neck jerked around, and he let out soft rumbling growls as he ripped into the meat. Watching and waiting, the raven sat on its branch.

Like all ravens, it was a scavenger and was hoping to get its nourishment from leftovers, surviving as an outsider as best it could. It was just a matter of time, and the wolf would be finished with his portion of the carcass. It could have its turn to eat what was left - it could reach what couldn't be gotten at by the wolf in the crevices between the bones.

As he indulged in his earnings, the wolf peered upwards at his observer.

He – the raven - looked directly back as their gaze met for the first time.

2

COMPANIONSHIP

The co-operation of wolves and ravens in the wild is a wonderful and curious phenomenon. The raven, one of the most fiercely intelligent creatures in the world, has long used the might and skill of wolves to their advantage in order to find food. Wolves, as wily and opportunistic hunters, rarely turn their noses up at the presence of ravens, who provide an extra set of eyes for these purposes. It's rare to see such different species operate so well together, but as both animals are each known for their complex and well-developed social habits, they make for a perfect and productive cross-species alliance. Their unity has been examined long enough for them to become connected through folk tales and old cultures (such as in Norse mythology) to the point where ravens have been nicknamed 'wolf birds'. In short, the co-operation between wolves and ravens is nothing supernatural or uncommon. What is uncommon, however, is the presence of a single lonely wolf and one misfit raven catching each other's attention in the middle of the open wilderness and stumbling into a less than favourable hunt, where the lack of numbers and poor cover made for a notable disadvantage, only for an impulsive interruption and a dash of risk to tip the scales in their favour. Even as far as wolf-raven alliances go, the meeting of this lonely wolf and this solitary raven had turned out curiously and especially well.

The wolf indulged in the lifeblood he had claimed – its colour, its vitality. It stained his lips like spilled cherries staining a grey rug, or like crimson paint staining a canvas. But by the time the wolf's stomach was full, more than half of the elk's carcass was still covered in plenty of flesh. Though he was tenacious enough to take down the elk by himself, its body was still much more than was needed to fully satisfy a young wolf. He often went for this kind of target; unassuming and simple. Leftovers gave the superficial impression that he could take down something much larger than he could handle, but the unthreatening and isolated nature of his prey usually made for a safe and certain success. He hunted in low flat areas, where only the dumbest and most unchallenging ventures would drift.

Yet he was content. He was confident here.

Bloated and gummy and having had his fill, he turned away and began to walk out of the grassy opening back towards the forest. The impatient raven wasted no time in noticing that the wolf was taking his leave and torpedoed down towards the corpse. He tipped his beak and needled through the air with a focussed dive before tilting upwards at the last possible second and plunging his talons into the elk's hide, perching on the carcass. He sat in front of a gaping hole that the wolf's teeth had hollowed out - the left side of the ribs had been pried upwards into asymmetrical shards protruding from the frame, with various other bones having been snapped off and discarded in a flustered, unabashed effort to access the innards. Clearly, the wolf didn't indulge in his spoils with any sense of shame or restraint. While he was proud of his accomplishment, he certainly hadn't taken the time to savour the reward. His goal was the satisfaction to be gained from achieving his results, not the fulfilment of the result itself.

The raven, however, chose his picking wisely. Aiming for the stringiest, juiciest sinew that was left over, he slightly opened his beak into two sharp tips and slammed them down into the meat. He forced them together, creating a tight clamp on the flesh as he crudely jerked his head sideways and upwards, ripping the flesh from its source. At intervals, he would peck rapidly to mash and soften the meat into a more edible pulp before returning to his indulgent guzzling. He ate the tough meat, the pulpy meat, scraped the bones and slurped the blood. He savoured the variety to be found in the experience as opposed to the plenitude of it.

Just before exiting the plain, the wolf craned his head around to look back at his dinner guest. There was a gaze in his eyes that could have been taken for gratitude. To him, they had both been major players, the game had been shared, the winning tactic a result of both their input and as a result, the prize belonged to both of them. In the middle of his chewing, the raven looked back up at the hound and caught the expression on his face. With a slight dip of his head, the wolf seemed to simultaneously lower his guard in an effort to show the raven that there was no animalistic hostility between them (as there so often was among the different species of the wilderness) as well as give him a jovial nod of gratitude and, more than that, invitation. It was as though he were telling the raven that they worked well together and, if the bird wanted to see more of the exciting promiscuous hunts that the wolf planned to get himself into, then he should keep watching. Among the danger that the sunlight lit up in the forest, the wolf knew the best shadows to find fun and comfort in. With that, the wolf moved on back into the forest. His wispy tail was still barely visible and slinking away behind a bush as the raven hurriedly lapped up as much as he could and fluttered away to catch up.

The elk was a sorry sight what with the plentiful amount of meat that was still wrapped around its remains. However, the bustling and resourceful inhabitants of the wilderness, whether they were as large as a bear or as small as a maggot, would make sure the rest wouldn't go to waste.

Weaving in and out between the crooked trunks and wavering piles of earth, the wolf approached a steep mound of dirt between a frame of trees. The hill was wide and high like a wave and as he climbed up to the crest, he looked out to where it crashed down into his local territory. Out there, likely, was all manner of beast trying frantically to survive at any given moment, yet there was so much isolation in this corner of the world that standing still on any secluded point would bring nothing but an eerie near silence. From atop the ridge, he could look out over the muted countryside he called home stretching off into the distance. It was the final weeks of September, and the creeping presence of autumn was evident as many of the less winter-favouring trees had begun to shed crisp ember leaves onto the ground. Though the greenery was withering, year-round pines overwhelmed the varieties of plant life and anyone looking out from a considerable height such as this would still see an unending emerald sprawl right to the edge of the earth.

Though he could look out over the forest from here, it was far from a lofty height when compared to the turbulent hills and peaks that he could see in the distance. In this mostly flat area of the world, this was as high as things got. His eyeline raised up from the tops of the greenery until the cut of the horizon interrupted his view of home and instead, showed him the mountains of faraway. Ivory-dusted slopes pierced the clouds, reaching unthinkable heights as they sat silhouetted against the sun, promising a glimpse of heaven to anyone that could scale to the top. Amid these admirable peaks, one monolithic mountain stood buried within the lofty range that, in particular, called out to him. It was distinct from the others only from the nuances of seeing it first-hand; a particular way the shadows dropped and the specific angle of the summit.

His golden eyes lit up. The peak seemed to radiate a particular hue that perhaps only appealed to wolves, or hunters, or any animal with bright eyes, or any other such classification.

As the raven hurried to catch up, he accidentally shot past the wolf. He tumbled onto the top of a modest boulder that stood on the edge of the risen ridge and in a single hop, spun around so that the two animals stood at eye level with each other. Only feet apart, the details of their eyes became even more apparent as they stared into each other again.

One had a pair of electric wild eyes, whose honeyed brightness put the adjacent sunrise to shame and highlighted two pinholes of focussed darkness. The other had two wide and glistening vortices of infinite blackness that captured an intense spark of reflected light, imitating the distant silvery moon in a dark night's sky. On quick glance, a raven's eyes seem too dim and too void of focus to hold any detail, however in gazing long and deep enough, the wolf began picking out definition within his eyes. Many animals didn't take the time to stare into the raven's eyes long enough to see these details, often preoccupied with either hunting down or escaping the little bird. But the wolf saw.

There was no ferocity between them. They were acknowledging their contribution to each other's satisfaction, appreciating the effect and reward of each other's presence. The raven wouldn't have had an elk to eat had the wolf not aimed and succeeded to kill it, and the wolf may have missed his chance to do so had the raven not created the opportunity. Wordless - through only the unity of their glance - they both asked if the delight ended here, with this one simple pursuit. Or could the combination of their efforts make more difficult hunts easier, make dim weather feel brighter; make longer journeys more agreeable.

The wolf turned and stared back into the distance at the mountain that seemed to beckon him. It looked like a beautiful peak, basking unrestrained in the flourished sunlight yet with plenty of shadowed spots to hide in. If he were a raven, he could simply fly to the top, he thought. Seeing the dog's distant gaze, the raven tilted its great eye to see what he was looking out at and peered at the same abstract summit. If he were a wolf, he could take on any foe he met on the way to the top, he thought. They turned back towards each other. Neither had the attributes they felt were necessary to reach the top, but maybe together, with their efforts combined, they did.

The wolf shuffled his two front paws into a wide stance, to display his proud and valiant form. He then dipped his head into a sort of bow yet maintained his eyesight with the bird. In this, he showed that he didn't view it as a threat or a nuisance, willing to lower his snout (and his teeth) in its presence, but at the same time was always wide-eyed enough to keep an eye on his surroundings, traits that would make any companion feel comfortable and protected. He was an indefatigable protector full of focus and confidence. The raven, on the other hand, began bouncing side to side. He rapidly jolted his head around in an energetic manner as if trying to perform a skit or dance. In a still, deadly and serious forest, the raven was a joker, breaking the quiet and peaceful surroundings with an impulsive attitude.

Amid his cheery dance, the raven let out a string of happy chortles towards the wolf like an icebreaker, as if to say things like "hey, good job back there!" and "we made a great team," behaviour that would raise the spirits of any acquaintance.

In response to his playfulness, the hound's head tipped to the side and his left ear perked slightly. In that moment, he was more akin to a harmless puppy than a tenacious killer.

His eyes were now wide and receptive, reminiscent of a child's eyes watching a cartoon show filled with colour and rapid movement. The raven's coat was an interesting colour – so black as to make him appear as a silhouette yet so silken that streaks of white rippled across his feathers whenever they caught the light in a particular way. The wolf glanced down at his own paws under him. The coat was a pure silver all over his arms that seemed gleaming white in the noonday sun, with spots of shade where the light couldn't pierce through the thick fur. Having seen him glance down, the raven settled from his dance.

They both resumed their sights on the possibilities of the open world, to the woodlands below. Directly below the ridge they stood on was a gradual and manageable slope that led down into the vast continuity of trees. In response to the wolf's invitation to join him moving forward, it was the raven who now made the leading move and twisted his body as he kicked off from the rock, taking to the air in one heavy yet smooth motion. The wolf stepped down onto the head of the slope. It was more agreeable than the one he had hauled himself up and as he broke into a sprint, he felt the momentum of gravity carry him forward at intense speed. The air wafted through his fluffy coat and made him feel like he was flying as well. The raven was ebbing in the air alongside the wolf as they both skidded to the bottom of the crumbling dirt hill, returning to the vast underworld of the forest. Once again, the greater view of the world had become hidden beneath a stretching curtain of wooden spires and rustling canopies that broke the sun beams. At the turn of noon, full of optimism and potential, the two trotted away from the hill and threw themselves forward.

Journeying through the budding trees, they crashed into a small meadow of lime grass and butterscotch flowerheads. A gentle breeze carried the raven across the field until he wheeled back around behind the wolf, making playful circles. He created a game where he would swoop at his follower's tail and try to harmlessly fling it up in the air, like lightly batting around a tetherball. In return, the wolf would try to swirl about and softly tap the bird with his snout or a paw pad. His claws weren't out, and he didn't seek to harm it, instead playing a game of tag with his fragile acquaintance. He let out soft grunts and huffs as he leapt joyfully into the air at his new friend, almost as if to laugh. With cheeky intent, the bird dived at the grey-plumed tail below, trying to pick it up and escape untouched.

They ran and flew, constantly closing in on and expelling from each other with exceptional magnetism, as if being one another's companion came naturally and essentially. The field was transformed into a windswept garden as the two paraded around on it. On the edges of the field, confused squirrels peered at them from trees and baffled quails tried to keep their distance from the two boisterous beasts. None of the other creatures around understood their games, or why they would play them (especially as two oddly distinct species), but their focus remained purely on each other. The wolf wasn't interested in hunting the other critters and the raven wasn't interested in flocking together with the other birds; with each other in that moment, they had found everything they needed from another creature. There was leaping and springing and tumbling and goodwill with not a single living being that could deter them from the feeling of freedom. It was their moment to be themselves.

After a good while of heavy playing, they expelled all the energy they had. They stopped when the raven first left to catch his breath on a tree branch on the edge of the field. Reciprocating the bird's suggestion to rest, the wolf slowed his movements and began to trot over to the foot of the same tree. They had settled into a pleasant and satisfied mood, similar to the feeling of bone-deep weariness from a heavy workout. The wolf bundled up into the bosom of the tree's roots. It was a thin, high-reaching spruce with spindly twigs that started from its base and grew in breadth and foliage as they went higher. He tucked his legs in and wrapped his tail snugly around his front. He blew loud bolts of air from his nostrils as his heartbeat raced from the physical activity while the raven's small chest puffed in and out as he tried to catch his breath. Sure enough, with a moment's rest, their heart rates came back down and the feeling of excitement in their bones was replaced with a comfortable fatigue as their heavy breathing returned to silence. Then, as they lay motionless, everything else around them became still too. The wolf's disposition grew tender as he felt awash with comfort. All that could be heard now was the sleepy whisper of a million leaves. For the first time since their meeting, the two of them came to a complete stop, fully resting without travel, hunt or play as they took in the quiet solitude of their own little world. It was the purest moment of peace. No rules, no safety, no order, no violence, no knowledge, no progress, no malice, no pollution, no judgement, no civility, no intrusion, no distraction, no schedules, no standards, no expectations; no other beasts. Just good rest and good company.

The wolf's eyelids began to droop. The shadow of the tree cast out with a chill relief over them both, cooling them down after their tiring caper. His head swung drowsily to the right, looking out at the meadow ahead. Out of the tree cover, the field still shone with rampant colours of jade and gold. Similarly, the tired creature on the tree branch above began to drift off to the slumbersome sounds of the foliage that rustled in his ears. With an over-abundance of time and comfort, they fell happily together into a lazy sleep.

3

THE THUNDERSTORM

The time passed smoothly, their dreams came easy. Only in the later hours of the evening was the wolf disturbed from his sleep as something damp began to patter down against the top of his head. The trickling was dull at first, barely disturbing him from his rest, but as droplets grew heavier and more frequent, his mind grew irritated and his eyes creaked open. Eventually the hissing sound of rain reached a disruptive volume inside the echo chamber of the field. Now awake, all his senses had been overcome with discomfort and a cold shudder seemed to strip the warmth from his body's natural blanket of fur.

He peered upwards. For however long they had slept, a dark sky had rolled in overhead and brought a speckling downpour with it. His companion had clearly been alerted earlier and was perched wide awake on his sleeping branch. No doubt the raindrops, which had grown forceful against even the wolf's pillowed body, had seemed much larger from the outset to the small sensitive bird. He had perched close to the leafage overhead where the cover was at its strongest. At first, they resisted the rain – an unwelcome but harmless shower, they thought. But as the shower was growing more violent and the tree they sat under failed to seal it out, the wolf became too disturbed to stay in his lying position, so he decided they should move onwards. It wasn't a moment after standing up that a violent flash stole the whole forest, turning the trees white from shock for a split second. A titanic crack seemed to come from everywhere at once, shaking the floor as it hit the young wolf's delicate ears. It startled the life out of him; he had never experienced anything as terrifyingly powerful before. It was as if some reckoning giant beast that could control the entire world had broken into a hateful fit, its rage translated through the shuddering ground and battering rainfall. But no foe could be seen – the danger seemed everywhere and nowhere – and to the mind of the young wolf, this couldn't be naturally reasoned or explained. All he could see around him was the dependable mother nature that he recognised and relied on, transformed into something dismal and scary.

Instinct told the duo to find better shelter. Immediately, charged into the forest behind them without direction. The wolf galloped across soggy brown trails and greyish-purple puddles that stuck to his paws like loose glue, dragging down his escape and making him feel even more dark and damp. The bird fled as best he could through the chilling air, with needles of rain pushing against him and harsh clashes making his nerves jump. Another flash of light exploded onto every element around them. Air vibrated over wings; ground quaked under paws.

The wolf, in his nature as a predator, felt that the force must be another giant predator trying to assert its malicious dominance over the entire territory. The raven, as an animal that often scavenged off other creatures, felt that it must be an oncoming stampede creating havoc as it closed in on them. Their imaginations of what could be and what may happen ran amok. Whatever the source of the storm was, it was bigger than they could handle, and it terrified them. Out of this fear, it seemed easier – instinctive even – to stick together. Whatever each of them was afraid of, it helped to have someone to lead them away from it. Despite each of them feeling that the other was the one leading the way, at least they were confused and scared together.

As they swooped through the maze of trees, the deluge grew even more hostile. The bird took the downpour the hardest. Unlike the wolf, he had no grounding in his lofty flight to put his weight against. The spattering rain pushed onto his back, trying to force him down to the dirt. Each shard of liquid made the bird's body dip as he fought against them to stay airborne. Even after a particularly soothing sleep, this took a lot of effort.

Minor puddles had grown to pools of grit and sludge around them. These pools rippled hectically as the shower hammered against the floor at every millisecond. The wolf would slip one way or the other as he tried desperately to stay upright and keep moving ahead, wherever ahead was taking him. Thunder strikes continued to echo out often and close by, feeding the fear that they were drawing no further away from the dangerous environment they were trying to escape from. Minutes seemed like hours as the two endured the disarray that was happening around their bodies and in their heads. As the powerful push of rain kept constant against the poor raven, he eventually felt too drained to resist its dismal intentions.

The bird could take no more. Defeated by the storm, he landed exhausted onto the sloppy mud, face drenched in grey drops of water.

He attempted to hop onward with all the might that his plucky little body could muster, but he was handicapped against the speed of his disappearing partner, who was much more adept at trekking through dirt and haze. The raven was a creature built to flourish in the clear heights of the sky; neither the miserable storm nor the restrictive ground were where his strengths lay. He let out a pleading and sorrowful chirp as he could barely see through the unyielding volley of rain, which was now so all-encompassing it made the world look unstill. Trees flickered in place and the ground itself crackled. The hammering rain kept the wet floor constantly in flux and obscured the earth, making the raven uncertain about his footing. He began to feel even more lost and confused as the world he tried to recognise sank away and fell out of focus around him. His eyesight turned into jagged flickering static, the chill and the noise of the hail seized his nerves and panic set in. He could no longer see much of anything, including the wolf. Presumably, the hound had abandoned the detriment that the raven's handicap was causing him and had run off to find his own cover. Their time was fun while it lasted, but the raven knew that during stormy times, it was every beast for himself. Terrified, he manically darted his eyes around in an attempt to see something, but his world and his companion had disappeared.

His chirping grew frantic, yet seemingly futile. He was alone.

The only positive was that, in a sudden moment, the rain seemed to get much weaker. Then, somehow, it stopped hitting the bird entirely. However, the rain could still be seen and heard as it was overtaking the rest of the world; it had just apparently disappeared from the raven's space. Though the forest was already overcast by the dreary storm clouds, a stiller and more secure shade fell further over the bird. The sound was now no longer abrasive and deafening but was now dubbed, like beating on a pillow. The world still looked hectic – there was still an unbearable noise - but it was suddenly obscured by drapes of damp grey hair that hung over his eyes, darkening his sight so that the chaos was partially covered. A powerful odour settled over everything, like the smell of wet dog. Oddly, the shabby stench seemed more comforting than the natural air; the same air that had just been trying to assault him. A soaking paw stood upright in front of his face. He turned his head upwards to see that the wolf was standing over him, defending him from the storm.

He hadn't run off and abandoned the little bird after all. The raven, while still largely full of dread and discomfort, felt a wash of bright relief. Yet despite them being together, they were still out in the open and needed to find safe shelter. The wolf took a preparatory step forward as incentive for the bird. Recognizing this as a signal to move, the raven hopped in the direction of the paw's lead.

One slow step followed the other. The bird couldn't move fast in the sludge, so the wolf was forced to lead forward at a snail's pace. While he was in flight, the raven could keep up with swift speed, like when they raced down the hill and across the meadow together. In fact, it was he who had to pull back and circle around to stay near the wolf.

But once brought down to earth, a disability became apparent. Walking was not his natural state. After all, why would he walk when he had wings? He struggled to keep up on the low messy flatness of the ground. The wolf held back his natural stride to meet in sync with his stunted cohort. He didn't like going slow and it meant he'd be in the rain for longer, but he made himself less comfortable to make his companion feel more secure, as was the affectionate dog's nature.

Though still scared, they composed themselves and tried to be brave. They walked with increased alertness through the noise and grey, keeping an eye out for somewhere or something to help diminish the trials of the storm; the dry hollow of a fallen tree or an outcropped root to stand under. They pressed on through shiver and shock, just desperate to find somewhere dark, quiet and hidden. The wolf's head spun about looking for any sign of hope.

There, between the trees, he found some. Obscured by a rising hill appeared to be some large rocky formation that curved over in an arching fashion, complimented by slivered roots and dirt that cradled a spot of sightless   respite. A cave?

In the hopes that it might be the kind of safe hovel they were looking for, he twisted right. He moved in a dramatic enough fashion to give the raven a clear sign of his changing direction. The raven took note of this and hopped to the right with him. The bird hadn't seen the possible hideaway that the wolf had spotted but trusted that he would lead them to safety (not that the poor critter had any other choice than to follow underfoot.) The wolf's steady walking style switched from a precarious tread to a purposeful and tense pacing, which the raven tried to match. His shoulders hung low and ebbed like mechanical pistons, his eyes remained frozen on the line of sight where his apparent goal lay. Now, his stance was almost reminiscent of his hunting style; deep in a state of acute focus, prowling forward with the intent of taking the most effective route towards his goal.

The raven hopped curious yet trusting under his friend along the same path, confident that they were heading forward to safety. But then, against the unsettling roar of rainfall and dispersed snaps of thunder, another unfamiliar and malevolent sound came.

Off to their right, a tree croaked and then tilted sideways. A loud series of clicks and cracks came out as its wood splintered at the base and its trunk was ripped away from the roots. The fierce wind pushed against its side until it gained momentum and fell slowly - it was clearly heavy and not going down easily, giving seriousness to the force that it took to topple something so mighty and stuck in place. It crashed down into a cluster of other trees which while chipped and shaken by the impact, remained standing. The fallen tree rolled off the netting of leaves from the surrounding pines and hit the ground with a tremendous clobber. The sound was earth-shattering and horribly scary. Their world had seemed constant, ageless and undefeatable. The fact that a force so mature and fluctuating could disturb the status quo they were so familiar with – could be so strong as to rip a piece of the world right out of the earth – was an all-new level of shock. The wolf swiftly turned his head back towards the direction of his goal, trying to ignore this fresh fear, and moved forward as best he could.

The potential cave was now hidden behind the hill that he had first seen it over. Being much closer to it, the rising earth now covered his line of sight, but his eyes pierced through the hill towards some hopeful point beyond it.

The wolf's coat hung like willow leaves that were sopped with water. Its silvery shade was tainted by a milky sludge that added a grim stain and a gross weight. With each step, his paws pulled away from the sticky brown goop of the soil. It felt like it was trying to tug him back from progress, back deeper into the storm. A desperate and incessant chirping came from under his chest. It matched the volume of the rushing rain and could either have been cheers of encouragement or frantic squeals of fearful impatience from his companion. Trying to repress his own fear, the wolf approached the foot of the hill. Though it had only been about a hundred steps, the walk there had felt like a million. The hill had seemed like a bump from a distance, but now stood in front of him as a tidal wave of sliding mud. The potential safe spot that he had first spied was now purely an uncertain wish hidden behind an intimidating obstacle. Ever the optimist and taking comfort in the idea of a dry cave ahead, he took his first step onto the tilted slope.

He began struggling against the sliding mud, trying to clamber upwards as it streamed down in the contrary direction. His energy poured out of his joints and his bones stiffened from the effort, all the while the constantly shifting earth slid around underneath him and kept sending him back down. But by nature, the wolf was a tenacious creature with claws that were stronger than most other animals. He was bred to dig in and not let go. So, after trying and failing and trying and failing again, he found his grip under the slippery soil into the more solid ground beneath and he pushed himself upwards with the will to hope for what was on the other side.

The raven had far less trouble climbing the mound. He had

flustered ahead when they'd reached its base and landed at the top to wait for his struggling partner. The time spent underneath the wolf's cover had cleared the warping water from out of his eyes, but as he stood out in the open air again, the world began to turn hazy from the clutter and everything fell out of focus once more. However, this time the anxiety stayed away; he knew the wolf was right behind, finding his own way up and back to the bird.

Through effort and strife, his snout eventually rose past the raven's face as he reached the top of the ridge. However wet and slippery the dirt was, he could rest his legs now that he was back on even ground and his companion was back underneath him. The raven gave a comforting croak, like a sigh of relief. More comforting, the wolf could now see that his tenacity had paid off. Just over from them was a cave etched into a rock face. The bird finally saw his guide's destination. In his desperation, he flew ahead to the entrance of the cave without waiting for the wolf, with his soaking protector scrambling quickly behind. He hurriedly flapped his way inside as if it were the inviting doorway of a warm cabin in a winter's snowfall. That there could have been danger inside - a similarly sheltering bear or mountain cat - didn't occur to him as the only thing on his mind was shelter from the storm.

Following shortly behind, the wolf stepped onto a smooth stone that complimented the entrance like a welcome mat. Despite being moist and dank, the interior of the cavern was still refreshing compared to what had become of the outside world. Its gloom was comforting, its silence peaceful. Craggy sodden rocks formed a crooked cocoon that while far from waterproof, kept out most of the rainfall and dampened the incessant rushing sound into a pattered drumming.

Trickles still managed to pierce through. Above the thump of rain, drips echoed around the cave. Miniature streams spilled in from the opening; not enough to promise any flooding but enough to deny them a break from the sight of water. The wolf's paws tapped down onto the damp stone flooring as he entered and made his way down a slight curve, deeper into the security of the slimy hole. The raven had hurried so quickly inside that he had already found a perch and turned himself around to watch his friend enter. The wolf turned to see the chaos that he had just escaped from. A weak wash of greyed light fractured in through the opening as the fizzing rain continued to pelt down outside. From the right angle, the shape and size of the opening looked almost identical to that of the tree that he'd woken from that morning.

The leaking rainwater had formed small puddles that caught the incoming sunlight. Though the sunlight was weak, the slick surfaces captured the reflection and passed it through their murky jade filter and projected back against the rocks that formed the walls. The rushing wind that plagued the forest air was tempered down through the small opening which turned it into a whistling breeze that skimmed the puddles, making them ebb slightly. In turn, this made their reflections waver and sparkle against the interior of the cave. The pair gazed at these flickering strips of light against the walls.

There was a newness to this kind of light. This green tint wasn't quite the dulling blue of a cloudy storm, or the dazzling gold of sunshine, or the deep silver of moonlight, but somewhere in between a mix of them all. It was as though they were looking at the water, but not the true water. Seeing light, but not the real light. It was formed naturally, but not the natural version of what formed it. There was an artificiality to the projection. It felt distant but within their reach, as though they could view the water without getting wet or view the sun without getting blinded – a safer version of enjoyable things, consumable from their dark little hovel.

They felt calmer as they stared on at the green glow that flickered against the stone screen. The wolf, with his delicate ears, wished the thunder outside existed in the same artificial form, but at least its roar was no longer painfully overbearing. The dome of rock provided a muffler to the frightening claps and its sleek surface gave a distraction from the dramatic flashing. The soft waves of jade reflections on the wall and the rhythmic beat of leaking droplets pushed the thunder and lightning into the background of his perception and took centre stage on his attention. He felt thankful to the forest for this kind of shelter.

Meanwhile, despite enjoying the distracting show of light on the wall, the raven found it harder to keep calm. Evidently, he was naturally a more panicky and emotional creature, and it would take more time for his nerves to settle. He had been brought down from his flight and forced into a constricted hovel, with his option for freedom and exploration taken away, something that would agonise any creature built to flourish in bright lofty heights. The wolf walked closer to the squatting raven and softly brushed his furry side against his wing. He took a seat on the freezing stone floor next to his friend, trying to provide some comfort. They were cold but together, he seemed to be saying. In response, the raven seemed to lean back against him. Calming the raven down distracted the wolf from needing reassurance himself. Wolves are naturally pack animals, coping with and caring for more than themselves and despite travelling alone now, the instinct of this one was no different. It gave him some vicarious sense of kinship to focus on the needs of this other animal.

There they sat together, with nothing more to do than wait out the storm. At some point, the last blade of sunlight that provided their show on the wall faded and left them waiting for sleep to mercifully take hold.

The night passed. The wolf's nose woke before his eyes did to a strong smell of dirty water and damp leaves. Then, his ears followed as chirping birds had replaced the clattering storm. As his eyes craned open, a beaming and invasive light flashed them immediately; the brooding clouds that had flushed out the sky were long gone, creating a blinding curtain beyond the cave's opening. His body felt sore and weary from having slept on uncomfortable ground, with his head leaned against the rocks and his legs dipped in dirty freezing water. The continuing rainfall had turned the growing puddles into a shallow bath that covered the cavern about an inch and a half high. If the den had been somewhat smaller, it could have grown dangerously high overnight. As the wolf glanced around, his fuzzy eyesight began to come back into focus. The side of his body where the raven had been sleeping felt empty. He turned to notice that the bird was gone.

If he weren't still in the middle of waking up, a stronger sense of anxiety or abandonment may have taken him, but for the minute he only felt a dull sting from wondering – worrying – where the bird was. The wolf wavered to his feet as he adjusted to the discomfort of a bad night's sleep. It must have been long past midnight when he was finally able to drift off. He moved his stubborn and creaky joints over to the entryway and stepped onto the stone slope leading outwards.

Having now adjusted to the gloom, his eyes were hit with a flurry of pure white which took a moment to dissipate into separate shapes and colours as the obscured remnants of the forest slowly came back into view. Among them was a hazy black shadow standing on a stony outcrop that lay just outside of the cave mouth. The figure's top half whipped side to side in a frantic blur. The wolf felt a joyful relief to see that the raven hadn't departed for good.

In the distance, other indistinguishable avian creatures weaved through the maze of trees. They were silhouetted against the harsh morning sun, all of them looking like black ravens, however their twitters and whistles sold them more as everyday songbirds. The raven stared out at them as they appeared flickering through the gaps in the forest, in some manner recognising their wings were similar to his own. He wondered how they'd coped in the thunderstorm; they didn't seem to be lucky enough to have a wolf standing over them to protect them from the rain. The wolf slowly stepped towards the bird to let him know that his companion was there. The raven twirled around, tilting his head down to the right as if a doctor were examining a recovering patient. The wolf did the same and they both deduced each other to be right as rain.

The intrusive morning daylight was trying its best to erase the previous night's showers, making the muddy floor gloopy and ill-mixed with unabsorbed water settled here and there. The rain had wetted everything it touched, giving the entire forest a laminated appearance. As a result, it reflected the light off every tree and stone, making this morning glow even brighter than the previous one, yet somehow giving the forest a diorama-like and almost artificial sensation to its appearance.

From a more optimistic perspective, the duo recognised what a dreamlike quality the woods now had, with a shimmering sense of newness and with that, possibility. Now the danger of noise and fury had subsided, the world reverted to a sense of natural momentum – a neutrality – where it was easier for the pair to imagine any potential outcome for the following day. In their youth and naivety, they imagined a purely positive outcome. If the forest was bright, then the day and the future would be too, they simply thought. The raven gave an encouraging squall and flapped lightly over the top of his new ally, landing on the dog's back. He turned to face the same direction as the wolf and tipped his head down again to look him in the eye. By this point, the wolf had craned his head around; he didn't seem in any way irritated or put out by the raven's attempt to ride his back, but simply checked to see if his new travel buddy was settled and ready to move on before he stepped forward. In the communicative method that they felt was best, they gazed into each other's eyes once again.

Internally, a shift was felt. The wolf had protected his miniature follower for a reason beyond survival or self-preservation. He had stunted his speed and risked his safety to make sure the raven wasn't left defenceless. The pair had been lucky in hindsight. While they huddled in their cave, rockslides had reshaped the landscape. Entire bunches of trees had collapsed. Water had turned into torrents that flooded away trails and pooled into hollows. Many animals were drowned in the wash or crushed by the falling world. Every second the two were out in the havoc was a chance that they could've been victims to a wave of rainwater, or a tree trunk toppling down on top of them, or a shard of lightning coming down to strike them. Any hiding spot they'd discovered could have already been claimed by a larger creature, temperamental and willing to defend its place of safety. But the wolf risked all of this to see that the raven wasn't left alone in a 'both of us or neither of us' act of selflessness. The raven, aware of the possible sacrifice, sought to repay this in the best way he was able; with staunch companionship. Looking out at the other birds fluttering through the trees that morning, he recognised a more standard crowd, but felt more secure and understood among the wolf, turning away from the uniformed flock.

Something like respect was felt. As they stared into each other, there was an unspoken transition from partnership to companionship. The wolf's eyes squinted; his cheeks were slightly raised in a manner reminiscent of a smile. An affinity beat through their hearts, a sense of empathy that transcended animality; something almost human.

Spark-eyed and aiming for higher territory, they continued their journey. While they were resolute in moving on, the weariness of the night still weighed heavily on the wolf. Despite his relief that the storm was gone and despite his hopefulness that the day wouldn't bring another, it wasn't easy for him to forget the random snaps of thunder and how they came so suddenly. This instilled a doubt in him, a worry that one could come again at any moment while he was unaware. He felt the raven was clearly still somewhat detached from his usual cheeriness as well (otherwise he would be flying), but they were equally determined to push on. They spent the first few hours wandering in one direction and though the two as animals were incapable of talking, they understood each other to have the same goal of distant freedom and hopeful opportunity.

There was a serene ambience ebbing through the rest of the wilderness, with all the other animals seeming fresh-faced and enthusiastic in the face of a new day. All living things around them appeared to radiate the very sunlight that lit up the world, with their social movements and their cheery moods. Trees stood placid after being rocked and battered only hours ago. Animals that had escaped death now bounded about with a carefree exuberance, despite each and every one of them having spent the night hidden away in a state of fear.

This confused the wolf and the raven as they loped on. The pair felt optimistic, but they were still affected by their experience of the storm. In their movement, they were wide-eyed but cautious. However, the other animals seemed to jump right back into their swift habits without any care or adjustment. It didn't seem like cautious optimism, more a blissful ignorance? Maybe these other creatures had all been through enough storms to get used to them and after enough terrible nights, the two would also be able to forget and re-adjust to their new mornings just as quickly. Or maybe the other animals feigned their confidence as they moved on, just like these two were doing, but were simply better at faking it?

Rodents dashed across fields and a spectrum of birds streamed through the air. The morbid clouds that had previously engulfed the sky had given their all to the storm and wrung themselves completely dry. Now there wasn't a single dot of grey left, leaving only an eternal sweep of clear azure. A prominent strip of light blue glided across the horizon like sea foam, then dipped gradually into a solemn hue as the sky reached higher and deeper. In the loveliness of the world, comfort began to slowly return to the two travellers. Each harmonious element around them gave a feeling that their home was strong and dependable and no matter how long they crawled away into a dark hidden hole for, sturdy woods and open skies would still be there through any hardship when they re-emerged.

On their way back out of the area, they passed a toppled tree lying beside their path; the wolf recognised it as the same one they had seen fall in their journey to the cave. In that tumultuous moment, the destruction of the tree had seemed so grand and nerve-shattering, hitting the other trees as it came down, giving a sense of intense power and importance to the stormy wind. But in the light of day, it turned out its demolition from the treeline hadn't affected the rest of the forest a single bit. It was a bittersweet realisation that the death and turmoil which such a great force could bring meant nothing in the grand scheme of things. Where one tree had fallen, a thousand more still stood strong around it. For now, the wolf was just glad that the same couldn't be said for the two of them.

4

THE SNOW FOX

Familiarity grew as the duo travelled, hunted, ate, played and rested together over the weeks. They continued heading for the lofty peaks that they'd spied on the first day they'd met, all the while feeling young and spirited through the consistently brisk yet sun-kissed season. As November came around and they trekked into more northern territories, flecks of white appeared on the floor around them. Flecks turned into cold patches, patches turned into trails, and over the days the two were eventually wandering across peaceful snowy hills. It wasn't a harsh cover brought about by a blizzard; just a natural sprinkling that occurred annually in these parts. The snow was shallow enough for the wolf to walk through as normal, kicking up sugary bursts as he marched ahead while the raven swept through the air above. The two of them freely glided forward in their own particular way. The bird held his wings straight against the breeze, his feathers ruffling as they tilted about. He had grown a tendency to still perch on the wolf's back during moments of exhaustion, but here in the wistful air, he was in his comfort zone where he could watch everything without blockages or restrictions. He kept an eye on the wandering wolf, often getting ahead of his companion's path and then circling back around like an orbiting moon never straying too far from the gravitational pull of its planetary partner.

It was as the two passed through the centre of a rotund field that the raven decided to give his wings a quick moment's rest. There was no urgent sense of danger about, so he pattered down onto the crackly snow blow. The bird would do this every so often to signify a rest for both of their sakes and the wolf came to recognise this in his behaviour, where he landed on the ground instead of on his escort's back. "We don't constantly need to be moving forward," the bird was saying. "Let's have some fun or take it easy for a bit instead."

The wolf came to an agreeable stop; he also felt that this was a fine place to rest. There was a bright purity to the snow on the field – it was as white as canvas. The travellers didn't see moving forward together as a survivalist necessity or a chore-like means to an end; it was something to be enjoyed and savoured like a passion, so it could be put on hold whenever they weren't in the mood or temporarily wavered from when a more immediate source of excitement presented itself. This source came after only a moment's pause when a disturbance broke their peaceful moment. A nearby scrunching sound hit their ears. It was quiet and unthreatening, but it soon caught their attention in the otherwise serene atmosphere. A short distance away, nestled between the sparse trees, a crusty mound of snow sat bunched up. It appeared to have fallen from the overhead branches of the pines and poured down into a single spot to form a miniature white mountain. Unnaturally, however, the surface of the snow seemed to ebb in and out, as though the snow pile was breathing.

They cautiously stepped towards its direction. It was in the wolf's nature to approach every new experience with intense forethought, so he tiptoed up to it prepared for anything, including a fight. He suspected something was hiding behind the snow pile, but it was about the same height as the wolf so he was sure he'd be able to deal with whatever might slink out from the cover. The raven, a more curious and optimistic creature, had a look of giddy inquisition in his eyes. He was sure that if there was something dangerous hiding behind it, then the wolf would be able to handle it, but still held a much more open-minded expectation for something fascinating that might reveal itself – a new animal they'd never seen before or element of the world they were about to discover for the first time. Either way, each thought process led them to the same conclusion; investigating the snow pile.

As they inched closer, the mound continued to pulse and rustle and scrunch. When they were only a few feet away, the wolf's senses were hit with an electrifying jolt as the snow pile suddenly burst apart, sending blobs of frosty shrapnel flying everywhere and making an adorable bumping noise as it exploded. There was a cloud of powder that obscured their view of the snow mound before it slowly dissipated. Beyond the powdery mist was a concave left in the now-destroyed mound. It resembled a volcano with a hollow bowl sat in the wake of its eruption. In a swift moment, a head popped out of the hollow. It was covered in ember fur and presented an expression of pure mischief. A fuzzy set of black ears perked up. They belonged to a peculiar fox who tilted her head at the duo as she glared at them. The wolf tilted his head in kind, as if to say "yeah, I can stare at you as well."

Even the raven, noticing the behaviour of dogs, tilted his head in imitation. An awkward moment of curiosity passed by before the creature launched out of her hole. The fox made a small splash into the frosted field as she crashed down. Apparently, she was incapable of keeping snow from flying about whenever she emerged out of or submerged into it. She ducked her head down and crawled towards them, mowing through the field with her elbows tucked into her sides, her belly lay flat, and her nose pushed into the snow. Like a plough, she cleared the snow in her path as she moved and in doing so, left a trench of green needles in her wake. The wolf had only left gentle scrapes and respectful paw prints pushed into the snow behind him. Where it had hopped around, the raven's little feet hadn't even pierced the snow. But the fox seemed intent on ruining the blanket's purity. She stopped swimming through the meadow some distance away from the two. They watched on, unfazed and confused by her lack of grace. The scene gave the impression of a bumbling pickpocket trying to sneak up on someone fully aware of them, banging about as they tried and failed to make a sly approach. When the fox stopped, she remained in a prone position, digging her nose into the thin layer of cover and attempting to peek over what little snow there was. The wolf looked at her as you would a nuisance; with an exhausted brow. Realising after an embarrassingly long time that the two were staring at her with perfect awareness, the fox raised her neck as if to say "Fine, never mind!" (Whether she was giving up on trying to liven their spirits with a joke or giving up on honestly trying to outwit them, was anyone's guess.)

The raven was far from cynical. At some point between her explosive entrance and her failed sneaking, he had begun to find her interesting and humorous. He hopped forward a little bit closer, ahead of the wolf. In return, she bounded towards him, getting slower as she did. She was much bigger than the raven yet much smaller than the wolf, fitting comfortably between them yet looked awkward alongside each one separately. She had an obtrusively fiery coat dabbled with a white strip running up her underside – some of it was natural fur, some of it was clinging snow from her low slinking. Her eyes were as clear as crystal and blue as ice. An inextinguishable smile lay across her face. As she approached, she ducked her neck towards the raven and once her snout was within inches of his face, gave him a sniff.

The wolf snarled immediately.

Both out of mistrust for the sneaky fox and out of protection over his friend, he let out a deep and foreboding snap towards her. She shimmied backwards, sticking close to the ground as her automatic state seemed to be. The bird never flinched, not even at the unexpected roar of his protector who he had his back to. He turned his head around to look upwards at the wolf with a total lack of fear on his face. The raven's soft expression seemed to say, "aw come on, she was only playing!"

However, the wolf was not so trusting. His expression loosened but his stance didn't, staying on alert for whenever the fox tried to get close again. She had frozen in a hunched position some feet away from them. Her gaze flitted from the raven to the wolf, to the raven, to the wolf. Eventually she slunk to her side, turning away from them and jogging off as if on her way to leave. Yet on her way out of the clearing, she would swing her head around at intervals or even turn herself entirely to look back at them. It looked like she was goading them to follow her.

The wolf showed no interest in the troublesome thing, but even as he turned his head slowly away, the raven continued staring out at her. It was just as she was disappearing into a thicker bunch of trees that she turned one last time. The wolf was walking away as well, but the raven was still looking out at her. She noticed a more willing intent to play in the bird's dark marble eyes. Her ears perked up and her head tilted back, like how a dog would beckon its owner to throw a stick for it to chase. There was a sense of whimsy in her demeanour as she whipped around and finally pranced off into the bushes.

The raven didn't hesitate to pick up into the air and follow in her direction. Hearing the soft patter of feathers taking off, the wolf turned to watch him flutter away. Before he could even think of the possibility that he was being abandoned in favour of the fox, the raven fell back onto the ground at the same spot where she had beckoned him to follow and in turn, tried convincing his cohort to follow in this endeavour. The raven thought that she was simply playful and questioning of different creatures – not at all different to himself – and wanted his friend to share in that.

The hound hesitated. Oddly, he felt it was much easier to keep up with the wings of a bird than with the four paws of a creature like himself. He'd had bad experiences with other canines and playing with birds seemed much more his speed. Still, he didn't want his friend to go alone, so he followed suit. Noticing that he was heading in the same direction, the raven now felt at ease knowing that his friend was following along and flew back off after the fox, with the wolf hesitantly in tow.

Clambering over the bumps of dirt and slipping between the spindly trees, the raven chaseed the trail of the fox as the wolf tracked the trail of the raven. A spectrum of flowers sprouted up between sodden roots; mostly cool blues and violets twinkling with dew. They broke the drab pallet of the snow and the birch trees. The fox gave some petals a sniff before rolling about in their patches, tearing the colours to shreds. She hung her tongue out of her smirking mouth with a sense of pride, like a child tarnishing their parent's pristine walls with painted handprints, viewing their destruction only as an explosion of fun.

She imbued a level of energy that was hard for the weather-worn and solitary wolf to keep up with, but the raven's natural curiosity urged him to follow, and his frictionless flight gave him the capabilities to fly further ahead as he found himself beside the fox. She darted left, but it took no effort for the bird to tilt sideways and keep up with the chase. Failing to match their speed, the wolf began falling behind. In short glimpses, he could forlornly watch the pair's capers flickering in and out between the gaps in the trunks.

The little red devil stumbled haphazardly over humps and charged through bushes with a fiery sense of glee. The bullet-like bird shot through the air, to-ing and fro-ing slightly behind and giddily drafting the path of the fox's disarray like he was trying to absorb the residual spirit that she left in her wake. He sped up to meet the side of her face and the pair began weaving between the trees together. As they danced, their fluency and interconnectedness grew. Soon, they weren't only weaving through the gaps in the trees but through each other from left to right by moving in a curving pattern, like the way a strand of DNA seems to cross over itself from whatever angle you look at it.

Their velocity and vitality grew. It was a blur of black feathers and red tufts knotted between each other. The fox's slinky body moved back and forth, matching the dextrous flow of the raven's flight. The bird had never flown so acutely. He circled in the air under and over the fox's torso as if wrapping around her waist. Their dance was heavy and reckless – the fox came close to tripping over roots a few times and the raven came so close to hitting the ground with his wings, it's a wonder that he didn't crash down. The two pushed each other to their limits of passion and vigour as if trying to clamber over and outperform one another. Once they were both heavily panting and felt like they'd fled enough, they both slowed down. In order to catch her breath, the fox skidded to a complete halt, with the bird doing the same not long after as he settled down beside her. The fox's tongue hung out of her grin. The raven's breast ebbed in and out from exhaustion. He often playfully bounded about with the wolf too, but there was a difference here. The wolf chased with a brash childishness, offering a silly distraction. But the fox seemed to test the raven in a serious show of his physical abilities; their chase was flexible and challenging. Exhaustive. One was a game, the other was a competition. Neither was better or worse than the other, just different.

Even before she had caught her breath, the fox rolled onto her back in a moment of jest. Her spirit seemed undefeatable. The bird, drunk on whimsy, let out a chortle at her liveliness. She rolled back onto her legs and stood upright. They shared a look between them only felt by two naturally mischievous creatures who recognised themselves in each other; feeling free from anxiety, aglow with the warm sensation of feeding one's own immediate fancies. The instance was only slightly disturbed by a deep gargling noise that emanated from the fox's stomach. Calmed by her show of familiarity and without the wolf to discourage her, the raven stood firm and unafraid as the fox made a sweet step towards him. In turn, he took two hops towards her.

A gap in the overhead leaves left a streak of sunlight peeking through. It illuminated all four of their eyes – two glistening blue pinholes and two gleaming black orbs stared into each other. The fox romantically dipped her head downwards. Her breath was close enough to blow over the raven's feathers. His dark coat wiggled ever so slightly from the hot air. It was quite intoxicating.

Now her nose was less than an inch away from his blissful face. The eyes of the fox subtly began to narrow. Her stance was prone with her snout lowered beneath her shoulder blades.

A handful of silent seconds passed until the fox slowly lifted her eyes back to where the two had come from. Noticing the broken link of their gaze, the raven turned his head in a moment of remembrance, back in the direction of the wolf. They had run into an area where the woods had begun growing noticeably denser, where shade ruled over sunlight. Still, among the slits between the trunks, a grey silhouette seemed to trudge towards them. Even from this distance, it was easy to tell that the wolf's walk had a certain sulk to it. The fox looked back down at her dance partner. She looked about his body, at his wing, his head, his breast. Then she slowly twisted herself around and continued trotting off in the opposite direction. The raven bobbed from left to right, let out a stifled caw and then fluttered away after her.

Meanwhile, the wolf stared out at them. He was intent on keeping a line of sight with the fox but struggled to do so as the distant pair slid into the thickening cluster of trees. He straightened his neck and altered his pace to a hurried trot. The fox was small compared to him – practically prey really – but not to his friend, whose high-tailed nature gave him an impulsivity that might, in the right (or wrong) circumstance, get him into trouble. Before he could reach them, the fox and raven had resumed their darting and dancing. A black and red blob shifted about in the far distance. As they carried on, the blobs turned into balls, the balls into dots, the dots into specks.

At times, the fox let out a crass high-pitched shout in honour of their youthful adventuring that seemed to egg on the raven's delirious swooping. The presence of the wolf gave him a sense of security, kinship and comfort, while being alongside the fox gave a unique sense of rebellion, impulse and above all, an empowering recklessness. The raven hadn't resolved to permanently choose one over the other but in the company of the fox, he'd found himself quite forgetful of his friend. Probably, when he was drained of energy, it would be better to settle in the stillness of the wolf's company.

In a quick moment, the fox shifted her pace back to a rushing high. She charged fast enough to get ahead of the raven's flight path. Taken by the fun surprise, he flapped his wings harder to get back to a frantic chase with the fanciful fox. She precariously and expertly hurdled over gnarled roots, uneven hills and slippery snow patches. It was oddly a far cry from the oafish behaviour she'd first approached the duo with. In the time it took the bird to match her speed, she'd gained a good bit of distance away from him. Once she was about twenty feet ahead, she keenly swept her feet across the ground, slid along her back paws and made a spin that left her completely facing the opposite way. She was now looking straight ahead at the raven. He was flying low but fast. She stretched her paws out and ducked her head down to glimpse under the bird as he swooped closer. Behind him, she saw no sign of the wolf.

She straightened her head back up. The raven was heading for her at an oblivious speed. She stretched her jaw, opening it as wide as she possibly could. Dense with saliva, she hung her tongue out to the left in order to move it out of the way, as if she were making room inside her maw; room for the naïve bird.

In a panic, his wings flustered cartoonishly in the air as he tried to pull back. He cawed out in distress and attempted to careen away from the open mouth. His body contorted into unfocused directions until he recollected his instincts and pushed both of his wings back with enough speed to swerve upwards, narrowly avoiding the fox's teeth by a feather. She snapped her empty jaws shut as the frightened bird continued to luge through the air, up into the overhead leaves and twigs.

He had done enough to avoid the worst but was still flapping uncontrollably. Half out of his wits, his breast smacked into a branch, causing him to spin erratically towards the ground where he thudded down. Cushioned by the snow and soft soil beneath, he didn't suffer any serious physical injury, but his mind was still in a state of shock. As he wriggled around on his back, he could hear the fox looking onwards and chortling. He rolled onto his front and picked his feet up, turning to observe the amused pup sarcastically laughing with an unattractive screech. The raven was on edge, but stopped to consider that this was just one of her jokes. But the bird didn't share the same sense of humour, refusing to chime in with her hysterical reaction. Her giggling died down as she noticed she was the only one enjoying the moment, until she was once again fell silent.

In an uncomfortably short span of time, her disposition had changed from silly to sly. She stepped slowly and menacingly towards the raven. An egotistical glare held the residue of her laughter. As she slunk into his personal space, the raven let out a meek caw as if to say, "Yep, that was a good joke, wasn't it? You sure got me!"

He hoped that this was all just fun and games. The ginger devil looked back up to the forest where she once again saw no movement and no wolf, just trees and privacy. She looked back down on the bird and bared her teeth... a grin?

No.

The grin turned to a snarl.

Her brow ruffled and her teeth opened, sliding against each other like kitchen knives being sharpened. She let out a sinister bark as she viciously snapped her teeth at the raven.

Thankfully, he'd spied her changing disposition and creeping grimace before she had a chance to lunge, and pushed backwards with his talons, propelling himself into the air and barely avoiding a toothy demise. He fled over the top of the fox as fast as he had ever flown before. She leapt upwards in a second attempt to nab her victim. Despite being way off her mark, her quick motion was a terrifying reminder to the bird of her sharp reflexes.

He darted away like a rocket, with the tenacious heartbreaker in pursuit. The trees, while thin, spindled off into an array of wooden webbing that would surely catch the raven if he simply tried to fly upwards, similar to how he'd crashed into them when he'd first escaped the fox's bite. He was trapped down here between the trees with her.

He tilted his wings in order to make an arc to the right, sharp enough to turn around but wide enough to not reverse back into the fox. His goal was to head back towards the safety of the wolf, but his pursuer was maintaining an admirable pace, refusing to let go of the lofty fool. In light of their earlier affair, it was unclear to the raven if this had been her plan all along; if she'd truly enjoyed their dancing but had grown bored and hungry just as quickly. Or was it that to the fox, her friends and her meals were interchangeable, each to be guzzled down quickly and then replaced by another once the hunger had set in again.

The wolf trod on some distance behind. He was almost trying to show a sense of non-concern but was still sure he was tracking along their path. Little footprints in the snow and fallen black plumage gave away the trail. This was a standout trait of his and what made him such a good hunter – intense observation that quickly assessed and resolved any situation. On the exterior he could portray a sense of calmness, while on the inside he reasoned and calculated. In actuality, he was terribly concerned about keeping track of the pair and knew that this show of coolness was only for himself. It would be immediately stripped away if there came a sign of distress, such as an irregularity in the trail or a drop of blood. That sign came soon enough.

Far off ahead, a black phantom swept in and out between the lapses in the trees. It was flying at an alarmingly fast speed. At first, the wolf didn't know whether it may be the same bird or not – his companion wasn't in such a frightful hurry the last time he saw him. But then the shadow let out a distinctive squeal of distress that the wolf had known well since the ordeal of the thunderstorm. Bewilderingly, the raven was flying off past the wolf. The panic of the experience had done more than disorient his emotions; his direction was also muddled, his bearings a few dozen feet ahead of where he thought the wolf would be. The hound watched as a red arrow shot quickly across the same path, not far behind the bird.

Another fearful shriek.

He put two and two together.

Instantly, he shot off like a bolt. He veered right to match their trail, pushing his paws down hard, trying to pierce the top layer of slippery dirt and get extra traction beneath. No effort was to be spared. He treated the chase the same way he would treat a hunt; a matter of life and death. He was intent on saving his companion.

In the raven's mind, a haze of anxiety continued to obscure everything but his focus on survival, so much so that he didn't even notice the rising sound of crushing water that he was flying towards. In a sudden minute, he had emerged onto a rough bank that overlooked a set of hazardous rapids. The water fled over punished rocks and stranded outcrops, beating them constantly with its icy flow. The above-most rapid had a distinctively steeper dip than the others, trying its hardest to imitate a waterfall. The bank was made up of large, jagged boulders that looked like they had taken their fair share of abuse from the river, presumably at times when it was at its angriest and had overflowed from the boundaries of its creek. The treeline had immediately come to a cut-off at the footing of the rocky shore - either they were unable to sprout beyond the pebbled flooring, or they didn't dare grow any nearer to the fury of the gushing river.

Flashes of the wolf's visage echoed throughout the lonesome bird's mind. He would be safe if he kept flying over the river where the fox couldn't follow. He decided instead, however, to drop onto the stony floor and scuttle behind one of the large boulders. The bird was uncomfortably close to the water's edge, hidden in the shade behind the rock and out of sight from the angle of the treeline. He remained there, statuesque from fear and without a single hop or head shake that might give him away. The only sign that he was still alive was the pulsing of his heart, putting the nearby rapids to shame in its speed and intensity.

His fiery pursuer slithered out of the trees. Pebbles rumbled under every footstep, acting as a crushing countdown of her approach towards the waterline. She looked up towards the open blue sky to consider the likelihood that she had lost her prey. She then looked back at the gushing water, recognising its treacherousness. To her immediate left, the ground sloped alongside the adjacent rapids and roughly dipped downwards. It was a gradual slide that an animal with sure footing and extreme caution could manage to descend, but a less than careful creature would more than likely slip on one of the loose rocks; in a worst-case scenario, this would mean tumbling not down to the bottom of the incline, but off to the side and into the pummelling rapids. The fox peered into the air. No sign of any fleeing birds. Then, she turned back to look at the woods they had come from. No sign of any avenging wolves. At the very least, it seemed she wouldn't face any repercussions from the raven's angered sidekick.

The raven stood frozen behind his hiding spot, with the fox just a few dozen feet away on the other side. He could just jet off into the air and over the river to escape the encroaching predator, but in the time they'd spent hunting and surviving, he'd come to associate the very idea of safety with the thought of the wolf so that now, that was all he could think of to flee towards. He knew they hadn't crossed this dangerous creek from where they'd come, which means the wolf hadn't come this way, and to find his friend, he'd have to head back into the forest. Flying up and away from the wooded area would also be flying away from the wolf's position, the opposite of what he wanted. He shouldn't have fluttered so far ahead to begin with but had gotten caught up in his own gullible excitement. The little bird was immediately bogged down by a sense of regret. His internal focus was suddenly broken when he heard the patter of the fox's paws inching closer to the waterline; inching closer towards the boulder he was hiding behind. He couldn't see her but heard two deep nerve-shaking inhalations. She'd caught a scent.

Her paw steps inched closer. They were followed by another set of deep sniffs. The raven kept his silence. His heartbeat thundered through his veins hard enough to rattle against his tiny skull, making it sound heavy and cavernous. The thunderstorm and all the panic it had once induced now found its way back inside the bird's messed mind. The fox's snout was practically pressed up against the rock when she took one last deep sniff. She snarled again. It was a raspy high-pitched tone that almost seemed to say,

"Got you!"

Then, in a surprising turn of fearlessness, the raven leapt up onto the stone from where he was hiding. The fox skipped backwards as she was caught off-guard by the raven's reckless appearance. Almost out of apparent madness, the bird then decided to parade around on the rock, squawking and flicking his wings about as he had once done to distract an elk. Her head tilted, focussing all her attention on the bird's dance. She responded with a similarly mad reaction, cackling along jokingly as she slid within closing distance. Their resemblance was apparent, and it was clear to the bird that in some way, she had enjoyed their short time laughing and dancing together. While she was a violent predator, they were both still oddballs to some degree. In the face of the end, the bird's last wish seemed to be sharing one final hearty dance. One last toast to the disastrous end of their romance. But the fox didn't seem to savour connections like the bird. She chose to gobble down their relationship like a meal and then quickly moved on to the next treat. In favour of her instant gratification, she'd chosen to stay alone, and this would always be the case as long as she put greed first. But that wasn't how the raven lived. His emotions were high, and his heart was full. Because of this, he had formed at least one close companionship that transcended the animality of the wilderness; one that he could count on.

While the bird had seemingly been seized by some maddening reaction to his own doom, in reality his panic had been relieved by a passing shadow. A known scent. The feeling of familiar company. A silver ghost moved through the trees. The raven had caught on to its presence from around the corner of the rock, prompting a relay of courage that led to his joyous display. It had become like clockwork in their hunts – the raven would cause an unthreatening distraction and draw the target's full attention as the wolf crept up for the advantage. Whatever advanced sense of sight or hearing the fox had, the raven sought to distract it with loud squawks and excessive hopping.

An image from behind the fox cradled the raven's mind with the comfort of living another day, and certainly not doing it alone. As carefully and silently as he knew how, the wolf inched towards the raven's assailant until his nose was as close to her tail as her snout was to the raven's rock. His golden stare glistened of an emotion different from either mechanical hunting or automatic survival. In his eyes blazed a look of contempt, pinpointed towards the fox like a burning sunbeam. This usurper had tried to hurt his friend and he loathed her for it.

She licked her lips, now standing face to face with the raven. She was starving and arrogant enough to give up questioning why he wasn't moving to save himself. He could just as easily try to fly off over the raging river that ran right behind him. But she didn't consider that. Not that she wasn't a cunning and observant creature, but she was steeped in an arrogant sense of reward. She hadn't just hunted a good meal, she'd gotten a good game out of it too, tricking both the raven and outperforming the wolf. She's played with her food, so to speak. Had her cake and was about to eat it too.

Every creature that hunts does so for necessity in order to survive. There's a natural urge that they need to satisfy to continue living. This is hunger. But some beasts have a perverse level of hunger. They seek to take more than they should or take what they don't really need.

This is beyond natural hunger; this is greed. It's a sense that arrests all animals who struggle to survive in the wild at least once in their lifetime, as their stomachs grow emptier, and their minds grow delirious and selfish. It turns patience into compromise, standards into desperation, and cunning into foolishness.

So greedy was the fox at that moment that she hadn't even noticed the shift in sunlight. A large grey shade now hung over her. The rapids continued to roar close by, but their tone began to shift, from a hissing rush to a broad and daunting tremor. No, it wasn't shifting. This new resonant tremor was separate alongside them. Though it was just as ferocious and treacherous, this sound wasn't coming from the rapids. It was a growl coming from behind her. She slowly slipped out of her self-indulgent fantasy and in a moment, the lack of sunlight became apparent. She suddenly felt the vengeful chill of this new shadow. Before she'd even had the chance to fully turn around and face her aggressor, he let out a smouldering snarl. Its depth and echo was something that the raven had never heard him make before. It was both a trait and an advantage of the wolf to make noise only when he needed to and when he did, he made sure that he was heard. His bark was mature and confident and full of acid. It was close and unexpected to the fox, genuinely convincing her that this was her end.

With sweet irony, the same level of confusion and fear and helplessness that she'd inflicted onto the poor raven now shot through her own bones, like medicine forced down her throat. Her first instinct was to run in the most natural direction – away from the danger. In this case, away was towards the raven, the rock, and the water.

The bird quickly paddled into the air to avoid the sprinting fox, but he needn't have worried about her making any attempt at him – her mind was only focussed on escape. In her disorientation, the instinct to vault over the boulder only came late and she clumsily tumbled over it as she tried to sprint away. She tripped head over shoulders, her hip bounced off the side of the rock and made a graceless splash into the sweeping river behind it. Water was thrown everywhere in the same manner as the snow she had first emerged from. After the eruption of her impact, the droplets fell back to the surface and returned to the mass of water that continued to violently flow.

The wolf and raven looked down into the chaos. They saw no sign of the fox as the coursing water rushed by. Moments passed. The same frenzied and freezing river that had caused her to hesitate moments earlier had seemingly become her retribution. That was until her black ears and sulking snout popped back up; soaking, spluttering and pathetic.

Quickly, the river dragged the fox towards the precipice of the first rapid to their left, the one that preceded the other gushing steps as the tallest and most intimidating waterfall – a deadly drop. Two flaying paws splashed around as she let out helpless bleats. The fox feared for her life as she floated closer to her demise, in some way calling out for pity from the surviving duo. However, the nature of animals is to give back only what's given to them. When treated with kindness, they show compassion in return and when shown hostility, it's only fair dues that they show no goodwill to those who were aggressive towards them. So, considering they had witnessed her own ill intentions towards the raven, her onlookers felt no remorse or sorrow for her. The fox wouldn't have felt guilty for the raven if she had succeeded in getting her own way. The factor that connected all three of them, as well all other animals like them, was the simplicity in their philosophy. Self-benefit drove all their actions. They felt no guilt for hunting or stealing or scavenging because it led to the ultimate point: their own individual survival. Even the wolf and raven, with their sympathetic alliance, were still each helping to feed themselves through the other, realising that their own hunger and their own goals could be fulfilled much easier with the other's help. Even when the wolf had saved the raven in the thunderstorm, he internally surmised that the play they had shared had made *him* feel happy and full of life. He protected the raven so that he could keep feeling that essence of liveliness and companionship.

Even selflessness, in some way, was a selfish act. The fox provided no benefit for either of them, and she couldn't see past her own short-term sense of self-satisfaction. So, as they heard one final shriek cascade over the highest rapid and out of view, they apathetically sat and watched in the belief that it was either going to be the fox's end, or the raven's. They proceeded towards the sloping pathway beside the rapids. The wolf carefully skimmed down the gradual slide until the floor straightened out at the bottom. The raven simply flew down onto the flat land below.

Once they were at the bottom of the bank beside the rapid's end, they both turned to look up at the daunting collection of falls. After the first hefty drop, the angle became more obtuse and sloped down into another three or four bubbling rapids. The water churned and parted around divisive outcrops of various sizes that stood stranded in the middle of the river. With them, the dazed and soaking fox had fallen into an unfortunate position, having rolled onto a small and sturdy outcrop. After a moment of unconsciousness, she came back to her senses and stood up, then tried in vain to shake the damp mass from her fur. Her eyes were drowned in ice water and self-pity. On either side of the outcrop, dangerous churning water confined her to her tiny prison of a rock.

She howled an ugly screech. She expected no sympathy from the two after her actions yet was desperate for rescue. Still, even if they were in a forgiving mood, they had no way to reach her. The wolf couldn't cross the water on foot and the raven's wings were too light and weak to carry the fox back to shore. The position she'd gotten herself in needed a different kind of help. Neither of them, in their particular species, had the ability to rescue her. Perhaps the right animal would come along for her. Perhaps not. The two companions took one last look at the fox, who never stopped her futile cries as they turned and walked away. Eventually, her whimpering voice faded, leaving the tempered beast and her devilish intentions stranded alone in the cold water.

5

FLYING COLOURS

The companions continued to trek through the rising woodland, heading northward against the wind. The high-pitched whistle of the breeze sounded almost like the fox's adolescent cries calling after them, until it too disappeared into the unimpeded air of open valleys. They crossed large pastures in an awkward contradiction to the other wildlife, who had hidden within the trees and buried themselves away from the decreasing temperatures. The two were almost oblivious to the shifting season and instead took each new day as it came, failing to realise that chillier days were growing more common while the bounties of large prey and lush greenery were growing less abundant.

Now and again, they would stop for sips of water at puddles and streams or catch a measly critter that would hold them over for a spell. Any sustenance was useful, plus they were sure that any dip in quality and abundance was merely a temporary moment of poorer circumstances and that their tenacity to go against the grain would eventually be rewarded with richer fruits. Most animals fled south or hid away to sleep through the rising cold, but pushing onward against the natural flow meant that anything left in the untapped parts of the world would be theirs for the taking. All they had to do was stay strong of heart and endure the cold until they could enjoy the plentiful air of the mountain tops. As shallow as their snowy blankets were, the plains were mostly empty of larger game and any deer whose path they did cross could see the disturbing dot of the wolf coming from a great distance. Still, they continued to hope that something would come along to break the monotony of the inspirationless fields and soon enough, their philosophy on perseverance was rewarded.

Over an empty pasture, the duo happened upon a picturesque pool of glistening water. It was fairly large in circumference but still humbly hidden away between a meadow and an inclining forest; something halfway between a pond and a lake. Behind it rose a steadily rising slope of slate rocks. They were dotted with trees that grew high and slender on sparse dirt patches in-between the stone. It was something like a natural set of benches, where the trees sat and watched the games that would erupt from the gathering animals around the water below. Past the highest point of the rocks, the slope turned back into flatland where the trees had full reign to grow and turned back into a forest that lay beyond the lake. The foremost pines that peered over the lake were in full view of the landscape that the wolf and raven approached from. Looking up at the trees, the wolf noticed that their greenery was broken up by an outlandish and plentiful amount of white, pink and yellow dots that could've been mistaken for bloomed flowers. In reality, these heights were home to thrushes, plovers, turtledoves, gallinules, woodpeckers and a symphony of other visually musical birds that stared down, twittering as the wolf and raven approached the lake.

The hound stepped up to the water's edge. Its surface was so calm that it perfectly resembled a single unwarped sheet of glass. Even the coming breeze that skimmed across the meadows seemed to swerve clear of the water in respect for its stillness. Peering down below its surface, he saw the image of another wolf. He had no criticism of its appearance – no blemishes he would remove, no fat he would add or take away, no bones he felt should be reoriented. As far as wolves go, it looked like a fine wolf (although he always preferred looking at birds rather than his own kind.) Its pupils glistened with a golden optimism. Its snout was perky and angled slightly upwards, sitting cutely yet awkwardly between a raised brow and a bold jaw. Its teeth were yellowed and large, goofy yet effective. It had ears slightly too big for its head that poked up and outwards like satellites. Looking down at the other wolf, his head made a quaint tilt and the other wolf mimicked his movement. After a moment of confusion, he recognised that what he was looking down at wasn't a real animal. It wasn't somebody else looking back, nor was it really himself. It moved when he moved and blinked when he blinked. He even determined that, because the image reflected his movements, it must also be a reflection of his appearance. That those were his large ears and cute snout and golden eyes. But he knew this was just a reflection of his image. It wasn't the real him.

He turned to see the raven, who also hopped up to the lakeside and similarly looked down into the water. The same bird appeared underneath the lake too. It looked how the raven looked and moved how he moved. Though he didn't know how it was possible, that was definitely the same raven under the water because he could see him and his mirror image moving together. So, he determined the other wolf must be him. He saw the raven experiencing a similar internal process as he also tilted, stared down and looked back at the wolf. He was going through the same curiosity in trying to recognise himself. The wolf thought that shortly – hopefully – seeing him and his mirror image together would help ground the raven's conclusions, as well as help him to realise that the other bird was an accurate representation of his own appearance too. The two couldn't see themselves separately, only their reflections, so being able to see somebody else stand beside their own image helped to rationalise this confusion. They were glad to have each other at that point, to help them reason themselves.

The two pulled from their reflections and trotted around the right edge of the pool. Perhaps it was time for another small rest, they thought, as they approached the rocky climb around the other side. Though its face was littered with many flat areas at different elevations, they were parted by smooth angles that were quite slimy due to regular cold mists and the nearby watering hole. This wasn't a problem for the raven who, either out of encouragement or thoughtlessness, chose to simply flutter up to one of the trees on the very top where all the other birds were perched. They had all craned their necks around to watch the newcomers. The wolf attempted to clamber up the side of the slates but already had trouble finding much friction. His paws scuffled around here and there as he jogged up the damp stones, taking a great deal of effort and energy to make any progress. It reminded him of the soggy mudslide he'd climbed up during the storm and hopefully, there was a similarly pleasant rest to look forward to once he'd reached the top. The other birds continued to stare on in fascination. Having no experience struggling with a climb, they were unsympathetic to the wolf's effort.

He aimed for the small dirt patches that would ease his grip, but these were few and far between and acted more as checkpoints than regular footholds. Amid his climb, the wolf failed to find any grip on the sleek slates. Suddenly his paw slipped, his leg buckled, and he tumbled onto his left side. The surface was so sopped with water that he slid frictionless down the rock face towards the edge that overlooked the lake and before he even knew that he'd slipped, he was flung off the side. A buffoonish splash sounded out, hitting the punchline of the wolf's watery humiliation. Seconds later, his head bobbed up from the water and he paddled clownishly back out of the pool with obvious frustration on his face.

The fall hadn't hurt, nor was it a far drop, but he didn't enjoy or expect to be soaked. Paddling back to shore, he heard the audience of birds twittering with laughs. He wriggled out of the lake and tried vigorously to shake the water from his fur. Once he had cleared off most of the moisture, he decided to give the hill a second attempt. With his legs burning and his tongue panting from effort, the third time was the charm as he finally reached the top where he took a seat on a flat step beside the raven's tree. Once he was settled, his gaze drifted upwards to the foliage high above. His friend was peering down on him from a branch along with some other notable birds that surrounded him.

On the tree beside the raven was a friendly-looking cormorant. This was a slender-necked bird with an impressive wingspan and a quiet disposition, yet when he did speak, his call was deep and comfortable, not unlike the raven's, though more mature. Nearby, a red robin and a blue jay sat on a lower branch. The robin was rotund and rosy like all ravens but sat with a stiff dourness, portraying mannerisms that contradicted the bouncy nature you would normally associate with the species. The blue jay looked unkempt and almost half-asleep as he sat wavering from side to side. The robin tweeted incessantly as if ranting, while the blue jay stood apparently ignorant to the noise, looking happy enough. Possibly they had travelled together just like the wolf and his companion – maybe for much longer – and it meant the blue jay was used to the constant yapping by now. They looked like an odd match up, but then so did the wolf and raven and similarly, the blue and red birds had an air of inexplicable compatibility.

Underneath the cormorant's perch sat a fierce cardinal with a burning red coat. He wore a stylish spike of hair plucked upwards between his eyes. He was snuggled protectively into the side of another bird sitting next to him; a plump warbler with a heart of gold so pure and bright that it radiated through the bird's breast and gave him a buttery jacket. From a distance, the two brothers formed the image of a single striking flame. The collection of birds sat in concert to a relentless knocking sound coming from far up inside one of the few dead trees. The beat came from the constant hardcore tapping of a woodpecker. Repeated jolting movements had shaken the small bird's umber feathers into a static flurry. He was the scruffiest looking bird you could imagine, unapologetically carrying on with his rattling music, but he provided a sort of rhythm that echoed and gave the woods a sense of ambience and liveliness.

Beyond this band, the numerous other trees provided a multitude of wondrous and unique misfits too dense to mention individually, but each with a pair of wings and a singular charming identity. Hummingbirds of indigo and sapphire; tints rarely seen so strong in the natural world. Titmice sporting tufted haircuts with the confidence of teenage trendsetters. Bluebirds and buntings so bright in shade that they resembled accidental splats of imaginative paint on a landscape otherwise dulled by realism. A collection of monochrome magpies gathered on a single long tree branch as if imitating a vintage black and white photograph. No matter what direction you looked out at the forest, a parade of vividness hung on the branches like confetti in a spider's web. The wolf sat in awe at their diversity and how much their differences tied them even closer together. This was just one of the reasons he preferred birds. His metallic pupils gleamed in their presence.

A sound, song or squawk would echo out from time to time – especially a complimentary beat from the nearby woodpecker – yet for the most part, the tree-laden lakeside had a muted solitude to it. It was oddly soothing, the kind of peaceful silence that he'd usually find in a dark hole. It was as if all these wonderfully artistic masters of aviation had gathered here to hide from the rest of the world, in case the drab realities of its life tried to fade their colours. Here, where the trees grew tall and their branches only started far up the trunks, they could sit in the lofty heights and never touch the ground. The light show of feathers was almost strong enough to reflect off the wolf's own empty grey fur. In a placid state, heavy with water but also gentility, the wolf felt as though he were safe among the birds and could be part of the flock.

Maybe he was just another one of the birds, except with a coat of fur rather than feathers and teeth instead of a beak. He turned upwards to see his closest of flying friends, the raven. He would have no problem fitting in with all these outcasts. He was an acrobat like them, a symbol of levity and unrestricted exploration. His flight was expressive, and his call was full of volume and melody. His personality was woven not just in his behaviour but his biology; he preferred having his head in the clouds and rebelling against the restrictive force of gravity, a goal unachievable by any other animal except a bird. The cries and pitches of the birds formed a slow-moving concerto of multiple notes and voices. The red cardinal bounced on his branch in a youthful dance.

The raven, one for shaking things up, decided that the energy of the surrounding pals was wasted sitting in the trees. He broke the peace of the soft song with an impeding yet inspiring croak to which all the other birds snapped silent and turned their heads. He took a mighty push off his branch then navigated between the few trees that separated their spot from the water's precipice before exploding out of the forest and over the lake. He flew towards the opposite side of the shore then turned around and dipped downwards closer to the surface. Then, he began circling and waving through the air above the still water. The light of the sun mirrored off the pristine surface, creating something like an upwards spotlight. The lake was transformed into his stage where he showed off his unabashed personality. Through the gaps in the trees, the wolf and the birds gazed at his confident gliding. They were in awe of his ability to fly ahead and play around on impulse. Before long, the raven's spirit inspired the rest of them to join in the fun. It was firstly the blue jay that followed the raven into the air, still ignoring the robin. He followed behind in the sky as he created a dipping and spinning that contrasted the raven's own pattern, where they would meet each other in the middle as they flew upwards and downwards respectively. The robin, in jealousy of the fun, was the next to take off. He flew in a wobbly uncoordinated pattern in the complete opposite direction around the same circle above the lake, puffing hard and very nearly bumping into the two as they eventually all passed each other.

The cardinal and warbler jetted off in unison with an instinctive timing that showed how naturally they flew about together. The cardinal's burning red coat joined the growing flock, moving with them but still embracing his own side-to-side pattern within the fun. Behind him, the small warbler fluttered and panted off, drafting his brother and almost tapping into his energy to join in the game. He also bobbed in his own funny way. The woodpecker almost seemed to double take as he took a moment to shift from his music towards the airborne dance floor. It took some focus for him to break away from doing his own thing before he grew eager to merge with the circle of birds. He kept his body straight as his head rocked back and forth, wavering about in the centre of the ring and paying little attention to whether he might cross the path of another bird. Looking on from the nearby tree, the cormorant turned to the wolf and gave him a friendly call of acknowledgement before slowly extending his wide wings and taking off to join the antics. He was much larger than the others and flew up and down with a steeper and more pointed arc, yet still fit in with the dance of the misfits.

Like a troupe of friends skating on a roller rink, the flock of free spirits circled around the edge of the water in their own distinct way. To the wolf, their instant camaraderie was intoxicating to see. In a sudden flurry, relentless numbers of other birds took off from the trees, creating a mighty rushing sound and shaking every branch and leaf as they fled past. The wind that they created swept along with them, blowing hard against the wolf's fur. He almost felt like he was about to take off himself. A monumental array of them - at least one hundred – was shaken loose from the forest's limbs and before long, an enormous galaxy of chromatic shards swam through the sky above the lake. Most followed the raven's circuit above the water while others went in the opposite direction. Some went up and down, a few skimmed the inner surface of the pool. Some water lovers dove in and out. Some daredevils reached for the clouds. Soon enough, it was impossible to discern any pattern whatsoever as the birds waltzed frantically over the surface of the lake. Now fizzing with chaotic colour, its slick reflective screen resembled clustered static, a different show to be watched within each unique bird. Among the gathering, somewhere, danced the raven; lost in a flurry of excitement, impulse and belonging.

Without wings, the wolf watched on. He looked down towards the slope he had climbed up from; the one that had caused him such great effort, while the raven had simply flown up. He then thought on the mountains they were heading towards and wondered if he would struggle so hard to conquer their slopes, while the raven flew on ahead. Though he felt some sense of comfort and intrigue among birds, he realised in that moment how vital the freedom of flight was in order to be one of them. They were all different in their own way, but they could all still fly free. None among them were as different and on their own than he was.

There was an impulsivity for the sake of impulsivity that was inherent to them, and it seemed their minds were as fluttersome as their behaviour. Meanwhile, he was a creature that needed to think before he acted, and it was more natural for him to plan a hunt than jump straight into a game. His personality was woven not just in his behaviour but his biology; he stayed grounded and had to earn his place among the heights through the struggle and effort of a climb. He was in adoration (and admittedly envy) of their ability to fly. Perhaps it was this admiration of birds that gravitated him towards the raven. Nevertheless, he sat watching their colourful fun from the ground, unable to join in due to his very nature. His lack of wings frustrated him greatly.

6

THE HUNT

To most animals, the idea of home is defined one of two ways: the place that they're most familiar with (usually the area where you spend most of your time or the den where you were raised), or is a concept applied to the position, company or state where you feel the most comfortable (hence the phrase 'home is where the heart is'.) The first definition never quite applied to the wolf and was one of the reasons he had taken to venturing alone, free from a pack. But although he felt content among the birds by the lake, he didn't feel at home among them either. This wasn't the place where he felt a sense of similarity; he sat on the ground while they perched in tree branches above. This was also not the place he was most comfortable, as he could barely move across the slippery slate rocks and had little more to do than sit and nap. While he could keep up with one little raven who still pulled back his flight to stick by the wolf, he felt out of sync in the company of an entire flock. If the raven weren't as taken with him as he was with the bird, he could just as easily fly off into the air where the wolf couldn't follow.

The raven seemed to have this strange ability to make everyone feel included, the empathetic and emotional being that he was. All other creatures seemed to gravitate towards him. He happily flew around with the other birds and rolled around on the floor with the dogs. No type of play was out of bounds for the scrappy young creature.

But to survive, no animal can stay in one place forever. The other birds had realised this. The colour in the trees grew sparser over the many days that the two spent by the lakeside as many of them had followed the direction of the wind and naturally flown south to avoid the oncoming chill. Without their joyful plumage to lighten the area, the greyness of the trees became more apparent, especially now they'd shed their naturally colourful leaves. Among the birds that had departed were the suave cardinal and friendly warbler, who had gone to find their own way. The wolf lamented their empty branch as he stared at it through a rising steam that rolled out from his nostrils. The air was getting even colder, and he understood why the two pleasant birds had to leave. Winter was around the corner.

But south wasn't his direction. Contrary to all the birds, mice, deer and foxes that gave in to the season and escaped to tepid climates, he still wondered hard about what rewards lay through the blizzard. He was set on continuing north; he was determined to go upwards.

A creaking noise and a heavy constriction rippled through his stomach. The lake's scant offerings of freshwater morsels weren't enough for him; the wolf craved some larger fulfilment. A deep hunger was setting back in. He turned from the cardinal's branch to look at the raven who was lying next to him. He'd nestled his head deep into the wolf's breast to quell the cold, with a miniature stack of icy breath floating upwards from his beak. The bitterness of winter wasn't something he usually had to bear - like the other birds, he was accustomed to flying south and it was only through the wolf's inclination to push north that he had to bear the cold at all. The wolf looked down at his shivering ally perhaps realising this, but he was confident in himself and determined to not only make it up the distant mountains but keep his friend safe and warm while he did so. The raven trusted him to do this as he ruffled his ally's fur around with his head.

The lake lay encased in a deeper silence than usual thanks to the lack of birds. A family of oblivious ducks floated softly along the water in a uniformed direction, reminding the wolf of how lovable a place this was, as he gave a look – his last look – toward the refuge of the lakeside. He then lifted his body from the floor with a slow reluctance. The raven jostled about as he moved and then tipped over as he stood up. The bird's half-dozed eyes and wavering head sprung into their usual alertness. He saw the wolf looking out into the deeper woods, ready to depart. He was also reluctant to leave as he'd found some solidarity in the gathering of misfits and felt a sense of security here. But unlike the other birds, this was a scavenger bird and he too needed to feed his hunger for fresh meat and inquisition, instead of languishing by a lakeside. Unlike them, he wasn't just a bird; he was a wolf-bird. Like his companion before him, he took one last look at his frolicking flock of friends (the ones that remained, at least.) Most of them were still asleep in the stiffening dew of the morning. After stealing a photograph of them for his memory, he hovered up to perch on the wolf's back and they set off once again into the wilds.

Behind them, the waterside hamlet began to fade away between the rising grey trunks until after a few minutes of walking, it had disappeared completely into the past. Further into the forest's depths, the trees became more winter-favouring. Most still retained their overhead canopy and the few leafless trees had grown thick plentiful limbs. Even without their foliage, it was difficult for the sun to pierce through the flurry of spindling branches. Less sun meant not only a lack of light, but also a lack of heat and the growing frost in the air became so apparent here that it had formed a melancholy mist. Though the two could see through the haze well enough, it was only to about fifty feet. It gave the journey ahead a dull and purgatorial appearance, where the following stretch of miles would pale in comparison to the vibrancy and comfort of the lake. Yet they felt obligated to push through the featureless woods.

For a while, their wandering stayed monotonous and without direction or play. The shift from steady comfort to droning progression had dampened the raven's spirits. It felt more like a task they had to push through rather than a passionate adventure they had thrown themselves into. The wolf didn't mind; although the tone was gloomy, this forest was an environment he was more accustomed to, and he was especially well-adapted to finding something warm-blooded to hunt among the woods. Where there were trees, there was life.

Once again, his stomach groaned.

With no sign of life around to quell their hunger and no light or colour to quell his restlessness, the raven grew impatient towards the lack of stimulation. In his anxiousness, he pushed off the wolf's back and scattered up to a leafless branch about twenty feet ahead, then turned to face him and let out a call in his direction. As the hound continued walking at the same steady pace, the raven started to caw at an even faster rate. The intention of these calls seemed vague - they were either cheers of encouragement for the wolf to keep going or yells of impatience for him to pick up his speed, implied through their increasing tempo.

The raven got into a pattern of fluttering forward a few trees, letting out cries until the wolf was underneath his branch and then flying ahead to another spot for him to catch up to. All the while, the wolf refused to quicken his pace. He strained his paws over roots and hoisted up steep hills. He was determined to move at his own speed. Besides that, it was a smarter move to reserve energy as it took him more effort to move forward than it did his flying friend and sprinting ahead may expel more energy that he might need later.

He thought back to the other birds; to their wings and the speed and freedom that they allowed. As he creaked his limbs forward and arrived under another of the raven's branches, the bird simply fluttered ahead again. He started up his impatient cawing; a caw that was beginning to sound irritating under the circumstances. Sometimes it didn't seem like the raven understood that the wolf didn't have wings like he did, or that it took more struggle for him to move forward. While he was an empathetic bird, he was also emotional and impulsive, sometimes lacking the correct approach to the context. He was sometimes a victim of his own sensitivity and at this point in time, had been overcome with impatience to find something interesting within the blank stale forest.

The trees here seemed almost of stone and sprouted without compromise from a crass terrain where tattered roots and bent saplings hung over mossy crags. Clearly this was an ancient forest where the trees grew monstrous and without compassion for the creatures and scenery around them. As the two strode on, rustles came from under short bushes and distant squeals echoed all around, planting the idea that there were living creatures about. But this was a weak simulation of life and on the outset, the forest always looked void of any movement besides themselves. The hum of a meek wind tried to blow through a barricade of redwoods, but the mist remained still, almost as if the breeze were just a feckless voice in the air that lacked its usual physical impact.

The friends floated through the fog of the woods almost as lost spirits trapped in a dream-like place, unknown to them not just in location but in essence. Forests, for as far as they could remember back, had been bustling yet restful, with wishful mornings and vibrant foliage. The age and overbearing grandeur of where they now were felt much more serious; almost deathly. They headed towards the growing sound of trickling water, the only familiar element that reminded them of the world's motions. They came to a gap where the trees parted, revealing the view of a timid stream only a few inches deep. It was flowing down a slope that was so humble, only the delicacy of water could sense the change in its elevation. But they weren't, they discovered, the only wandering creatures to stumble upon this forgotten watering hole.

Alone and greedily partaking from the stream, there stood a

world-worn and arrogantly large creature – a moose. Its visage came as such a surprise through the tightly clustered curtain of trees that the wolf had accidentally wandered out into the open by the time he saw it. Luckily for him the moose was preoccupied, lapping at the stream with its enormous tongue. The wolf did the first thing that came to mind and stood as stiff as a statue. He hoped, considering the moose hadn't seen him yet, that he could avoid its gaze by appearing motionless. Though unable to move, he eyed and analysed the beast as it kept still.

It drank with a gluttonous slurp, neck dipping down as though it couldn't get enough of the richness of the crystal water. Its eyes hung solemn and bulged with liquid as though they too were greedily drinking what sustenance the pure stream offered. Its eyelids drooped in the manner of an elderly man. A once snug and earthen-tinted coat of fur was now short-haired, tattered and silvered around the edges. The greatest tell of the moose's age was its stature, towering and bulky to an unrealistic extent that no other creature could hope to match. As the wolf stared on motionless, his stomach gargled with a wicked ache. To his own ears, the rumbling sounded obnoxiously loud and surely must have echoed through the clearing for the moose to hear. A thought wormed its way into his mind; the courageous possibility of taking down such a grand beast. In his usual way of overthinking and overplanning, he considered all the positives and negatives of the situation and how good his chances were.

The cons: the creature was muscular and probably difficult to take down, having managed to reach an obviously great age in such a wild world. Meanwhile he was short and light-footed and, more importantly considering the animal's size, alone.

The pros: he was confident, energetic, calculating, patient and tenacious whereas the moose looked clumsy, complacent and unaware considering it hadn't seen the wolf standing in plain sight. Besides that, he was healthy and spry whereas the moose looked like a victim of its age, with creaking limbs and apparent soreness whenever it made a movement. He had youth on his side.

The wolf stayed still and didn't attempt to move up on the beast in case he lost the element of surprise, but events moved on once the moose finished its drink and turned around to walk away in the opposite direction. As it took its tongue out of the stream, it raised its head upwards. This quick glance was its best chance to see the ravenous animal standing ahead. Instead, its eyeline simply dismissed the general colourless image it saw ahead of it, likely interpreting him as another grey rock. Contrary to the moose's poor perception, the wolf's head steadily panned with mechanical focus at every wavering tilt of his prey, tracking even the slightest gesture. After the moose had moved onto a safe distance, the hound followed. He decided it would be better to get in a position alongside it and cut a curve around the trees, fleeing like an assassin behind one trunk to another. He stayed out of sight, yet close by. Deep in thoughts of hunger and function, wrapped up in his element during the hunt; it was the side of the wolf that the raven loved to see the most. The side that would lead to fresh meat for the bird.

He had gone about his natural tendency to observe events from the greatest possible vantage point among the branches, with an excitement growing in his mind over how things would play out. In his giddiness, he seemed to misplace their dour setting; the forestry was dense, the air was murky, the contenders slow and cold this time around.

The moose's creaking stride gave the impression that its limbs were made of wood, with joints that seemed to break through splinters with each step forward. It was as if one of the ancient greyed and dying trees had refused its stationary fate, torn its roots out of the ground and sought to leave. The two newcomers keenly drafted the moose's trail. The wolf was starving and almost impatient, but in his intelligence knew that this was not the time to give into impulse. He needed an open area where his prey was steady enough for him to approach, where he could hit a vital point with certainty. This was no meagre chance for a small reward; this was an advanced challenge that required full focus from start to finish. He needed the right moment to snatch up the opportunity in his jaws.

The raven also began growing impatient. Since their meeting, their hunts had become like clockwork – with the raven making the first step to distract their prey while the wolf took over once the difficult first step had been made. But their prey had also become clockwork – weak isolated creatures like small mammals and goats and, on occasion, a lost deer or foal; anything that a lone wolf didn't have to put much effort into clashing with. This situation was vastly different and required a much more skilful approach, if he was capable of gaining an advantage at all. The moose needed to be brought down to his level with the first move. The raven wouldn't need to interject here.

The trees began to thin out, but with that came less chance for the wolf to glide behind one trunk to the next without being noticed. Another variable for him to consider in his ever-changing thought process. Always calculating, always careful, always thinking and thinking and overthinking, predicting every route that the events could go down and preparing a game plan for every possible outcome that might happ-

"CAW!"

An alarming and displeasing noise.

Both animals came to an immediate halt at the sound of the raven's cry. The moose turned with a sluggish wonder, the wolf with an electric panic. The bird had disturbed the silence of the woods, the hunt, and the flow of events. The wolf couldn't see precisely where his perching comrade was sitting, but still gave a look of wide-eyed intensity at some symbolic spot in the trees. Had it assumed that because such a strategy had worked once, it would work again? The circumstances had changed now; the details were different. The moose glanced through the mist, questioning where the sound had come from until the raven began noisily jittering on a nearby branch. He caught the beast's attention enough for it to look upwards, but it wasn't captivated or intrigued. All it saw was a silly harmless bird having some strange fit in a tree. So, it craned its head back around to dismiss the raven and continue walking. However, it didn't get a chance to take another step. In an act of unprepared anxiety, the wolf immediately dove with open claws and voracious teeth into the side of the moose.

The great creature grunted in shock. The push of the wolf caused it to lope sideways slightly, but the moose was so huge and steadfast that he failed to topple it. His fangs tried to pierce through the monster's hide, but it was too thick, causing the grip of his teeth to slip. The wolf fell away from the moose and onto his back against the ground. A jet of steam bellowed from its heavy snout, and it tried to hoof away, but moving quickly was not its strong suit. The wolf uprighted himself and gave chase. He nipped at the side of his prey, trying to cut slashes into its side and taking snaps at its bony legs in an attempt to bring it down, but each attempt was like trying to score through a thick sheet of leather with a blunt bread knife. He could feel the density of its hide and the strength of its stance. Meanwhile, the raven excitedly chortled from behind. From his perspective (and with more than a hint of presumptuousness), his instigation had worked. All he could see was a predator attacking a prey. It couldn't see what the wolf could feel.

He chased alongside the moose for a short distance until soon, they headed into a cul-de-sac of tightly knit trunks that created a claustrophobic entrapment. Even more now, the raven predicted victory. He eyed the closed-in environment as a similar setting to the circlet of trees that formed the meadow where his ploy to confuse the deer had previously worked. The wolf, still uncomfortably winging his attacks, saw things very differently. This moose was not a helpless young idiot. It wasn't intimidated by the wolf or scared to put up a fight. No animal with a plenitude of meat on its bones made it to such a long lifespan without fighting to keep it. It hadn't sprinted to escape the wolf, rather sprinted to try and gain space from its attacker so that it could get enough room to turn and prepare a charging attack. He couldn't risk taking such a swift hit from its massive antlers, so he tried staying in close, cutting the moose's chance at movement by going for the legs. It was his only option now. But having run into a dead end where the trees were too tight for it to continue, the moose was forced to turn anyway. It would surely stop and, having been backed into a corner, go all-out to defend itself. The raven envisioned victory. But the wolf was fighting against failure.

Sure enough, having been blocked by a barricade of trunks, the moose cantered around to face where they had just come from. The wolf butted and slashed against it the best he could - at times his effort would be rewarded, and he'd manage to scrape some blood from its skin. But the moose was a monolith that shadowed his size and though his body was a natural weapon, his claws were small against the grand canvas of the moose's hide. No matter how tenacious he was or how much he tried to think out his next attack, the sturdy old moose never seemed to go down. It only continued to huff and snort with contempt until, predictably, it swept its antlers down in an effort to bash the wolf. It didn't have the freedom to build up speed and charge them towards him, but still threw them down like a giant hand trying to crush a fly. Still, just as a hypersensitive fly can usually predict this and escape being squashed, each swipe of the antlers was keenly avoided by the dextrous wolf.

As it flayed its weapons around, it tried to cut back around the circlet of trees, possibly attempting to double back down the opening they had come from. All the while, it twitched and winced at each new gash that the wolf tore open. His tenacity began to pay off as more and more blood began to drip out of the beast's body. The liquid in its eyes became denser and like uncontainable tears, rolled down its jaw. As a last resort, the great creature turned its neck into its own body and charged with chaotic effort towards the wolf, who simply leapt away from the rushing moose with ease. It came to a halt as it spewed cold air out of its nostrils then turned to face its foe. Each contender now stood at either side of the circlet.

The wolf was panting with fatigue, his shoulders ebbing up and down with each great breath. Blood speckled his lips and teased his tongue with a warm vitality that would soon fill his stomach and end his irritating hunger. Literally tasting victory, he was once again optimistic that he would succeed in his hunt. He crept tactically around the side of the moose, away from the exit in the trees. This meant that the moose began slowly treading back towards the opening once more. The intelligent hound was hoping to utilise the moose's attempt at escape. Sure enough, when the exit was near enough against its back, the moose let its guard down and began to whip around to leave, exposing its side to the wolf; the side where he had inflicted the most damage. One good attack and he had the chance to tear an opening big enough to bring down his opponent. An audacious bark rang out as the dog pounced through the air towards his target.

The moment dragged on for the wolf. Despite the panic and the uncertainty of diving in headfirst, going without a plan had seemed to work out fairly well for him. He had acted just as he had seen other wolves act – they would get their pack together and all jump in, putting their want and hunger ahead of forethought. No hiding in a bush for minutes on end wondering about everything that could go wrong and how to correct for it. No frantic eyes whipping every which way considering the pros and cons. Like a raven diving from a branch in an unabashed instinct to dance in the air, all the other wolves that he'd known would often dive forward and let the wind and the emotion guide their hunts. For the first time, he felt that sense of impulsivity and it'd worked out for him. For the first time, with all four feet off the ground and a lofty assumption of victory in his head - unrestricted by the gravity of what could go wrong - he felt what the birds felt. He felt like he was flying.

The moment passed by.

His flight was brought down in an instant. It ended in the worst possible way.

On its own chaotic whim, the moose swung its antlers around to the side once more in an uncharacteristically flexible motion. Unlike a bird, the wolf couldn't control himself in the air – he couldn't flap himself out of the way. In all its strength and luck, the moose had made a random decision to swing back around at that moment and an antler met the trajectory of the wolf. The impact was intensified by the wolf's tempestuous speed as he careened through the air, making for a disastrous result.

A crack emanated from the wolf's chest. A cold shock immediately ran through his nerves, immobilising him with pain. Like a solid oak bat hitting a soft ball, the great swing of the antlers caused the wolf to soar frictionless through the air. He suffered further hurt as his back met the side of a tree, shaking the leaves above and causing the wood to creak. Another gross sting ignited inside his spine and pulsated through all of his limbs. His limp body slid down the trunk and thudded against the stiff roots. Above all the disgusting and visceral sounds of the impacts, the wolf made a noise that the raven had never heard him make before; a high-pitched whimper of pain.

The raven was in immediate distress. To him, the wolf had been undefeatable. He saw everything as an absolute; deer were larger than the wolf, moose were larger than the wolf. The wolf had defeated a deer. Therefore, the wolf would defeat a moose. But this was like watching a shield crack, or a mountain crumble. In response to the wolf's fall, the bird incessantly cawed and babbled as if crying out "oh my god!" over and over again out of confusion.

Witnessing its foe's demise, the moose gruffed its nose and scraped its hoof through the dry dirt in a confident show of aggression. The wolf was now at the mercy of the titan, lying crippled on the ground while the moose had turned into the attacker. At the sight of the ego that flashed in its eyes, the raven feared for what might come next and in a frantic impulse, did something that he'd never done before; he took part in the fight.

His typical nature was to lie in wait and see who would come out on top, then take advantage of whatever was left. But now he had a preference for who he wanted to win. He had a friend. As usual, his emotional intuition overshadowed any logical moderation. While aggressively snorting and wondering whether it would finish off the wolf, the moose was caught off-guard by a black shadow darting down at it from above. The bird went for the only part he knew his small talons would have any impact; he went for the eye. Unlike the rest of the body, the eye wasn't protected by a thick shield of fur but was instead open and tender. He tried pushing his talon into the pupil of the moose, whose confident snort instantly turned to a hoarse groan. It wiggled its skull around trying to shake the raven loose. Its colossal antlers were now more of a hindrance as their weight made swinging its head back and forth a lot more difficult. All the while, the bird squawked like a hysterical teenager in the middle of a rebellious outburst.

But despite finding good footing enough to hang on, he had just as much trouble piercing through its huge gunge-filled eye as the moose had trouble shaking free of the flapping pest. Eventually his talons slipped away, and he was flung away from the moose. Unlike the wolf, he was able to correct himself in the air and land with ease thanks to his wings. The moose's eye hadn't been gouged but the bird had managed to scrape and poke at it enough to leave an uncomfortable sting.

Having been snapped from its offensive state and realising it had nothing else to gain here, the moose turned towards the opening they had come from, charged off between the gap in the trees and disappeared into the mist. Like other scars, the ones left by the wolf and the raven would heal over and the fur would grow back. Eventually, any other animals that attempted to take it down wouldn't even be able to see them. They would assume that they were the first to stand up to the moose and the only ones strong enough to succeed, as had the wolf and so many others that had come before him.

In the beast's absence, the raven flitted over to the side of his fallen friend. The wolf stayed lying on his side and grasping for breath. His eyes were in a frenzy as they darted around at nothing in particular; hectic and full of dread. The bird resumed his uncontrollable babbling. There was a hard minute where the two of them were still in high panic, with the adrenaline and confusion still arresting them both. On the wolf's part, this minute came with a flesh-splitting level of agony as something loose inside his body rattled around every time he took a breath. After a while, the harking and wailing of the raven started to die down and the only sound that remained was the wolf's laboured breathing.

The rest of the world around them held no sign of life or help. There they stayed, grounded amongst the mature wood and motionless fog. The wolf's eyesight started to calm down as he settled his view on one direction: dead ahead. With his head lay down, the trees appeared horizontal. A grey careless forest stretched endlessly up into the sky as high as any mountain and bottomlessly down, deeper than any valley or pit. The ground was stuck to the right side of his face. The foliage that was previously above him now lay to his left, as if he could walk along the trunks, off the top of the trees and keep on walking into the sky, into the clouds – into heaven.

His view of the world had turned on its side.

PART 2

ADOLESCENCE

7

THE HEALING AURORA

A bracing upset had overwhelmed the raven as he stared in disbelief at his protector lying broken in front of his eyes. He hopped over to the wolf's back legs, looking up at his stomach as it inflated then deflated with a terrible shake. On the other end of his body, the wolf's eyes continued staring out into the stale mist. He seemed to have gone very still - whether frozen in pain or languishing in defeat, the raven couldn't tell.

The bird let out the quietest of croaks in the same manner as a person trying to find the right thing to say in a difficult moment but tripping up at the first thought. What could he say? An anxious amount of time had passed, and he'd just lay there motionless, long enough to make the raven assume that he might not get up.

The wolf struggled to move in both body and mind. All he

could do was stare ahead in the hopes that he might recognise something to comfort him, but all he saw was a curtained world that he didn't understand. Everything was baffling. Every experience had taught him that the lessons of his youth - his enthusiasm and his creativity, his intelligence and his patience - would lead to success in his hunts. Yet he lay with broken confidence and a fearful head. The mathematics of how he was bested by the flaying mindless luck of an elder constantly bounced around in his mind and never equalled up to a sensible solution. The raven, fearing the worst, lightly tugged at the fluffy tether of his friend's tail. He yearned for a physical response; some indication that the wolf would recoup. He didn't want to be alone in this forest of maturity and hopelessness. He didn't want this to be where the wolf's journey ended.

He scurried up to the other end of the wolf – to his face – and began chirping at him in a steady squawk. The call was controlled, something like a chant or a cheer, with patient breath and formidable volume for such a small creature.

He was encouraging his friend to get back up. He was begging him to keep going.

The wolf had gotten stuck in himself to the point where sound and sight had become dulled, but the raven's cries reminded him that wherever he was, he wasn't there alone. Like a lasso, the stirring calls pulled him back into the real world. His eyelids flickered and his pupils scanned around as if a dormant machine had started back up. He saw the raven's feet to his left, he heard non-stop rally cries in his ear, and he pushed the complicated thoughts of how and why into the back of his mind for later. For now, he focussed on the present moment; on the beckoning raven cheering him on.

He didn't want this to be where the wolf's journey ended. Neither did the wolf.

His nature was built on ferocity and fighting instinct. He was determined to get back up if he still had a droplet of blood and effort left to do so. He rolled from his side onto his belly when a sudden jolt of agony punished him for the motion. Lying in one spot, the pain of his injuries subsided into a throbbing tremor, but moving around was like provoking a hornet's nest, where he was stuck with a sharp sting on every muscle he put to use. As he rolled frontways, he could clearly feel something unfixed and wiggling about in his upper chest. The adrenaline had worn off and he suffered the full weight of the hurt, but at the very least, the view ahead had reoriented to a comfortable familiarity - trees were vertical, the sky lay above, and up was up again.

Once his feet were back under him, the next step was to push himself upwards. This would be a greater sting than just letting his body roll. This would be pushing through the pain. He fixed his paws to the ground and tried pushing up with the muscles in his legs. Just as his vision had started normalising, the struggle of lifting himself up caused it to fracture again. The world split into a rotating clone of itself where one tree became two and danced counterclockwise on their own separate plains. The view started to make him feel sick. To deter the feeling, he looked down at the floor, but it did little to settle his motions as the stones under his paws quivered to the same tempo as the nerves pulsing in his body. It was a brutally long endeavour to lift his own weight. His bones felt tarnished, and the last few inches took a powerful push that extended his limbs to their limit. Ignoring the repeating images of the spinning floor, the wolf lifted his first paw and placed it forward in the trust that somewhere underneath him, there was still a true and solid plain of earth. Thankfully, his step into the unknown was caught softly by solid ground. His second paw quickly loped forward, nearly buckling as he put weight onto his injured side. Then, the dog repeated the painful steps. He did so again and again until they began to resemble something like walking. His ego had been shredded, but his will to move forward was still intact. The raven didn't fly ahead. Seeing his friend struggle put the limited capabilities of his footsteps on display to an exaggerated degree. At once, the bird understood the hindrance of a life on the ground. He hopped beside the wolf, stunting his flight to keep earthbound beside his forlorn friend.

Progress was slow. Even though they'd only travelled a short distance, a change in light became apparent over time and though the sky was obscured, the two noticed a grey-tinted dusk encroaching on them. They were determined to make it out of this cursed forest before nightfall, but their speed was splintered, and they had no idea if they were heading in a direction that would take them out. Still, the raven refused to take flight. The mist seemed demonic, and the bird feared he might lose his cohort if he tried to take a look up or ahead. He would rather stay lost in this hell with a friend than make it out to the clear skies and fly alone. Losing the raven would leave the wolf - who was already suffering with a broken body and mind - with a broken heart. It was the raven's turn to now stick by the wolf through his hardship, through a turbulent and trialling storm.

The craggy uneven flooring of the forest didn't make the wolf's recovery any easier. Over time, his wavering eyesight meshed back together into a consistent form of the world, but the stabs of agony didn't subside. Hopping on in front, the raven would frequently turn towards the wolf and tilt his head. As he noticed his companion's pain and unhappiness, he would jog over to him, go under his legs and push sweetly upwards as if trying to hold him up and take some of the weight for himself. The wolf's eyes trained forward in a seemingly dismissive fashion, but he wasn't being callous, nor did the compassion of the raven go unnoticed. It pained him just as much as walking with broken bones to see his friend disable his own freedom to stick by him - imagine having wings and purposefully not using them. The wolf wanted only to get out of the forest as soon as possible for both their sakes. So, he stared ahead and walked on with that goal in mind.

The spectral tone of the woods seemed to go on forever, yet only drew into existence a few feet ahead of them. A grey wall of fog gave miraculous and sudden birth to tree after tree after tree again and again and never anything else in a seemingly unending stretch. The trunks rose in row after row like infinite bars imprisoning them. If he'd had any comprehension of what spiritual belief was, the wolf might have assumed he hadn't gotten back up at all; that this was purgatory. Cloudy, silent, grim, and infinite.

The only indicator that grounded him in life was the presence of his surely-living companion beside him. But as otherworldly as it seemed, in reality, the forest was just a forest; tangible, passable, and certainly finite. After what felt like hours of treading on, he gradually noticed how the trees had begun to space out like cracks in the cell. As the trunks thinned out, so did the foliage. As the foliage parted, so did the mist. The raven looked up and saw flecks of deep indigo between the dulled greens. The drops of indigo turned to larger pools that bled stronger through the leaves, eventually becoming big enough to glint with pearly star drops, a thing of beauty within the maze of trees. The shards of open air came through greater and greater until there was more sky than foliage. It gave the bird a reclaimed sense of life and hope, like finding a sparkling lake after trekking through a dead and arid desert. The bird was reminded of the waterside oasis that they had abandoned for more promising and unexpected pursuits.

The woodland faded out so gradually that there was no definitive treeline. As the forest passed into obscurity, so too did the mist that it housed. It was like a dark enchantment that had been placed upon a dominion, constantly blanketing it in death and misfortune but that held no power beyond its borders.

They had walked through trunks clustered by the dozen, then the handful, then the couple. Now, lonely boughs stood inside chill open fields, thicker and healthier than those in the woods as they had the chance to sit solitary in rain and sunlight.

The pair had unknowingly journeyed north in the direction of wintry rises. With the fog cleared, it revealed an untainted white eminence backdropped by quiet and unspoiled mountain vistas. Buried within the peaks was a familiar one, distinct only from the nuances of seeing it first-hand; a particular way the shadows dropped, or the specific angle of the summit. It was the one that the wolf had eyed when he and his friend sat looking out from their bright hopeful hilltop after their first shared meal. It was now noticeably closer; a hint of progress that gave some small sense of compensation for his struggles. Making it up the peak might now be much more of a struggle, but they had made it through the hell of the woodland and come out even closer to the mountain, making his goal seem - while certainly more difficult - surely achievable. A final whisper of copper daylight flared behind the summits.

The friends inhaled the breeze of the fresh openness. It grazed their fur and feathers, covered them, cradled them; cleansed them. The murky shackles of the forest's limbo had fallen away, though it left wounds that wouldn't be so easily shed or forgotten. The forest had stood for a great age, unable to be felled by any creature who prowled through with childish disrespect. It had no definitive end and curved and dotted indistinctly around the landscape to the point where far ahead, at another time, they might wander into its disgusting depths once again without even knowing it.

As they limped on, kinder and more wistful trees continued to spring up from the snow. Out of the proverbial woods, they were in need of rest for the night and chose a scenic oak tree to collect themselves under. The wolf's legs wobbled as he settled down at its roots. Trying to lift or lower himself made his face curl with discomfort. He kept his right side elevated and lay on his left arm in a casual manner. As soon as he was still, the raven took the immediate opportunity to nuzzle itself into his neck for a proper show of affection. The wolf delicately lapped the bird's head with his tongue to say thank you. He had a lot of thanks to catch up on. Thanks for being concerned. Thanks for sticking by through the pain. Thanks for showing thanks.

He had seemingly completely dismissed the notion that it was the raven's actions that had ruined his hunt and probably tipped the scales out of his favour in the first place. There wasn't time for that kind of blame. They needed each other when things went badly just as much as when things went right. The raven then hopped over to the other end of the wolf to bundle up into his tail, using it as a sleep blanket. He let out a sentimental croak as his eyelids dipped.

"It's going to be okay," his sleepy caw seemed to say.

The raven, who was obviously strained from the day, seemed to drift away with ease under the rustling of the friendly oak tree. But the constant constriction in his ribcage left the wolf restless. The bird slept adorably with his chest puffing up and down. While he slept, the wolf stared up and out into the stars, still famished and aching and now contemplating, in his own instinctive way, his failings. He looked back down at his resting buddy. No doubt he too was hungry. The wolf had assumed a sense of brotherly responsibility for the raven. Where he succeeds, his friend must also succeed. Whatever he enjoyed doing, his companion would be safe in joining along. Wherever there was love to be found, he would ensure that any passion discovered by him would be shared with his companion. If there was an achievement to be made, the rewards would be split evenly between them. In this, if their efforts led to failure, then both suffered. The wolf, in his failure, had let down his counterpart. If he was starving, the raven must surely be starving too.

He stayed reeling in a wakened state for a considerable time. The final remnants of sunlight eventually faded away and the truest night sky came in overhead. But thanks to the depth of its darkness, any show of light became that much more luminous. Stars were no longer just white dots but a flashing display of spotlights. Fireflies rose from the grassy thickets like small floating lanterns. On top of these lights, a soft and eerie glow began to shower over the world. The illumination grew strong enough to spill over the hound's face and dance across his features. It cloaked the snow, the great tree and his sleeping friend. Curious as to what could've painted the world so vividly and suddenly, he looked up into the sky.

As if having formed from a miracle, a great shining wave that wasn't there before was now slithering through the sky. It was comprised of ribbons of exotic jade and aqua blue – maybe a soft ivory in there too? It was hard to tell as the strands were wafting about and their hues ebbed between each other. The lines meandered this way and that like a winding nature trail or the bounding hilltops of the earth. As the ribbons swayed, he noticed that they seemed to be woven from burning fractal lines jumping up into the depths of space. But the whole aura also moved forward across the sky, like the light was journeying somewhere itself. It curved like valleys, burned like fire and ran like water. Its winding and flowing nature reminded the wolf of a river, but far purer and more refreshing. This must be the river that angels drank from.

Its nebulous motion and colour were beyond any intensity he had seen in his life. It distracted the wolf from thinking about recent events, or his pain, or even about thinking about much at all for that matter. The aurora had captured his attention with its glinting display. The only thing that came close to its spiritual affection was a glimmer of light that once played a soft show for him on a cave wall. It gave the same sense of intrigue and comfort without needed a dark wet hole to facilitate it. It had become clear that the wolf had a disposition to expressive movement and vivid colour. He was drawn to things that embodied passion and excitement in their aesthetics, like the raven with its shimmering ebony coat and vivacious fluttering. Now, this great spectacle of light captured his interest enough to anaesthetize his anguish.

It was out of reach and would be untouchable even if it were right next to him, but its glow changed the colour of the snow and his fur; that made it real enough. Its emerald shine danced over his smitten golden eyes, giving them the filtered appearance of fool's gold. He stared unblinking at nature's film reel playing against the screen of the black sky, forgetting himself, his surroundings, his senses, his pains and his failures.

When he lowered his gaze, he saw the real world ahead, but the great stream continued to stretch over the top of the distant mountains and beyond. The wolf imagined that making it to the top of the mountains might bring him even closer to the reel of light, so close that he might actually be able to touch it. That, he thought, was now another push to go on; a resurgence of motivation to make it to the top of the mountain. The complexity of the aurora's nature was too great for the wolf to fully explore in his young and simplistic mind, but he nonetheless loved its presence. Hours past in a hypnotised state as he stared into the vast illumination, until he finally waned into a hard-earned slumber.

That evening, the wolf dreamt. In his dream, some essence of his awareness fell to a silken cloud of minty smoke that took him away from the spot where he lay. It carried him to a holy place high up in the air where he felt not only light of weight, but also light of burden. He didn't know what flying felt like, but he knew what clouds looked like from the ground and he assumed he was travelling through them - even though all he could see around him was the billowy mist, it whizzed past him and gave the impression that he was travelling high and far away, a great distance from any harm or upset. Eventually the smoke dissipated to reveal that he was looking down on a vast lush valley with great shimmering lakes in the distance and titanic mountains resembling a giant throne, where the lordly creatures residing on the peaks could sit and observe the entire kingdom below.

One of these stone spires looked mightily familiar. The wolf's mind flew down to the summit of this mountain, which from a distance had looked like it simply ended in a snow-drowned point but as it drew closer, he saw an entire forest of trees reaching up from the peak and climbing even higher into the unending sky; higher than he could see or go himself. Instead, he hovered down to the mountaintop forest that they grew from, weaving in-between the trunks and coming down to an entirely new place.

It was as perfect a habitat as any animal could want to live in. The earth beneath him was crumbled and intensely deep in colour, like coffee grounds. The trees had rich barks that implied nutrition and health, each one stretching up so high that they disappeared without end into a white flash that filled the air overhead. Running up each bark was a plentiful number of sprigs that seemed to curve in ways that let the light stream into the grove from above; in fact, these branches *were* bending away with sentient movement, to purposefully dance in the wash of sunlight.

And it was the sun up there, but it wasn't contained to a single permeating circle in the sky. The most pleasing essence of its whitest and brightest point was everywhere all at once. It took the place of canopies and clouds and sky and like a waterfall, it cascaded through the trees then flooded out in all directions, bubbling over rocks, frolicking down slopes, splashing against trunks and sweeping across the earth, covering everything with a sense of life and vigour.

The leaves on the branches first appeared to be painted in colours that couldn't possibly grow naturally from trees, with tints of gold and cobalt, but on closer inspection it became obvious that there were no leaves at all on the thousands of branches that sat overhead. Instead, each one shuffled and fluttered with the presence of hundreds upon hundreds of luminous birds of every species and tone. In contrast to his earlier retreat in the real world, the birds were no longer dotted through the trees' vegetation but instead created it. As if that was their purpose, they imitated the constant liveliness of leaves rustling in the wind. Birds sat on top of more birds to mimic the natural manner of foliage; a great white owl hooked onto a limb at an impossible angle as two doves sat unbound by gravity on its shoulders and on top of each of their heads, three small warblers casually perched. The forest was literally made of an unending palette of birds that stretched on into the distance and up into the light. Each and every one had their own individual uniqueness.

Somewhere buried in the rainbow flocks were the previous birds he had met; the great grebe, the duo of the cardinal and warbler, the pleasantly noisy woodpecker, and the silly pair of the robin and the blue jay. Each bird added to a relaxing orchestra of tweets. There were sparkling watering holes that drew in a cultural deluge in the form of rodents, ruminants, canines and amphibians. Frogs sat on bobbing driftwood, slapping at flies. Foxes chased each other through the legs of bison. Though the waters were full of demand, they all indulged with respect so that the surface remained calm, enough for everyone to observe each of their reflections clearly and without distortion. The grove was the epitome of plenitude. It seemed to eternally be midsummer – warm and budding with new life.

Then the wolf's essence drifted down and a mighty shadow glazed over a spot on the ground. It belonged to an unknown form but held a scent all too familiar to the wolf. He couldn't see what it was, but he could feel it because he was inside of it – the unknown form belonged to him. He knew it was himself and his dark-feathered friend too, but they weren't individuals. He perceived not two natural forms side by side but one magnificent creature. It had the snout of a hound yet was covered in sleek black plumage and displayed an immense pair of wings. It had dog's paws, but somehow also the talons of a bird. Its eyes warped and pulsed as two different sets – one made of ebony glass orbs, another of ferocious golden lenses – simultaneously existing at the same time. The beast and the bird were one entity, with the flaws of each having been eradicated by the strengths of the other.

The wolf no longer needed to struggle to climb anywhere now that he had a pair of stunning wings capable of flying as high and far as he could imagine (perhaps these wings were how he flew to this wonderful place). The raven didn't have to rely on the skills of others to provide for itself now that it had a powerful set of teeth. It was confident and adventurous, yet clever and aspiring at the same time. They integrated perfectly as one being and with total security, this new creature – this Merger - looked out over a pristine kingdom filled with potential.

As tranquil as the forest was, it was still a perfect catalyst of natural order where the hunt was still on. Spiders captured flies, birds in turn ate the spiders, the birds were gobbled up by all manner of mid-sized critters, and they were then stalked by the grandest predators. Nothing compared, though, to the will of the Merger. It fled like a mower through the bodies of elk and rams, never having to stop in place to consume them. Each was simply absorbed through its gnashing mouth and all that was left in its wake were polished bones. Even the greatest beasts – the likes of bears, cougars, conventional wolves – simply faltered backwards and whimpered as they fell to its razor talons. Any animal that thought it was smarter, stronger, or better; their egos shattered under the hammer of this new species. It was the very idea of a flawless predator.

But the Merger's indulgence was brought to a halt as it saw an insulting visage in the distance. Something that stood guard beside a picturesque waterfall, propping its front hooves up onto a fallen log and soaking in a flash of holy light. It was the moose that had escaped their grasp. Its boisterous stance almost seemed to mock them, displaying itself as some undefeatable victor. How dare this creature of ignorance and luck - with an expression of undeserved pride spread across its face - stand at the highest point of the forest's most beautiful spot as if it were untouchable?

Clearly, the moose believed strength came from its size and its age and its brashness. But back in the real world, it was the tiny bird that had driven the large moose away. It was caution that kept the young wolf from alerting the deer. It was thoughtful reservation that kept him from underestimating the fox. So, the Merger knew that it was stronger, because it had the right elements to overcome every single obstacle. It had a wolf's eyes to track down a cave within a storm. It had a raven's wings to glide across an otherwise impassable river. It had a thick coat of feathers to keep warm even in the wettest climates. It had a dog's snout to sniff out a prey from a hundred yards away. It had bird's talons to target their vital spots. It had hollow bones to make a move on its target with impossible swiftness. It was so swift in fact, that as the Merger fled forward and the moose made a swinging attack with its antlers, it was able to simply flap its grand black wings and dart out of the way, then immediately come back down on top of the moose.

The old beast only had a moment to realise the folly of overestimating itself before its killer had leapt up onto its body. It toppled onto the ground hard enough for several snaps of bone to echo out. The burst of shock that the wolf had felt during his fall was now inflicted a dozen times over on every rib of the moose. The Merger's talons pushed down against the monster's formidable antler with immense force; enough to snap it off.

Though it could have shredded through the moose with the same lightning speed as the other animals it had devoured, the Merger took its time, biting and crunching into its prey's humongous body with its silver teeth, ripping easily through its hide with hooks of black ivory, breaking apart all the definitions of the moose until it was nothing more than pulp. When it was finished, not even bone was left. The old form of the moose had gone, and its luck had run out, overcome by this new beast. There was suddenly an almighty flash of light more powerful than any sun or fire. It only lasted a second before the glare evaporated away.

The grove was as perfect as it'd always been, but wherever the Merger had left its footprints in the ground, mushrooms and flower buds had now spontaneously sprouted so that wherever it had stepped, other animals could graze and grow. Sure enough, foals and wolf pups and even some of the birds gathered around to take from what the wolf's hunts had left them. In moving forward through these beasts, he had also fed others, not just continuing the cycle of life but excelling at it, creating beauty and sustenance for the young creatures that came after him. The fluorescent plumage in the trees bustled and twittered with immense applause.

The Merger now took its place atop the picturesque log where the moose had stood with its front hooves up, displaying its dominance with pride. It felt this pride was deserved – it had proven itself beyond luck or circumstance to be the apex predator. It turned its head out towards the forest that it had fled through, now even livelier and more vibrant than before it had stepped into it. The Merger now sported a wondrous set of antlers which it had apparently assimilated from the species it had consumed; another element of its might to proudly display. All the birds around, including his familiar flying friends of the lakeside, sang out in awe and tussled their wings about. Some took off in flight, whisking into the brightness above and venturing into the unknown as their songs reverberated out.

The Merger turned its snout up to the blinding sky. With a powerful whooshing sound, it extended the entire span of its ravenesque wings. Grains of earth were playfully tossed up into the air and in a hurricane of wind and sound, the Merger flapped its wings back and forth. It prepared to fly away, on to a new adventure with the possibility of anywhere and anything ahead. All four of its paws shot up off the ground, and just as the Merger took flight...

Blackness.

The blackness quickly opened like rolling shutters to an intrusive flare of light that soon dimmed into the image of the homely oak tree, and a clear snow-covered landscape beyond it. The sky above was bright but washed out, with the beautiful aurora nowhere to be seen. The wolf realised, as the gripping throb in his side became real again, that he had woken up from his dream.

8

HEARING MUSIC

The first thing the wolf did was look down at his snoozing counterpart. Back in reality, he no longer felt the absolute strength and potential that their fusion as the Merger had brought, but he did feel the warmth of his companion emanating through his side. The raven woke up shortly after, his eyes winding open and drearily looking around their musky hilltop environment. The sunlight was buttery and invasive with the strength of noon, a signifier that they had clearly slept for an unusually long time. Snowflakes were twirling through the air. The transition from autumn to winter had tipped into colder favour as now, the power of sunlight couldn't stave off the thickness of the frost which barrelled out of their nostrils as they breathed. On the plus side, the cold that was rolling across the northern territories was so deep that it had helped numb the ache of the wolf's injury like an anaesthetic. Even so, it hurt to try and stand up, even if he knew that he had to.

The wolf remembered his dream. He remembered being flawless and free from oppressive challenge or pain. He remembered being able to overcome any hardship and how nothing as small as a step or as large as a moose could oppose him. Strengths that he possessed as a wolf now seemed puny in light of the strengths that he lacked, now that he wasn't amalgamated with the raven. Even though in reality he was still a wilful and admirable creature, he lamented over all the things that he wasn't. For a moment, being awake felt like an unfairness, or like a lesser experience than his dream, but a glance at the distant mountains helped him refocus on the rewards and luxuries that potentially lay in his future; new preys that could be hunted, unchallenged by all other predators that weren't strong enough to make it up themselves, the lofty open heights to play around in, the great scale of the aurora in the sky. It would all surely feel much more visceral and wonderful than any dream, if they were able to reach it.

As the wolf stood up, it was clear that the marks of the previous day's struggles would stay with them. He clenched with sudden turmoil as he lifted his body from his lying position. Putting weight on his leg was unpleasant to say the least, but he still moved forward with determination. From then on, he got more accustomed to the pain with each step, though his journey from there would be accompanied by a distinct and problematic limp. With each broken step, the memory of his dream and the beast that he was – its potential, its victories, its freedom - stuck with him too. Even though he knew becoming this creature was out of the realms of reality, attaining a position at the top the mountain and claiming ownership of its unseen splendours might give him a similar sense of superiority and hard-earned pride. Now he not only aspired for where he wanted to be in the world, but also who and what he wanted to be. As they moved on, thoughts of these goals and aspirations pushed him forward, drove his direction, fuelled his tenacity, and fully preoccupied his mind.

The raven wasn't accustomed to walking so much, but didn't feel much like flying and didn't want to trouble the wolf by riding on his back. Besides, hopping handicapped against the wolf while he was in his own currently dishevelled position kept them pretty much in tempo with each other's movement. Jumping slightly ahead, the bird would sweep his eyes backwards at regular intervals to check on his friend. This was no doubt in commiseration, but there was also a widened anxiety to his gaze; something like a concealed sense of distress. It was difficult for the bird to see the wolf in his current downtrodden state, just as it always is to see someone you care about in agony. It was equally shaking to his confidence, however, to see someone who'd always seemed so strong and impenetrable – someone he'd relied on for security - take a hit, whether physically or emotionally. The raven wanted to be a presence of comfort for the wolf, but he also felt a little less secure himself, as though his own body had been weakened.

Ravens are among the smartest and most empathetic of all the creatures on earth. In the wild, they've been known to display sadness towards the loss of friends, provide a comfort in the presence of their kin, show suspicion towards any abnormal activity from other animals (including fellow ravens), and go through the similar emotional life steps that humans do; they progress through group learning in their early days onto youthful teenage rebellion before settling down, for life, with a single partner. Other birds try and fail to outsmart them and in turn, they outsmart others of their kind, seemingly completely oblivious to how smart they truly are. This raven was no exception; he'd shown time and time again that he was a deeply heartfelt little critter with a fair amount of intelligence (if sometimes stifled by his youthful impulse) but who never really acknowledged or recognised himself how bright he truly was – humans might describe it as humility.

Progress was slow. The bird looked up to see that the wolf was in a trance-like march, fixed on the subject of survival and progress. He envisioned some final point of comfort and security that lay ahead for them both. The raven would have a place in the sky as high as any bird could perch and would always know how to make his way home. Remembering back to their excursions of playing in fields or co-operating in hunts, the raven felt an odd sense of nostalgia; one that didn't lament a time from long ago but the time before a dramatic shift. He knew now, with the pain that inhibited the wolf's freedom, it would be much harder for him to play about. There was a shift in mood as the raven felt the forlorn impediment that dragged through the wolf's limping footsteps. The raven couldn't see exactly what was going on in the wolf's mind. All he felt was that it had been a very long time since they had done anything fun together.

In a surprise move, he spun around on the ground, bringing himself to a halt in front of the wolf who also stopped, in turn wondering what had caused the bird to pause and face him. They stood still for a while; the wolf had tensed up as he wondered whether there was some kind of danger ahead, something that he hadn't seen but that the raven had. Then in a flutter - apparently for no reason at all – his chirpy little friend impishly burrowed himself down into the snow, flinging it all up and waggling his small legs as they sunk inwards. In his place now stood a little cotton mound into which he'd fully disappeared. The hound looked around with a wide-eyed bafflement. His friend had vanished! Had he dug away somewhere, like a mole? Though he was confused, he had just the thing to find the raven. He bent down and hovered his nose over the snow, then took a deep sniff as he tried to catch the scent of damp feathers and dusty bark. He walked around in an indiscernible pattern, all the while inhaling rapidly like a detective trying to find a clue. The smell of a distinct species grew closer. He tilted off to the left and followed it to a patch in the snow no different from any other. Slowly, he approached where the odour was the most powerful and took one last big breath, creating an almighty sniffing sound above the ground. It was then that the raven erupted out of the snow. The wolf jumped back; at first in his instinctual defensive stance, but then in the realization of his friend's emergence.

The snow exploded out like prize confetti and the bird let out a celebratory "craw-craw-craw!" whipping his wings about. The playful animal looked up to see the expression on the wolf's face.

His look of surprise had first broken through a troubled brow that had been there since their later days at the lakeside and seemed to hold the physical weight of his concerns for the coming cold, his impatience for better positions, his frustration over setbacks, his anxiousness over his failures and all the stressful expectations that ticked away in his head. In that instance, his brow bloomed upwards as all that tension released and his eyes returned to a gleaming and playful fascination. The sides of his jaw opened as he panted in excitement and a playful tongue hung out of his mouth once again.

The wolf's dream was of an immaculate collaboration of their formal being, optimised for success and domination. But if they were one entity rather than two, how could they play together? If their goal was always towards progress and improvement, where would they ever find the time to play? This was the raven's dream for them. Not one perfect amalgamation of a creature defined by power and confidence and flexibility and freedom, but two. They could play any game together on equal ground or go anywhere side by side so that one could always be capable of following the other. Two equally great, yet separate minds. He revelled in their individuality. He appreciated how the wolf was a wolf and the raven was a raven, each different enough to be fascinated by each other's differences.

The raven dug itself back into the marzipan blanket below. The wolf, ready for round two, sniffed about again. How good was his nose, the raven wondered? He was still heading towards the patch of snow that the raven had tunnelled himself to when the bird pre-emptively popped out before he reached it. By the time the wolf had jogged over to the spot, the raven had already burrowed back under the snow, chortling away as he went. The hound spun his head about, realising he'd have to think ahead. He'd barely set off sniffing when the raven re-emerged some feet away and then before the wolf knew it, he was hiding again, popping up and down at random places like a game of whack-a-mole. The raven seemed to emerge in bogglingly distant spots. At first, the chasing pup simply spun his head around in mystification at the raven's magic act until he realised what his feathery friend was doing.

So, it was a challenge, the wolf thought.

He pressed his nose down intently and his eyes burst open, alive with a copper glow once again as he rediscovered a sense of whimsy that had been bashed out of him. The raven bobbed here and there, and the wolf tried to detect the route he was taking before he had a chance to reveal himself. As they faced off, thoughts of their experiences flew through the wolf's mind. The grim severity of their encounter with the moose. The sleepy rest of the lakeside and his sombre show of the flying birds that he was longingly unable to join in with. The maddening nuisance of the fox and the frustration she'd caused. The frightening tribulation of the thunderstorm. Had so many of the world's trials really gotten in the way of them playing together for so long? The rush of joy and peace that they felt together overshadowed all those other thoughts at that moment, as they finally played once again. What's more, the raven had designed a game that took his new limp and the nuisance it caused into account, so that he could happily track along the ground without running around or straining himself. Their game had changed – it had needed to change because of what they now were – but they were still playing together. Tunnels of cold fluff now weaved in-between each other under his paws. The raven's darting was without pattern or direction, constantly creating new holes by bursting out from a flurry of snow. Yet as fast as he was, there came a point where one of his cloudy explosions dissipated to reveal the wolf's snout overhead, already looking down on him. In a gentle tag, he tapped the top of the bird's head with a soft bump of his snout.

"Found you!" he was saying. He had won the game.

With that finished, the raven clambered out of his tunnel with snow clumps clinging to his coat. He tried to shake the flakes free but missed a few, so the wolf helped him by licking away the excess crumbs of ice. What the wolf did next was wholly unexpected; he bent down slightly (still with a stiffness in his front leg) in an invitation for the raven to hop onto his back. Knowing it was an imposition, the bird hesitated at first. Were he able, he would've gladly been the one to carry his caring friend on his own back and instinctually, the wolf knew that. He also knew that it would add a little extra strain on his already aching side, but by now he had come to feel like it was his lot in life to carry his little friend, especially if the burden was only a slight soreness. This was a responsibility he took up with no resentment, just great enthusiasm. Carefully, the bird hopped up onto his guardian's lower back, nearer to his tail where the wound was less prominent.

Finally, they once again set off, together again.

They passed by icy creeks where the raven caught a small squirrel and dropped it by the wolf for him to devour. For itself, it found a bush bearing some juicy red berries that it nibbled on. It was hardly sustainable, but they could survive for a while on snacks like this. Neither knew how long the wolf would be unable to hunt for or how cold the season might get. They entered woods once more, set against a fair slope with immature trees that barely offended their view of the sky; a place that barely qualified as a forest at all. It was also far from dead, with perched birds observing the strangeness of the pair's partnership as they passed by. A wandering badger spotted them before diving into a tree hole in fear of the wolf's form, unaware that he was in no condition to keep up with it.

The wolf turned to his friend on his back and the duo each made a shrug with their eyes, indicating their disappointed acceptance of a missed opportunity.

The day was by far their slowest and least eventful. Still, the wolf trotted brazenly on with something of a resurgent confidence. He felt the raven on his back. The comfort of his warm feet felt almost like a small massage on top of his soreness. The raven himself bobbed about with calmness, shifting about on the rickety ride and accepting that he had nothing to do but enjoy the journey and wait to reach their destination. A straight trajectory compensated for their lessened pace, and they were still able to cover a distance of a dozen or more miles under the light of day. Over the hours, the wolf had seemed to grow accustomed to walking with a limp, but a natural fatigue eventually began to take hold. The strong ebb of the sun diminished over mere minutes, drowned out by an early nightfall and giving everything a contrast of overpowering depth with a slightly blue tint, like the darkest and most undisturbed parts of the ocean. A relief of yellow spotlights passed across the wolf 's gloomy coat as a parade of fireflies floated by them. Apart from that, the wash of foliage above them gave little in the way of light from the moon or the stars. The raven began to cower slightly out of worry, thinking back to the last time they were bereft of clear sky. But his attention, along with the wolf's, was suddenly captured by something else, a strange and unaccustomed addition to their senses.

They were warmed by a faded amber glow off in their peripherals down the hillside. It would have been indistinguishable within the yellow varnish of sunlight but now permeated through the woods, splashing against the navy-blue barks. The light wasn't silent either; it emitted an unnatural tone that dropped in and out again within a second, forming a steady beat. It was too heartfelt to be thunder, too vibrant to be the wind, too consistent to be some random shuffle of rock or leaf, too mellow to be the cry of some other animal. The sound seemed impassioned with intent yet kind in its nature and so full of purpose that it moved even too steady to properly resemble footsteps; something wholly synthetic.

The duo was long done with trampling through the cold dark, so they turned left and loped down the hill towards the flushing warmth of the light. As they headed on, the phenomenon grew. Its glow intensified as its buttery comfort fully engulfed the trees, save for the streak of their shadows on the soil. The sound became more distinct to the point that it tickled the hairs on the wolf's ears. For a moment, it reminded him of the thunderstorm they'd endured. But that had struck his ears with violent chaos enough to confuse and hurt him. This, instead, had order – it had a rhythm. He could predict when the strikes were coming. They were not coming from all places at once, but resonated from one spot outwards, turning into a gentle echo before each pluck softly crept away. Just as the rain and lightning had made the sound of frenzied strikes, perhaps all weather made a noise, and this was the sound that the sun made - something pleasant and soothing - yet it was usually too far out of reach to hear. Perhaps that's what they were heading towards; the resting place of the sun after it had sunken from the sky to sleep. It made sense, as the light beamed brighter the closer they walked, and the noise grew stronger too. Maybe this was the sound of the sun snoring, or dreaming.

Fascinated by the anomaly, the wolf became loose minded as he was pulled towards it. In its mystification, he briefly forgot his loping limp, his weary bones, his dissatisfied stomach and his backseat passenger. He placed his foot against an unexpected dip in the floor and with the skip of a heartbeat, found himself collapsing to the ground and sliding aggressively down the gradient hill. Taken aback by the fall, his feathered companion fell off his back and followed down the hill in a cry-infested rolling. They snapped small, uprooted branches and toppled over uncomfortable mounds as they tumbled down, unable to ground themselves on the slick snow. They came to a stop only when the slope began to ease back into even ground and there was no more hill to spin down.

The raven was the first to reorient himself, tussled and shaken and covered in snowdrops but no worse for wear. His immediate instinct was to check on his injured friend. He hopped over to the fallen wolf, who was trembling and whimpering as he lay sore on the ground. His face muscles twinged, and his eyes were scrunched. The raven tilted his head towards him, wondering if he was okay in more ways than one. Through caring croaks, he urged his fallen friend to stand back up. He knew the wolf was capable of getting back on his feet; he'd done so after being defeated by a monstrous moose, so a tumble wouldn't be the thing that kept him down. Still, he seemed almost resistant to get up. He made the coos of an abused pet; an apt sound to make, for in the wolf's head he felt as though he *was* being abused, by the fortunes (or rather misfortunes) of the world. Self-pity had hurt him as much as the pain, feeling handicapped by his own body and trying his best to cope, but failing at each step that wasn't even ground. No matter his effort, his inability to move as freely as he once did had already started to hinder his quality of life – he couldn't eat what he wanted, couldn't travel how he wanted, couldn't run and play how he preferred. Even here, his fascination to investigate something that seemed kind and beautiful had left him falling down and worse off for trying. His pains had flared back up as punishment for his spontaneous inquisition. He reluctantly pulled himself back to his feet, worrying over what he'd have to endure next. By that point, the raven's concerned crowing was no longer aimed at him but instead towards another point off to their right, as though directing him to look somewhere.

Slowly, he careened his throbbing body around to see that there, some feet ahead of them, was something peculiar. They were standing at the foot of an unnaturally pristine cliff of intentional design. It was the most confusing rock face they had ever seen - it had a blunt straight rise with no bumps or outcrops as a usual cliffside would, and it ended with an immediate edge at the top that was cut smoothly and flawlessly. It was also a pointlessly small cliff, only rising about twelve or so feet, but the uniformed red rectangles that it was comprised of were so slick and gripless that climbing over it would be impossible even for an adept mountain goat. The cliff was obstructing the light they'd been heading towards. Though it had flowed over the top and against the woodland slope they'd come from, they had tumbled down into the shadow of the red ridge. They tried walking around the left, but they were blocked by what the wolf first feared was a large creature sleeping in their way – it did seem to have two glimmering eyes that stared unblinking at them, four oddly circular feet made of a sturdy cushion that was similar to the pads on his paws, and its body was covered in a sleek solid shell. But as the wolf sniffed and poked at the beast, he noticed that it didn't seem to be breathing. At the very least, if it were alive, it was asleep. Walking right, they trimmed the edge of the strange red rock face until without warning, it cut away from them. Suddenly, they found the source of the unusual light, something unlike any forest or valley that they'd ever crossed.

Ahead of them rose strange-looking caves that stood alone outside of any hilltop or mountainside, with razor-straight edges defining their sides. Many of them were strangely coloured much like the red cliff they'd come past – blocks of scratched green, blotched cream and slatted crimson. Some had seemingly captured the blinding luminescence that the wolf had seen in the sky, which was now tethered to the sides of these structures. Instead of an unruly stream, the glowing ribbons had now been curled into purposefully weird shapes; shapes that looked like 'B' and 'A' and 'R'. The wolf wondered why the powerful illuminations of nature would be constricted to such small and specific ropes of light rather than spread all-encompassing through the air as they had freely done before. What's more, these mysterious monoliths had managed to contain the light of the sun well past its disappearance behind the horizon, emitting an intensely rustic shine from within.

Light also radiated from clear orbs hanging off the top of sickly-looking trees, all of them thin and grey and stiff. They reminded the wolf of the backs of fireflies, some of them even flickered intermittently as though a heartbeat were running through them. Though separated by these apparent cells of cubes and stalks, all the lights met in the openness, meshing to form the one singular glow that had drawn them to this place. The ground that this bizarre valley rose from was completely flat beyond any measure of difference, like one giant rock surface polished down to the edge. The wolf had never walked so evenly across any ground; it certainly helped to quiet his recent ache. After processing the sight of their strange new whereabouts, the pair became aware of the inviting melody again. It emanated from a den more soothing in appearance than all the others. It was brown and flat-sided just the same, but the sunlight that flowed from its angular panes was humid and steamy. On its side, this den bore the exact hue of emerald as the great aurora in the sky had, lassoed into shapes that formed something like 'HAPPY HOUR 5-7PM'. Of all the hollow dens around, this one seemed the most lived-in, with jovial shadows stumbling hither and dither within.

They heard not only the pleasant rhythm reverberating outwards, but also clear movement and calls from some yet unseen group of creatures. As they headed cautiously forward, they kept alert for any other living beings that occupied this valley. Crossing the even ground, they passed under one of the grey trees' shining orbs that hung overhead. Its splatter of light highlighted how out of place their wild forms looked inside this alienesque landscape. It also lit up a strand of soft material that was suspended above their heads, like a large stretching of animal hide. This too was embossed with a strange line of symbols, yet these ones didn't glow by themselves. Only by the light of the poles was the cryptic pattern 'WELCOME TO THE TOWNSHIP OF

TAYLOR!' made visible.

They approached the hollow brown den from its right side, staying out of the light that flushed out from its rectangular entryway. More of the apparently sleeping beasts sat in perfect rows next to the den in a variety of shapes and tints, all their glinting eyes staring dead ahead. The pair sauntered up to the side of the den where a transparent opening was set into its wall, much like its entryway but smaller and higher up. On closer inspection, streaks of dirt gave the impression that the square opening was closed off by some transparent material, like a completely clear sheet of ice. It was a few feet too high for the wolf to look into from the ground, so instead he stood under the opening and listened. He could hear the harmonious strumming coming from inside, now blaring loudly and resonating with a tinny echo. The sound had to be loud at the source, because it was trying to overpower the howls coming from the unseen beings inside. From the variety of noise, the wolf surmised that there was a massive group of something in the den, all simultaneously making the most complex and confusing calls that he'd ever heard an animal make. The opening was too high for the wolf to see through, but the raven was able to flutter up and settle on a lip that protruded from beneath it. The dog stared at the bird as his neck tilted sideways and forward in a way that signified interest. He remembered how he'd reacted similarly to the aurora in the sky and how it had gripped him with its wondrousness. He wanted to know what had astonished the raven and whatever unique element of the world had produced such a transcendental sound.

What he couldn't see – what the raven saw – was a crowded cave filled with a lively ensemble of some new thing. Much like birds and their feathers, there was an array of different shades and lengths to their plumage, but like birds and their beaks, all bore similar enough features to belong to the same class of creature. Like the wolf, they had four legs, but at the ends of these limbs they had distinctly protruding talons like the raven and, most curiously, they stood balanced upright on only two of their legs. They had fangs like the wolf (although most of them were somewhat blunt) set inside neither a beak nor a muzzle, but a sunken maw in their faces that opened and warped and stretched in many peculiar positions. What was most recognisable to the raven was their behaviour, which was not unlike that of the flocks he'd flown with. Some sat silently observing, others danced around chirping and whooping, some focussed on drinking and eating while dismissing any others around them. Some made obnoxious calls and bellows of no particular purpose. Some were entranced by powerfully iridescent lights coming from rectangular boxes with transparent faces that allowed the creatures to look inside, much like what the raven was doing now. But these ones were small; small enough for these beasts to pick up and observe in their paws. They seemed equally entranced by the unnaturalness of these boxes, picking them up, turning them about, looking at every angle of the things and tapping repetitively upon them like dumfounded magpies entranced by nebulous shininess. Perhaps they'd also just discovered these strange light sources and weren't yet aware of what they were, or what exactly their point was.

What seemed truly unbeastly though – something that the raven couldn't comprehend the purpose of – was a central figure to these creatures settled on a high perch and separated above all the others, with a light selectively shining down on him. All the others were focused on this one individual. Possibly it was the pack leader that all the others followed and looked up to, and with good reason; he was able to do something that all the others weren't. He sat on top of a decorative pedestal, holding some freakish oddity that seemed too complex to ever grow naturally by itself; some miniature portable tree with a hole in the middle and thin vines running across it. The lines vibrated as he washed his hand against them, causing the tranquil rhythm that they'd heard through the trees. There were also large ebony obelisks behind this alpha. As he made his sound on the odd relic, these monoliths appeared to replicate the noise with cacophonous volume. It seemed to boom artificially throughout the establishment, loud enough for its floors and sides and ceiling to shake; loud enough for it to have tremored out of the den and into the nearby forest. Similarly, it shuddered the sill that the raven stood on. The alpha also made a complimentary howl like some kind of romantic cry for a mate that peaked up and fell down with high screeches and deep groans.

The raven heard upturned snow shuffling behind him and was interrupted by the sight of the wolf nudging a barely stable but effectively large wooden box alongside the window. He intelligently moved it beside the raven's viewpoint to create a step for himself. Once positioned, he pounced up onto it then lifted his front paws up onto the same sill where the raven sat.

He was now able to see all that the raven had seen; the lights, the whimsical creatures, the alpha, the source of the sweet sound, and in a shared moment of admiration and bafflement, both of them watched the crowded den. The fundamental intentions of the room seemed so simple to them – these creatures ate, drank, socialised, rested – but in its outward display, it all seemed to have been made so complicated and they couldn't comprehend it. They drank by clasping weird containers that carried tiny portions of liquid, rather than just lap at a lake full of water. Their muzzles moved a mile a minute in long runs of odd movements and baffling sounds, as opposed to conveying instructions to each other with a simple squawk or a distinct look in the eye (as the wolf and raven did.) A ludicrous amount of them gathered singularly into this one den at this precise moment of nightfall when it seemed every other part of their valley stood desolate and avoided. Many of them bore fur coats that were vibrant and unnecessarily outlandish, while others had bland coats covered in dirt and stains, which he felt was fair enough; by coincidence, some animals tended to get dirty through their activities while others led lives that kept them well-groomed. Yet despite drinking from the same watering hole, these two distinctions seemed to separate the creatures, as the vibrant ones would steer clear of the dirtied ones. It all seemed so confusing.

The wolf only had a second to try to rationalise their unnatural and absurd behaviour before the flimsy box that held him up began to crack under his weight and his view of the den quickly disappeared. It crumbled softly and thanks to his reflexes, he managed to safely hobble off it before falling over himself, but his view of the creatures had fallen away, and he had no more boxes to see them with.

The intricate sounds of the beings inside and their melodic plaything carried on as he stood out of view contemplating what to do next. The duo marvelled at the beasts, but still refused to get any closer to them through their natural caution of the unknown. The raven floated back down onto his partner's back, and they strode out onto the path they'd come from. They were on the edge of this odd community; a dry icy trail lay out to their left which stretched onto an eternally dead and dark ridge. To the right, more rustic dens were spread out, offering a new sense of discovery and exploration. The duo remained on their guard, yet the design of the world around them exuded an aura of structural purpose and with it, security. It wasn't a jagged quarry where darkness obscured their footing or a wild forest where tight-knit trees hid potential threats. The brightness of this place lulled them. Steadily, they trod deeper into this new world, hoping for more delights like the music they'd discovered. At this time of the evening, all the residents would either be slumbering at home or sternly nestled inside a place intended for relaxation. They had the place to themselves. Just as it had quivered through the trees, the music continued following behind, but it began to evaporate into the air as they walked further down an open empty lane. At first, they stuck to the leading lines of the paths they'd started on but ended up cutting behind homes and alleys as they were unaware of the purpose of these paths. Most of the dens they passed were characterised by a particular smell, but most were darkened with inactivity, their scents simply residue of whatever purpose they served in the waking sunlight. However, one that they passed was brightly lit up and still occupied by a handful of individuals. Exhausted, these final strays sat drinking their last relief of the night from their containers. They seemed soothed by their drinks. Some of the liquid was tinted a sickly yellow, some was a deep earthen brown. The wolf reasoned this must be more than just dirty stream water. It put a warmed expression of indulgence and satisfaction on their faces with each sip. He watched as they bit into rectangles with yellow sap oozing out with each bite. He didn't know quite what it was they were eating, but it reminded him of how he hadn't satiated his own hunger in a long time. He licked his lips.

A female with a buttery mane and frilled violet plumage on her body lifted small structures into the air and baffling piled them on top of the ledges they'd been shuffled under. What a strange ritual, the pair thought. But they also recognised the wildly unaccountable dexterity and capability that one of these beings must have in order to *lift* something. Paws were used for moving and striking, simple motions. Even the wolf's paws – even a great moose's hooves – couldn't *lift* something. She continued as if it were a simple routine for her. They used their bodies with such adaptability and, more than anything, variety. The entire side of the den was a transparent pane and the light blared through it, yet they stood at a distance in the middle of the street. The glow only grazed against them, keeping them out of sight from the tired occupants inside. The companions moved on.

Another pane with its lights on. This time, a pair of beings stood on the other side, staring right at the duo as they walked past! But they couldn't have seen them – the wolf recognised that this particular pair didn't seem to have any eyes. Didn't have mouths, or any faces at all. They stood completely still, not even appearing to breath; no puffing of their chests or anything. The wolf wondered if he and his companion had been spotted. For an embarrassingly long time, they stood in a freezing contest with the two porcelain figures, but they never seemed to move an inch and the two animals grew uncomfortable.

"Rhawk!" moaned the raven, as if to say, "screw this, let's

keep walking!" and the wolf turned with an immediate sensation of disinterest, plodding away.

The valley of blocks was infinitely intriguing. Shining symbols and intricate formations arrested their vision, doing much the same to their ears with clattering and squeaking from here and there. At one point, the wolf's suspicions about the large mounds with glassy eyes – that they may be living creatures – was confirmed to be true as one of them growled and spluttered its way down a street past them, rolling along on its paw pads, its eyes flushed as brightly as the lights on top of the grey trees. Occasionally, some of the occupying creatures would step out of various burrows or walk by at a distance, spewing their elaborate garbles. Noises seemed to range from hearty guffawing like that of the raven's chuckles, to harshly snapping at each other like the wolf's intimidating barks. No matter the disposition, it always accompanied a hieroglyphical tangle of 'oo's and 'aa's and 'im's and so many more elastic sounds. Soon, it was more than just sights and sounds that enticed them. Their sense of smell was also overcome with newness and culture. Something ten thousand times stronger than the raw smell of newly killed unaltered flesh. It was, by the very nature of its scent, obviously warm. Not warm from recent liveliness – it was warm to a sinful degree. Plus, the base stench of meat wasn't alone. The aroma was as indescribable as the nuances of colour would be to the blind. It was something that animals never need to describe, so there never came a word for it. Years of primitive rawness was instantaneously overshadowed by the convoluted concoction of something else. They drifted magnetically toward the scent. Behind a wiry obstruction left open through carelessness, round the back corner of an adjacent den, they sunk into a narrow alley. A sudden slam made the wolf jump backwards as he caught the last glimpse of an entryway snapping closed, just as somebody disappeared back into their home. Next to the entryway was a cluster of large grey containers. What they'd left behind – the thing that was drenched in the fantastic odour that guided them here – was still-warm food, abandoned for whatever wasteful reason inside one of the containers. Sweet-smelling and gooey strings trickled over the edge. A slab of hot browned meat trimmed with a ruby paste was nested on an overflowing mound. Some kind of thick liquid, black and rich, dripped down the side of the pile. Scattered throughout was an inedible mess including ruffled cloth and discarded bones, but to the two undernourished scavengers, it was all churned up into one smorgasbord of delight and gluttony. The raven barely contained his excitement as he hectically flung himself up onto the lip of the large container.

Without etiquette or consideration for what he was digging into, his beak snapped at strips of hot rind and pools of sweet orange stickiness. He didn't stop to wonder what magic or skill was used to make it taste so different to the usual carcasses and carrion, he just buried his face into a long-awaited and much-needed feast. His talons rocked in giddiness until the can he was perched on rocked with them. Then he suddenly remembered his partner. Looking down, he saw the wolf nudging the can with his snout. It was filled to the brim with waste that weighed it down. As he was already tired and weak, his attempt to tip it over was futile. But suddenly, a meat slice was dropped on his ear which then slid down onto the floor. He looked up to see his sympathetic friend dropping portions of food over the side, trying to feed him. If he had the ability to contemplate, the raven might have recognised the irony that he'd joined forces with the wolf so that he might hunt larger game and make it easier for himself to eat, but now the bird was the one feeding the wolf. Regardless, the raven continued dropping cuts of cooked food over the side for him. He began to ravenously snap them up.

Impossible flavour.

Absolute ecstasy.

After broken bones, cold skin, long nights, shaken confidence, a dry mouth and a loss of ability to hunt for himself, the wolf felt the satisfaction overwhelm him. He lived to hunt and eat, but right here he had found something he didn't have to hunt for yet was as prized and tender as anything he'd previously tasted. Without moderation, he guzzled down his morsels, free of the ideas of judgement and manners. He would have loved to bury his mouth into the large can as deep as his hunger would take him into it. He imagined that it was never-ending in depth. The raven kept pushing slithery ropes and slightly moulded chunks over the side. As he swallowed down everything that fell to his feet, he began to fill with a comfortable familiarity. The fur around his mouth was damp not with blood, but a sticky sweet sauce. As opposed to raw flesh, it was now gourmet delicacy that was tangled in his teeth. The raven took his own bites of course, as he slipped every other scrap over the side down to his friend. But every time he turned to drop another piece of food, the last one had already disappeared. While the voracious dog's stomach filled up, he still ate and ate, seemingly with unquenchable greed. Then, the steel door beside them swung back open.

Out stepped one of the creatures, short in stature with a black mane sweeping low behind her back. She had a flap of white fur around her waist stained with the sauces and goop that coated some of the food in the can. She had a heavy sense of aggravation in her step as she hauled a bursting black sack around the door, quite probably filled with the same bounty that she'd already dumped inside some of the cans. She was in the middle of a muddled thought but as her eyeline rose to see the wolf stood at her door, she was taken aback. She wasn't, however, gripped with fear or fluster, and made a quick yip of demand towards them.

"Aye!" she snapped.

The pair didn't even flinch. The human turned away as though they were just another problem added on top of an existing stack of stresses. It's possible that in the darkness of the alley, she didn't quite register the wolf as a wolf; that she saw two fluffy ears, four legs, a furry tail and a snout, and assumed it were just a fox or some other less fearsome animal. She re-entered through her door as the two stared puzzled, but it hadn't even fully closed again before she came bouncing back out with a set of objects – some large round thing with a handle and a shiny stick with a bulbous half-globe on its end. She ricocheted the large stick off the back of the round apparatus repeatedly, making a hateful echo. It seemed similar to the artificial object that the human in the warm den had used to make sound, but this was decidedly more violent, and it was obvious she didn't mean well. She barked in her species' usual string of gibberish.

"Aye! Aye, noe noe noe, geyowt! Shooe! Menjimut! Gawawey!Algitagun! Shoo!"

They couldn't understand the distinct syllables of her bark, but its tone immediately rubbed the pair the wrong way. It sounded wholly aggressive, and the clanging of her tools seemed filled with the intent to harm, at least from the two wild animals' perspectives. It was reminiscent of the godawful striking noise of the lightning storm but didn't instil as much dread when it was coming from a small, sassy, frail-looking being with a noisy stick.

The purpose of the noise was not a warning; the wolf had no concept of that. To a wild wolf, aggressive movement and harsh noise was territorial contention. She wanted the food in the containers.

A fight hadn't been on the wolf's mind, but she had interrupted his singular moment of joy, which had been such a long time coming that having it disturbed immediately enraged him.

He bared his teeth, buried his paws into the snow, and snarled. Defending the food he had claimed, he lunged at the oblivious beast's calf and bit into it. Her indecipherable syllables immediately turned into one harking string of "Aaaaaaaaaaahhh!"

Her arms flung up into the air on impulse but came back down as they brought their utensils onto the wolf's head. There was no softness in her arm movements anymore; she was slamming down with the forceful intention of saving her own life. The wolf tugged left and right and winced back whenever the solid bowl came down on his skull, but he still hung on.

After a dozen or so times, the strikes to the head began to affect him and he released his clamp, backing off with a sore skull. The expression of terror that had been absent the first time she encountered the wild dog was now struck across the female's face. Her leg was indented with teeth marks, streams of blood running from each one. Her lower leg was coated with the same red spill that expelled from every animal that the wolf bit into. She immediately made a limping lunge for the door, dropping her tools in favour of stretching for the handle. The familiar tang of blood was on the wolf lips. He dove after her with the rumbling of a greedy stomach, but she swung around the other side of the door and bent back on her knees as she pulled the handle as fast as she could. As she did, the wolf caught his snout in the gap, gnashing and grizzling while trying to squeeze through. The sight of a roaring muzzle rabidly snapping between the crack in the door caused her to scream in terror. All the while, the raven squawked frantically in the background. It seemed that the bird, just as much as the wolf, felt defensive about their prized pile. He egged the wolf on once again as his little cheerleader, with him in the throes of a hunt and the raven beckoning on his victory. His jaw eventually slid back out from the gap in the door and through tearful cries, the female clicked the heavy seal closed, safely separating her from the supposed monster outside.

The wolf's adrenaline calmed, his breathing (while strong) slowed with his heartbeat and his top lip dropped back down as he put his teeth away. The two fell silent, save for his heavy panting. They heard the creature's muffled panic continuing inside. It was followed by the calling of another voice, and then another. Objects inside clattered. A huge uproar began as dozens of voices started heckling and spluttering. Through a barred and vignetted pane on the high wall above the cans, a silhouette looked out at them and then returned down. Either due to sensing oncoming retaliation, or simply not wanting to stick around any longer, the wolf turned and signalled the raven to follow him. In his resourceful thinking, the bird grabbed one last big cluster of chow from the top of the waste pile. As he settled on the wolf's back, he leaned towards his friend's face and let him casually pluck a portion out from his beak as they left; one last splendiferous mouthful.

They moved around the back of dens, staying in the shadow and away from any concentration of light. They could always hear clusters of noise disperse from the front entrances as the worry of a wild and vicious animal spread fast through the valley. However, they were gone by the time an authoritative group of beings were investigating the spot where their violent encounter had taken place. Clusters of these creatures formed together in distressed groups. Small, directed lights that they held in their paws began to track across the trails. In their natural talent, the two blended into the night and stayed out of the way of any oncoming retribution. The uproar grew quickly. The two were ducked behind a ledge and staring around the corner when they saw the pathways becoming littered with search parties and beasts alerting other beasts, door to door, to stay in their dens. The duo had lost their direction in the forest of blocks, but thought it was better to get out sooner rather than later. As panic spread among these creatures and they scoured the streets for the dangerous predator, the two friends slunk furtively back out to an adjacent forest, returning to nature and relieving this confusingly civilised world of their unfamiliar wildness.

These peculiar things – these humans – with their incredible assortment of objects and oddities and lights and liveliness, were left searching for nothing.

9

EATEN BY WOLVES

Once they'd escape the lights and the noise, the two strolled on through a comfortably silent patch of woods, accompanied by a new-born breeze made audible by creaking pines. Their hunger was satiated for the first time in a while and the soreness on the wolf's head, brought about by the human's utensils, paled in comparison to the joy of his long-awaited nourishment. Besides, he'd put up with much worse than a sore head. The raven was almost brought to sickness by the overpowering expanse of sugar in his throat but enjoyed the sensation immensely.

From here on, they knew that if they saw any mysterious light with a yellowed artificial glow, it would be a signal for respite and indulgence among their troubled travels; their drink of ambrosia at the end of the world. This new idea of flavourful trash and calming music was a fresh and much-needed avenue of happiness, considering the wolf's injury had barred him from some of the motions and merriments that he'd previously derived his joy from.

The wolf felt more himself than he had in a while. To his own mind, he had exercised his nature. He'd fed his stomach, appeased his animalism and proven his valour. Blood on his teeth was blood on his teeth, regardless of whether it had come from a worthy contender or from an unsuspecting buffoon. A satiated stomach was a satiated stomach, regardless of if it had come from a fresh kill that he'd made himself or a pile of trash that had been dropped into his mouth. While flavourful, the meal wasn't the hearty slabs of protein that he was used to, yet regardless of whether the feeling would last, the unnatural concoction that he'd indulged in certainly felt filling now. He'd once again felt protective of the raven, but against what? Some small woman who didn't know what wild creature she was up against. They seemed content enough with the outcome, like wandering hoboes who were satisfied with their scavenger lifestyle, having done away with traditional customs and making the best of their shameless lot in life.

Passing a puddle, the wolf caught a glance at his reflection in the muddy water. He'd been through an ordeal since his last glimpse of himself at the lakeside respite and it had started to show. The current surplus of fatty leftovers had made his stomach look bloated but other than that, the weeks of languish and small scraps had taken its toll on his body. Now, despite having a generally wiry frame to begin with, it had grown even more frail than it once was, with ribs embossed against his chest fur. His fur was now scrappy and patterned with mud and dust. His grey sheen still came through, but it was like a fancy silver coat that had worn down over time, then been fixed up with ill-fitting patches of scuffed brown and oily yellow.

On the contrary to the wolf (and though it didn't visibly show through), the raven's legs were getting stronger as it held itself straight on the wolf's rickety back and, here and there, walked around more. It began to get used to being grounded like all the other animals, as opposed to floating in wistful mindlessness on a separate plain from everyone else. Rest came easy that night and though the weather was far from toasty, they found warmth in the crevice of a tree quite similar to the hole where the wolf had slept the night before they met. It was small and slimy and buried in simple darkness.

They both fit inside perfectly.

The next morning, they emerged from their crevice to what seemed like microscopic starlights trickling down in the daylight, but it was only ice particles in the air catching the bolstered sunshine. Now in the light of day, they could see something beyond their sparse wood rising from the earth into the sky, separated by shadow as it stood with its back to the sun. Without the presence of mind to intend it, they had made a full journey through the town and come out the other side, making enough headway on their northern trail to reach the foot of the mountain valley they'd been heading towards. The first of the mountain peaks, that months ago had seemed as small as a tooth on the horizon, was now close enough to stand ward over the whole landscape. They would reach it before noon.

Suddenly, an influx of adrenaline and drive compensated for the wolf's limp. A glimpse of the stone monument ahead reminded him what he was walking forward for – something better than trash. He walked faster than he ever had since acquiring his limp, much to the giddiness of the raven. He crowed like an excited sports fan whose team was just about to sweep a victory. The return of the wolf's youthful disposition seemed to reactivate some idea of their dynamic within the raven's head and rediscovering his fluttery self, he took to the sky in his usual dreamful manner. He circled overhead, blaring out a cheery call that echoed for all creatures to pay attention to.

"Make way for the wolf!" He seemed to yell. "Here we come, everyone out of the way, we have somewhere to be!"

The ground transitioned into a steady incline as the stone of the mountains tore through its soil shell, like fangs piercing through skin. As the trees disappeared for the most part, stubborn boulders took their place atop sloping volatile rock. Around a cliff face here and a granite hill there, the two threw themselves into the veins of the mountain range, hoping to reach its heart. They were journeying to the top of the highest summit that currently hid itself among all the other high rises, but the wolf would know it when he saw it. The pass was like a giant stone mansion made of darkened corridors and rickety uneven steps, but large open rooms still dotted the crevices in-between. Choosing a direction was more difficult now than it had been during their deep forest excursions. They were blocked from travelling in some directions until they could navigate themselves back on track; up didn't always necessarily lead to the top. They walked up and down and slid and clambered for what seemed like a good few hours, right into the late afternoon, until they reached the naturally formed equivalent of a crossroads. The wolf swivelled his head, wondering which path to take.

A lone and stalwart mountain goat appeared against a smooth rise of rock, standing on an impossible slant. They had seen sheep before but nothing quite like this animal. It was strong and shaggy and fearless of its apparently precarious position, giving credence to the hope that this location held some magical essence that the pair had yet to fully explore. Like a knowing sage, the goat bleated and stared upwards with its large soapy eyes to a peak above from where it stood. This peak was distinct from the others only by the nuances of seeing it first-hand; a particular way the shadows dropped and the specific angle of the summit. The wolf remembered this as the mountain he had spotted from his hilltop view on the day of the duo's meeting. The highest peak. The pair turned a corner around the wise goat, the wolf meeting its stare with a thankful gleam as they passed. Beyond that, a slope turned into a beckoning pass that spiralled around the mountain. This would surely take them to the very top.

The pass was characterised by wide precipices that marked the growing delicacy of their footpath. Overhanging rock formations led into obsidian tunnels and passages deep enough for the mountain to close them in with rising walls on either side. These paths were much narrower than the two were comfortable with, but they were quite familiar with taking their time by that point. The raven, once again, commandeered a spot on his partner's shoulders. Every so often, they would see something like another mountain goat galloping by or a robin taking a shower in a water drip, but some odd sense of direction deterred them from tiresomely chasing pests about, as though they were being pulled somewhere else. Perhaps there was some other great purpose or reward waiting for them up the summit.

The wolf stepped down a casual ramp into another corridor that closed them in with more sharp stone walls. These ones were tall enough to drown them in shadow; tall enough that the usual wash of snow had trouble touching its inner depths. Despite the height of the sun and the affectionate clarity of the sky, they were submerged in the shade of primordial cliffs. The wolf's eyes had adjusted to the brightness of daylight at that point, and it was only once they had wandered deep into the trench that he noticed something emerging from the darkness ahead. A spectre bearing a familiar form was walking towards them on a set of paws just like his. Though unknown as an individual, the wolf recognised the scent as that of his own. For a second, the world seemed mirrored as the trench they had walked through still stretched on ahead and the wolf's own black shadow marched towards him. But it bore differences, like how it lacked a crick in its step or how it held its head proudly up as it strode with a sense of dignity and dominance. This was a different wolf treading towards them.

It was soaked in a stunning macabre that was far deeper than the shade of the trench, like it had rolled around in the blackened coals of a burnt-out fire. Its aqua-green eyes put every sun-soaked pool they'd ever drank from to shame. Its oblivion pupils stared at them with fixation, reminding them that if they moved an inch to the left or right, their eyes would follow. While unblinking, the black wolf's eyelids sat without tension, portraying a sense of relaxed confidence. This was contrary to the grey wolf, whose eyes always remained wide with a sense of concentration and presence. It conveyed the idea that this wolf's response to an event came without the same level of anxiety and forethought; unlike the grey wolf, it wasn't on high alert in preparation for every outcome, but would (and could) fearlessly handle anything that happened, *as* it happened.

It proudly stepped towards them and stopped. But it wasn't alone.

It was supported by three equally harsh-looking pack members. One had a dusty timber coat and stood muscular and straight, as if it had found a comfortable equilibrium between filth and self-esteem. The other two had grey coats with much darker tints than that of the lone wolf, yet they were distinct from each other in that one had a bland lime hue in its irises and the other a dulled shade of hazel. They all stood there, motionless, the travelling duo included. They didn't attempt aggression, at least not in any physical sense. But the language in their stance highlighted the difference in their dispositions when compared to the young grey wolf. Their personalities seemed almost like a show of natural separation. They didn't try to approach or befriend or familiarize themselves with the dog and the bird. They only stood and stared.

The black wolf kept his head in a dominant upright position, making the visitors too uncomfortable to move. The wind careened over the edges of the cliffsides that boxed them in. Its whistling was the only break in the silence. The raven had always imagined his companion to be the archetypal image of a wolf, tenacious and confident. But in this moment, he had his first chance to compare him with others of his kind and noticed how much of a difference the outside details made. The black wolf and its gang stood with high heads and straight backs, structural and masculine. Their eyelids hung easy and with a sense of ego. Each of their coats were short with not a hair out of place, as they clearly regarded their grooming with high pride and had other wolves to help maintain that standard.

His friend, however, looked different. His shoulder blades were tense and his head hung low with agitation and readiness. His eyes were widened with effort. His fur was tussled and somewhat dirtied, yet with a naïve sheen of silver dominating his body that conveyed a lack of physical experience, even despite his recent calamities. While his outward appearance to these beasts might have been largely similar in foundation – the snout, the paws, the teeth – his details separated him from the pack. No one saw and felt those details of separation more than the grey wolf himself. While the raven had the pack of wolves on his mind, the wolf thought first and foremost of his friend. He knew the nature of wolves and their approach to strangers and while he had the advantage of bearing some similarity to them, the bird was a different species entirely. They would notice, he thought. He'd known wolves like this before – wolves that didn't like difference. They may not even like the basic similarities between him and them enough to let the two pass. It was entirely their call. The pair of misfits were at their mercy.

In an extremely cautious manner, the black wolf backed up and craned to the side. His followers did the same in response. It was as if they were giving the duo permission to walk through their territory, but they kept their sinister gaze on the wolf and raven, giving their show of goodwill an underlying sense of fragility. Their kindness could break at any moment. The wolf naturally considered the possibility of a trap, making his nerves tenser than they already were. The raven dared not make a sound but was eager to chirp in an effort to warn the wolf, to plead him to turn back and not lock them both into a corridor of doom from which they couldn't turn back. The wolf stepped ahead with clenched shoulders and knees. A shudder ran through him. He knew how he looked to them; even a wolf who was blind in one eye could see how weak he appeared, shuffling forward with his head lowered like a scolded pup. He took it one step at a time. The wolf pack never broke their gaze as the pair wandered past them. It was as they passed the fourth wolf that the raven finally blew out a small croak. He tried his best to make a sound as quietly as possible, but he had to communicate with the wolf somehow. He had to alert him, to make him look upwards; to make the wolf see what he had seen. Whether thankfully or not, his beckoning worked as the wolf finally tilted his head up enough to look at the edges of the low cliffs that boxed them in. Now, he witnessed something that made his heart feel as though it were going to vibrate out of his chest. There were dozens of wolves - maybe thirty or forty – perched on the bluffs above.

They all sat in silence, looking down on them. The mood was in the air as clear as if it were spoken out loud – they watched on not with benevolence, but with silent scorn. All were mechanically keeping watch on them, unflinching like owls gazing at scurrying mice. The intruding outcasts didn't know whether to feel judged or endangered. The wolf felt like they could see through him; they saw his limp, saw his broken rib, saw his different mind. Somehow, they knew that despite having four paws, a snout and a set of teeth, he was weak in comparison to them. The raven felt equally small, stuck in a world of viciousness that was unfamiliar to his free and cheerful self. Even if he wanted to escape and leave his friend alone, the land they now travelled through was narrow and closed in. If he tried to fly out, the monsters around them could easily swipe at him in the air and send him plummeting back down into their dark world, where retaliation would be harsh and he would be punished for trying to fly so carefree. The wolf felt like a joke, and the raven felt like a foreigner. But they were now stuck in this den of anxiety; they just had to tremble and stress their way through it.

Memories of old habits and habitats tracked through the wolf's mind. He wandered back to a time when he was, by all accounts, a baby of the world; his feet pattered clumsily, his howl was meek and cute, and he was still learning to chew on a stick, let alone hunt in the wilderness. He was surrounded by other pups just like him, with wide eyes and a penchant for playing, as the mature wolves tried to mould them into focussed hunters. At first, the elders provided food for the young ones and licked their fur clean and straight, keeping them innocent. But over time their lessons turned the pups into a mirrored generation of themselves. The eyelids of the other pups drooped; their lessons turned to automatic instinct. But the grey wolf's eyes remained wide, and his mind kept busy. In line with their teachings, he learnt to groom himself and keep his coat sleek, learnt to harness his hunger as a tool of survival and progress, no longer expecting others to take care of him and instead launching out into his own hunts, becoming somewhat wilder for it. But while the other wolves dove head-first into a hunt with their gut guiding their actions, his hunts were methodical and thoughtful, measuring every outcome and every angle before each and every step. All expressions of life, whether as tumultuous as a fight or as inconsequential as a nap, remained a pressured event full of questions and concentration. His desire to play games hung around for far longer and at a much higher intensity than what was useful for a beastly survivor, to the point where it kept him agitated in the other wolves' more docile or restful moments. He never stopped chasing butterflies even when he knew he had to chase deer. More notable than anything, through it all, his eyes remained golden.

Wolves are uniquely examined, able to be referred to as both a tight-knit group or close family (through the term 'wolf pack') as well as a solitary individual who prefers their own company (who we refer to as 'lone wolves'). The grey wolf's disposition couldn't be so easily explained as to categorise him as either a lone wolf or part of a wolf pack. He enjoyed play as well as the hunt. He felt comfortable in the timid solitude of darkness as well as the baffling chaos of sunlight. At one time, he grew with a conventional pack just like the one that now looked down on him, but something inside kept him from feeling a kinship with them. Despite now standing to the same height and age as these other wolves, a familiar feeling still reverberated through his senses. The feeling of being a pup among wolves; a child among grown-ups. He had the hunger of a wolf and the spirit of a bird. He didn't belong in a wolf pack, but he didn't belong as a lone wolf either. Just like him, the other wolves had trouble identifying this contradiction. They watched and judged that he was like them, but not enough like them. He trod through an uncanny valley. This is all the watchful hierarchy of wolves saw as they looked down on the unexpected duo - difference.

The wolf snapped out of his reminiscing mindset at the feeling of the bird's talons gripping on his back with a nervous constriction. To the wolf, this was an unnerving trip into a life he had never quite fit into, but for the raven, this was a stroll through death row lined with an excessive number of executioners. Never mind having different fur or a strange perk in his ears; he didn't have fur or ears at all. Predators like these ate up any creature that didn't have the skills or tools to fight for themselves, like the raven. To the bird, everyone was larger, faster, smarter and more furious. He spoke different, moved different, and thought different. Every individual around them felt like they were licking their lips at the prospect of eating him alive. This rocky metropolis was claustrophobic, and its residents were monsters. These were the kind of wolves that had not gold in their eyes, but bloodlust. Their society was built on the beneficial tactic of dragging things down into the shadows; they completely lacked whimsy or the freedom to fly. The raven had grown familiar with speaking to the wolf mostly through the look in their eyes, as expressive as each of them were. But here, the language of choice was violent barks and predatory sniffs. Their eyes said nothing. They were cold, but in that coldness, he still knew what they were all saying - he knew what they were all thinking. The differences of the grey wolf were exemplified, for better or worse. How odd of a wolf he must be to even be here, carrying a bird on his back. As both of their minds flustered over their own concerns and anxieties, all that the other wolves continued to do was stand motionless and stare at the pair as they hobbled through their territory.

They both wondered why. Wondered if they were being taunted or tricked on top of the clear intimidation. Regardless, they stared dead ahead as they walked, desperate not to offend the wolves with any unclean looks or movement. The breeze continued crying through the constrained path. Slowly loping forward, the walls grew shorter and the number of watchers in the grey wolf's eyeline fell from dozens to one dozen, to a handful, to a few. The end of the pass came into sight as they remained unharmed. The only attack had been what their anxieties and imaginations had conjured. They had seemingly passed safely through to the other side of the wolves' den. But then, a harsh growl pierced the wolf's ears. The raven squealed in distress. He spun down to the floor in a panic and the bird followed, tumbling off his friend's back.

The alpha wolf had followed along behind them, keeping them pinned to their trail just as much as the immovable walls had. In its unsympathetic beastliness, it had waited right until the point where their anxiety had cooled – until they thought they were safe – for the moment when it cruelly lashed out. It jumped beside the wolf, letting out a vicious bark as it swung its paw against his face. A hard and unrestrained hit, but its claws weren't out. It wasn't looking to start a fight; it didn't need to. It knew it was stronger than the young wolf, but in its ego, wanted to display that strength. It wanted to send a message. This was their turf, their territory, where it was the strongest and most ruthless. The grey wolf hadn't even set out to challenge this ruthlessness, but while he had grown up with wide eyes and a love of play, these mountain wolves had been brought up in a world where aggression ruled. After barely managing to avoid squashing the poor raven under his falling body, he clambered up to his paws, whimpering. The bird scrambled to his own feet as well and prepared to take flight and escape (as desperate an act as abandoning the grey wolf had become). But then it noticed that the black wolf hadn't made another move towards them. It just stood there again, snarling callously and staring coldly. So instead, he hopped towards the back of his only ally - who now stood face to face with the black dog - and hid behind his leg.

Inflicting fear had been the intention. The grey wolf had timidly walked through the pass with a hung head and the black wolf wanted to see how much lower he could hang it. It had gotten its wish as now shaking in dread, the poor pup backed up apologetically. The black wolf didn't follow them but raised its head and howled with a grisly sense of gleeful cockiness. It was as if it were laughing at them. Following suit, all the other wolves raised their jaws and howled one by one. The howls reverberated through the mountain pass and echoed out like the boisterous hollering of a hundred hooligans, hot-blooded and hopped up on over-confident virility. The society of wolves seemed not only to agree with but enjoy the teasing and terrorising of the two outcasts. Before the riling of the crowd convinced the black wolf to push its antics even further, the raven cawed as a warning signal to the grey wolf, as if instructing him to run. They were at the foot of the steady slope on the other side of the pass, where it turned back into even ground that they could run up and dart around. So, the raven took to the air and flapped his way up in a fright. Following his friend, the wolf took the opportunity to spin quickly and even with a limp, sprinted as swiftly as he could back to the weaving grounds of the mountain, around the corner of another rocky outcrop and away from their territory. He didn't know if the other wolves would follow, but he didn't care. The only thing on his mind was getting somewhere safe – whether a dark room or a fresh environment – to escape the apathy of other wolves, as he had done once before.

None did follow. They stayed in their den, spurning any territories other than the cold crevice they had grown up in and shunning any creature that didn't belong to their tribe. They had no use for the insignificance of the raven and no respect for the habits of the grey wolf. The black wolf turned around, the other wolves settled, and they all went back to sleeping in the shadows or fighting over scraps. Not even the coming winter had seemed to deter them from the grim canyon they had resigned themselves to. They had grown used to the cold.

10

THE MOUNTAIN PASS

As night came, the two companions found a stony nook to rest in. It remained fairly well-protected from the elements by an awning of stone that sat overhead. Icicles hung over the entryway like the wet teeth of a giant creature that concealed them inside its damp maw. They had climbed high by that point and from their hovel, they could look down on the expanse of forestry that they'd overcome. Though shards of green pines could still be made out, the whiteness of winter had draped itself entirely over the valley. The blank of snowfall that they'd walked into was unavoidable, as prevalent on the forest floor as it was on the mountain range. At least here it was predictable; from a distance, the wolf had already seen the cold that washed out the slope of the mountain and he knew that making the journey upwards wouldn't be easy. But its highest point reached far through the clouds that the snow had fallen from, and he hoped that the very top and all its wishful luxuries were out of the cold's cruel reach. Much like with the quiet stillness in the eye of a storm, there may still be some high point of warmth and plenitude past all the harsh rocks and icy emptiness, where only the most determined and tenacious animals deserved to be. The wolf believed himself to be one of them. The settled state of the other wolves had given him pause for a moment – they seemed so use to their environment and they'd adjusted to a perpetual winter as if the mountain was cold and dead all over. But that could just as well have been the result of stubbornness or ignorance. For all they knew, there may well have been an Eden at the top of the mountain, past all the fog and hail, a mere walk from the place they'd remained in for so long, but they'd grown used to the harsh blizzards and granite slabs, becoming too set in their ways to risk any change in their arrangement.

The ridge they had journeyed to was full of crags and ice clusters, built up by crumbly grey pebbles that made it difficult to find footing. While from a distance the mountain seemed to be one solid form, the imposing tower was made of individually feeble stones when seen from up close. Seemingly, their sole purpose was to add to this one great structure; insecure individuals pretending to form one unbreakable system to any audience that was far enough away from it. Meanwhile, the beasts here that did have heartbeats were of immense fortitude, with tough feet and steely demeanours; the likes of bighorns standing firm against a skewed platform and rugged eagles lucky enough to be bred with both the freedom of a bird and the killer instinct of a wolf. Extreme spikes and drops in the landscape resembled the erratic rope on a heart monitor attached to somebody in the midst of a panic attack. It jumped from high open ledges that overlooked the boundless valley to tight ominous hallways where passers-by were blinded by rock. The sierra had its own not-so-little world contained in its edges and peaks, with many secret homes and alcoves, including the inlet where the two now found rest.

They had both kept silent during their walk here. Their mood was caught in a confusing gap between their demoralising run-in with the other wolves and the optimistic realisation that they were nearing the top of the mountain. The walk had been filled with a contemplative tension as the wolf thought about himself and the raven thought about him too. Over the period of time they had spent together – a whole season and then some by now – his changes had been too spread out and gradual to notice. But seeing him side by side with a strong and average wolf, the change became apparent.

Still, the raven wasn't without his usual empathy. He was reminded of how small he felt compared to everyone else; the wolf, creatures such as deer that he couldn't hope to take on alone, the humans, and almost any other being they came across. Knowing what it's like to feel small had made the raven grow even more akin and heartfelt towards the wolf. The bird watched over his woeful guardian as he slept. A perpetual whistling wind waved by, curving into the alcove with specks of snow riding along its current. The frost snapped at the raven, who shivered slightly. He looked down at his wing covered in satin feathers of black. It was streamlined and immaculate, though his feathery coat was much easier to keep clean and sleek than a mammal's fur one. He looked over at the wolf's coat. The knock to the floor by the black wolf had thrown gristle over the wolf's fur and it was now blotched even further with dull dust, thrown about in a multitude of unmanaged direction. With that, the whole coat had darkened, giving it a crude greyness more similar to iron than silver.

The bird peered back down at his own coat. It was a striking ebony like the commanding darkness of the alpha wolf of the mountain, who had also kept its coat slick with maintenance. The pack leader and its allies were fierce, mature and without injury. Lucrative hunting wouldn't be difficult for even one of them, let alone a whole pack. With such a force of strength, the raven might never in his whole life have to go hungry again if he stuck with the optimal pack – the general pack. With an army of wolves, if one fell, he could simply move to another and in its stature, it seemed the indomitable alpha wolf would be incapable of faltering anyway, forever keeping a sleek and glistening coat of black even in a harsh environment filled with blank white blizzards.

However, more thoughts crept in. Faults in the system that contradicted survivalism and basic nature. Remembering unique elements of his partnership with the wolf pushed the raven into an emotional state of mind. The other wolves were clearly a reckoning force, a production assembly of eating and resting and not much exploration in between. They might not like to play and run and wag their tails. It seemed they had a mechanical position within the space of this mountain; this was their staying point from which they never moved, picking off wanderers at the mountain's base and never daring to venture upwards themselves. Wonder and inquisition was more than likely cast aside for rules and normality. They probably cared more for tradition than freedom.   The raven was instantly soured off the idea of never using his wings to go adventuring again, seeing the same trees and rocks every day. He looked at his friend again, who had travelled all this way by his side and always provided adventure. Staring at him reminded the bird of all their similarities and experiences, all the stuff that tethered their hearts together. This sealed his choice. This wolf had thrown himself in harm's way for the bird, and vice versa.

He would die for the raven, and he in turn would for the wolf.

He watched the breathy fur of the wolf's chest move sweetly up and down, up and down, lulling him into a soft hypnotic relaxation where he eventually drifted off himself, nestled beside his best friend. By this time the following night, they'd be drifting off on full stomachs and a bed of greenery atop the summit of their deserved Eden.

Some hours into the morning, they awoke to a tremendous wail. It was the banshee-like howl of a ceaseless blizzard that made boulders judder as if on the verge of rolling. For a brief moment, they contemplated staying in the alcove of the rock face, but they would have to exit sooner or later, and it wasn't as if it protected them any more from the volume. They stepped out. The gale was hardly a hurricane that threatened to pull them up off the ground, but it was very uncomfortable to walk through. A harsh snowfall now intruded along the stream of wind, no longer gentle specks that grazed their coats but a hail of offensive pellets that needled at them. Winter had come in full force. Their eyes winced as their eyelids tried to guard against the flurry of snowdrops. The wolf's impressive eyesight kept them true on a path uphill, still heading towards the peak. Though the wind wasn't strong enough to knock the bird over, it kept him from being able to fly. On top of that, the craggy uneven floor of pebbles sometimes became taxing and caused the tiny being to lose his balance. A couple of times, he rolled sideways in a stumble with a panicked yet clownish bleat. The wolf helped him back up by pushing his small friend to his feet with his snout. Each time, the raven looked foolishly unaware of where he was and what had happened, sometimes resting on the wolf's nose with his feet dangling and swimming about in the air until they found the ground again.

The raven tried standing under his friend again, but it didn't work as well as with rainfall, as the wind fled right underneath the dog's body. He stayed under him anyway as they now walked at the same speed, and it kept them closer together. They pushed against the wind as they ventured through the peak's twisted ridges until they reached a slanted open side. Here, the mountain opened to an expanse of unimpeded air. Because the hard breeze wasn't being directed towards them through rocky tunnels and pinning precipices, its force grew a little bit weaker. They scurried to a flat rise sitting at the foot of a slope that led directly up to the summit, beyond the fog and the snow and the clouds. They stood in the wind a moment, looking at the trail ahead and contemplating that for all they knew, this could be the final leg of their dreamful journey. The slope upwards was a white carpet that led into an alley of granite. Its interior was marked with fallen trunks wedged against each wall like jumping posts. Brambled hedges and eroded piles of rocks lay on the sides. Leading up to the trail were tall and jagged stone spires that looked like discarded spears of the gods that had been petrified over millennia. These spears and pillars ran up to the sides of the trail's entryway, making the alley of rocks and trunks the only way through, the only way up to the peak. The site was daunting, but the crevasse looked like it provided cover from the blizzard by natural design, so they rushed onwards into the shadows of the great spires that hung over them.

Immediately, the inhospitable aura of the trail hit them. Now their concern was slinking around the prickly dead bushes that hogged the alleyway and ducking under the unsecured logs that were wedged between the cavities above them. It seemed like things from up high had fallen and tumbled down into here, giving credence to the thought that past the point of the cold wet clouds, there was a land of greenery and lush trees beyond. All they could do was have faith in the idea. Still, the hollow was a scary place, like the skeletal remains of the earth's body. They clambered over its stone ribs and weaved between its wooden bones. The floor was littered with rusted twigs that had fallen from dead trees, surprising them with snaps under their feet. Each step felt as though they were activating some precarious trap. What seemed like the ivory remains of an unfortunate goat lay smashed and trapped under a curtain of stones, implying the poor animal had lost its life to a rockslide. The dead stare of weeds and timber was almost as ominous as the watchful wolves, the tempered gale as daunting as their judgemental silence. Despite this, the two didn't walk precariously, trying to get out of the place just as quick as they could navigate it. There was no exit in sight, lost inside the oncoming clouds and taped up by the intrusion of wooden scaffold. The wind here didn't whistle like on the ledges of the mountain but bellowed and moaned as it bounced off the soft and unstable walls. All the stones around them quaked and jostled like grains of sand atop an erupting volcano. The deeper they stepped into the frosty fog, the harsher the weather grew in revolt of their progress; it was as though seeing creatures from the dirty forest floor trying to reach the shimmer peak was cause for an uproar. This, thought the wolf, was the barrier that separated the lowly floor-dwellers from the strong and tenacious mountaineers. The unseen divide between the highs and the lows. As they pushed on, the whirling weather turned into a furious boom. At first, it laughed in their faces for pursuing the summit, but now that they were actually attempting it, it sought to put an end to their efforts and tried to push them back – quite literally. Whether the pair had made a misstep that disrupted the alley's precarious arrangement, or whether the fragile structure had chosen this unlucky moment to give in to the harsh weather, the two were caught inside when it all started to come crashing down. In a turbulent rage, the walls ahead began to disintegrate and slide away at the will of the wind. Solid soil turned to grain. The grain turned from walls into piles. In a terrifying instant, the window ahead of them seeped away, closing quickly with loose earth. This brought the two to a fear-struck halt. In the wake of its power, a creasing shuffle came that sounded like a flame igniting on gasoline, but instead of fire there was only a cloud of dust. Ahead of them, one of the overhanging logs began to slide down from its fixing, falling away with the fickle wall that had held it in place. It rolled to the ground with a heaving thud before being consumed by the oncoming earth rolling over it. The walls weren't just closing; the path was coming down with force and taking everything inside with it.

Not just a cave-in, but an avalanche.

There was no hesitation. The pair experienced their most instinctual moment yet as they turned hard and fled. It was a long way back through the canyon where they had come from, past a course of many obstructions that they'd casually braided through. Now they had to run the same route as a gauntlet of hindrances that might trap them in or slow them down with fatal results. Behind, a destructive dominoes of rubble and wood pursued them. Every bough and rock that the wolf hurdled over and slid under was then left in their wake for the avalanche to consume. The raven had instinctively taken flight but stayed beneath the torrent of wind that spewed over the top of the trench, ducking around the wooden beams as his friend did. The pair were never too far away from each other, staying close out of panic and camaraderie. Nature's destructive power was not unknown to them, but it had never before chased them down with an apparent sentient malice. Dust rolled after them ceaselessly like a tide of molten magma cascading down a hillside, disintegrating everything in its path. The wolf struggled to stay agile, fighting through his limp to overcome barricades and blockages. Raining gravel made the raven's dodging unbearably difficult as stones were flung from the roaring maw at high velocity.

They knew the barrage of earth was growing closer as the logs ahead began to shudder, forcing them to push harder to stay alive. This only added to the exhaustion and confusion that started to affect them. The world collapsed all around and fumes of powdered rock enveloped the corridor as they fled ahead in the hope of escape.

An uninvited shock hit the bird. His lower back froze as a sensation ran through his nervous system. He felt as though he'd been petrified. In turn, his body tensed up. A shard of flint had shot out of the running rubble and scraped against his body. The motion of flight was replaced by a stunning seizure as he plunged downwards, twisting through the air and dashing against the rough ground. The wolf heard his painful creak but was still in a hectic sprint as the raven hit the floor. It took a moment for him to stop running and pause as he looked back to see his friend's downfall. Calamity continued to barrel closer to the fallen bird, threatening to bury him with the rest of the trench. The wolf hoped he would clamber back to his feet and dash ahead into the air, but the raven stayed down, motionless.

The wolf knew he was about to damn himself as well as his friend, but he also knew what he had to do. His loyalty was indefatigable. Seeing his companion falter had frozen the heartful hound with icy shock, but a brotherly fire melted through the ice, and he sprang into action as he vaulted back towards the bird in a race against fate. When he reached him, he nudged his ally's immobile body with his snout for a sign of life. He received none, but didn't wait long for a physical response. He had mere seconds to do something. Tension ran through his nerves, but overthinking in a moment of tension was his forte, whether for better or worse. With the last seconds afforded to him, he opened his mouth and mindfully lapped up the tiny creature, carefully pushing his lips around the bird to secure him in place but relaxing his jaw as to not bite into him. He tasted a pile of bitter soil that was scooped up underneath the bird's body on his tongue. The wall of death was rolling quickly up to him as he spun around and sprinted off again.

Every muscle in his body insisted on tightening out of panic and urgency as he ran, but he fought against his instinct and moved tender enough as to not harm his friend any further. His sympathy for the raven forced itself into his priority. He now cared more about protecting his companion than the obstacles ahead of him and the effective measures he should take to pass them. Various twigs scraped against his body and he recklessly butted against the sides of the rocks in a haphazard effort to escape. He was usually so careful and sure with his footing, but when it came to protecting the raven, his mind became clenched with emotional response. He was heavier now, and less careful – less streamlined. The landslide continued to rapidly gain on them.

He could see the entryway they'd come in from marked by teeth of stone, but his view of the exit became vignetted with clouds of dust that spewed out from the crushing earth behind him, just as smoke scolds your eyes and lungs before a fire engulfs you. He knew that the more his vision became deadened by debris, the closer death drew.

He ran blind yet heroically pushed on. Any hurdle or mound now appeared as a surprise from the sandstorm, and he bashed unknowingly against them all. He felt the rumbling of ground intensify under his paws and the avalanche chased close enough to push a breeze across his back. He took each problem as it came; there was nothing else he could do when he couldn't predict what was coming. Despite not paying much attention to the tangled weeds and startling boulders that came his way, he still noticed when they stopped appearing. He sprinted on, and the indecipherable air began to seem more transparent. The walls that ran beside him became shorter until they were level with him. His legs burnt from pushing forward, but he felt assured by his inevitable exit from the hole as the ground began to rise up as if exiting a trench. Beside him, a stone spire whizzed past, the same stone spires that formed the entrance. He turned sharply to follow them around, back to the foothill that they'd started on. He was panting heavily, trying to inhale oxygen in the little spaces between the body of the bird, as he turned to see whether they had escaped doom. The mass of rolling slush that followed behind had come to a heavy and resounding halt. With the walls beside them growing shorter, there were no more walls left to cave in and though an outburst of dust spewed from the remnants of the tunnel, it failed to pick up speed or volume past the trench, eventually fading away and cutting the avalanche short. His friend still lay limp in his mouth, but he could feel the poor bird's heart beating against the wet sensitive spots of his tongue. He was, at the very least, alive.

The wind still assaulted them. He looked at the mass of desolation left from the landfall; a barbed ruin of the valley that had closed their pathway to the summit. It was now impassable with disarray. The splintered shells of the logs and boulders now protruded up from a hostile pulp, looking like the aftermath of an active minefield. Beside them were the crooked spears that looked down over the edge of the mountainside. The passage had been their only way up to the peak from this side, but it had now been permanently clogged. The mountain was expansive and surely must contain another way up, but it wasn't this way. The harsh gale forced the panicked wolf to make a decision. Due to the rocks and daggers around him, the most useful path away from this fateful exit was back down the ledge; the way they'd come from. At the very least, it was familiar. That direction held the safety of the nook in the wall that they'd sheltered in; a knowing place where he could wait and keep watch over his friend until he woke up again. He headed back into the air of winter and reversed over their progress of the day. A morbid feeling hung over him as he focused on the idea that he had made no advancement, yet had ended up with a hurt friend and a head full of worry. Despite feeling so close to their goal, the day had been all loss and no gain – if things had gone to plan, they would have been at the top by nightfall, but now it would be the end of tomorrow, or the next day, or the next day. Just as it had grown inside the alleyway, the wind outside was still rageful. Travelling back, he kept his head turned into his body and away from the wind to protect his little friend from the cold. The alcove they had stayed in was easy to find again. He ducked inside it with tired and shivering limbs. His tongue let out a gentle sloshing noise as he released the limp wheezing body of the raven onto the ground as far back against the wall as he could. Then, with his own body, he rolled himself around the open side and hung his jaw over the top of the bird, creating a seal of fur around him. With any luck, the wind couldn't get to the raven now.

He looked around at the inlet they were in - a sterile and joyless hole, but it was less hostile and uncomfortable than whatever was outside. Ironic for the wolf; he'd once enjoyed both states of staying inside dark holes and leaping out into open air, but for the first time, he enjoyed neither. In exhaustion, the wolf managed to find sleep while the snowstorm swept in and battered against his back. Tomorrow they would search for another trail up the mountain. If that closed up as well, they would look for another. If that one was too precarious to traverse, they'd approach it from another side. And then try another, and another. They just had to bear through the stale winter and keep trying when they could until they succeeded in their goal. Because – just as he'd been taught as a puppy - the most lively, tenacious, proactive and heartfelt beasts were always rewarded for their efforts. He would surely reach the top.   That night, the wolf dreamt.

11

THE DESCENT

An indeterminate number of hours passed. Eventually, the wolf woke to the sight of the meek raven staring up at him. The thankful critter blinked his wet distraught eyes. His head was sore, and his mood was solemn, but he still tilted his neck around in a regained manner of self. While the wind shrieked outside, they lay still in each other's gaze without consideration for the harsh world they'd hid from. Their visual link was filled with worry and uncertainty, but behind it lay an abundance of comfort, knowing they saw the same worries within the eyes of another, a contradiction that gave an intensely necessary feeling of kindship within a situation of otherwise numbing frailty. It linked them in their moments of fear as much as their playfulness did in moments of freedom and whimsy. It was obvious that even when the world collapsed around them, whether in a physical sense as it had in the trench or an emotional sense as it had after the moose's attack, their main priority was and would always be each other. They didn't want to move from the hole – they cherished its knowability and security – but they knew that they wouldn't reach a better place if they didn't leave. By pushing through hardship now, they'd be out of the cold sooner rather than later. With a deluge of unease and reservation pushing back on them, the pair mustered themselves out of the entrance and trod on back the way they came, down the ridge side, with the wolf keeping an eye out for any offshoots and outlets that may lead to a safer route up to the summit.

Recycling their efforts, the two wandered by hideaway pockets and unremembered passes, but none led to anything fruitful. In a less mean-spirited season, these slopes and circlets may have been beautiful, with pooled water trickling from springs on the high rise and dandelions trying desperately to bloom through cracks of limestone that were warm to the touch. But as it was, each one was a frozen duplicate of the other, drenched in snowfall with only unwelcoming crag faces showing through. The snow here wasn't crisp and glinting like it was in the fields they'd pattered through. It was a drab and suffocating cover that abolished the world of colour. It bore no source of life or inspiration, warmth or respite. Despite the dry mood of their visual surroundings, they found a hopeful rise of tight-tunnelled steppingstones. They didn't go all the way past the clouds and to the peak, but still led upwards. Following the steps up, they came across a matted cul-de-sac adorned with sitting stones and a sliver of what was once a pond; frozen. A fatherly precipice hung overhead that may have held well against rain but had failed to protect this place from the all-consuming bleakness of frost. It was perfectly shaped - an oasis waiting to happen - but it had fallen prey to the same deathly winter that had taken the life and creativity out of everywhere else. A pit fell in the wolf's stomach. This kind of place was eerily similar to the mountaintop garden he'd expected to find at the summit, the one he'd dreamt about. This was the kind of place that had room for a field of flowers to play in, where prey and other animals could gather and graze, where fresh water could keep them hydrated and relaxed, and where tall trees could house the most admirable of birds in their rightful place among the clouds. But here, snow drowned flowers, animals abandoned the bluffs, the water was frozen solid, and any trees had toppled and rolled down the hill, becoming more liable to crush birds than accommodate them. This was exactly what would have occurred if the thing he hated the most (the dead cold of winter) had destroyed the thing he most desired (a bountiful paradise). That potential thought was worse than if the oasis didn't exist at all; at least then, it would be his own fault for dreaming up something entirely off the top of his head. But to see that the place he dreamt of was real and have it not appear the way he'd hoped – to have it be corrupted and killed by a blank merciless scorn – was the worst possible outcome.

He pushed the idea out of his head and clung to the baseless (and possibly foolish) hope that what applied here didn't apply everywhere up the mountain. The plateau had no other exits to lead from – this was as good as it got under the clouds. They took one last chilling look, thought about what might have been and turned out of the dead-end, returning to their desperate journey.

The wind and snow were admittedly not as aggressive as they had been during the strife of the previous day. The weather was now characterised by a pestering wail that fled through the mountain's crannies. It was reminiscent of a child ceaselessly tormenting its exhausted mother. The twists and turns of the mountain now twisted and turned more than they had on their first leg through, thanks to any waypoints or markers having been vanquished under snowfall. The way they'd come from became unnoticeable among new pathways that they hadn't yet ventured down, until they found one familiar arrangement. One they wished they hadn't rediscovered.

Two domineering cliff faces trailed either side of a tight and unwelcoming corridor. Had the sun not been blotted out by the drab clouds, these stone walls would still be tall enough to drench them in shadow. As harsh as the snowfall was, it had trouble touching the inner depths of this pass. It was the wolf den they had shamefully slunk through, but it was now void of wolves.

Even with their resilience and fortitude – even though they despised the idea of venturing out from the bitter crevice they had grown accustomed to – they had still hidden away from the ruthless weather. Sitting in frost was one thing, but having it batter down on them was another. The lair was no longer neutral for them, so they'd left for somewhere more comfortable, much like the wolf and raven (although what satisfied the pack's comfortability was probably much less aspirational than the paradise that the wolf and raven were hoping to find). Somehow it felt just as hostile without all the wolves looking down on them. While they were an army of unfamiliar and unfriendly animals, they were at least still animals; a sign of life. The duo continued on with a cautionary feeling. if their more instinctive and stern-faced peers had considered it wise to move on, they definitely shouldn't still be here.

The wolf stared out to the other side of the tunnel. To travel back to the other end would be travelling back through the home of aggressive degenerates and reclaiming a place at the bottom of the mountain, underneath them. He turned away in refusal. There would be more pathways to explore that may lead upwards. However, as much as he tried to find an opening, there was no easy passage - whether through gloom, blockage or danger, each one held a grim challenge. They hoped this one wouldn't cave in and try to destroy them. They hoped that one would be too steep for the wolf's strained step to be able to reach. They hoped another wouldn't meet them with stone claws that obstructed the way. They never did come across another peril as great as the avalanche they had first encountered, making them feel particularly unlucky and foolish to have experienced the trench's downfall. The harshest thing they found was a dead tree fallen across the way. It was so great in size and slick with snow that it was hard to clamber over. They mostly clung to the safety of the rock face, much like a mountain goat who made the best out of its situation to the point of impressive adaptation. While the corners and crevices they now travelled through were subtle and isolated, they were humble. However, this way was ultimately just as fruitless as if they had put themselves out in the open. No matter the angle they came from, they never saw a way to the top. Sometimes they sought to compromise, thinking that if they came across a set of rocky steps leading downwards, it may eventually carry them to a position that would take them higher. But the difference never evened out and they would always end up at a lower footing than where they'd set out from. Without realising, they'd descended the mountain just as much as they'd risen up it. Eventually, they slipped off the last chunk of ice-dotted stone that comprised the body of the sierra and stepped onto dull ground once more. From here, the wolf could look upwards and notice the sheer scale of what they had tried to overcome, as well as realise they had made no progress on it. It wasn't exactly the same spot as the crossroads where he'd first looked upwards, but the view now looked very similar. He was still, either way, back at the foot of the mountain.

Their discovery of the dead oasis had planted a fear in their minds that perhaps the peak above the clouds was just as desolate as the rest of the world, but now another fear overshadowed it; the thought of never making it up there to find out. The thought of miscalculating the difficulty, or even the impossibility, of making it up the mountain at all. The idea that it didn't come down to tenacity but breed, and that only certain kinds of animals had the necessary tools from birth to make it up to the top. Or worse, that there were only two type of animals; ones born above the clouds and ones born below, and no-one could ever pass from one position to the other – no-one could ever make it *up* the mountain.

As they focussed on climbing, they'd put food out of mind, but the grievous strain in the wolf's stomach became apparent and now needed immediate attention, especially considering the scarcity of food sources left in this climate. Despite his resolve to scale the mountain, looking up from the base of it gave the wolf some small assurance in coming away from his goal for a while. It wasn't as if any progress would be lost. Nevertheless, doing so invoked an understandable sense of defeat. So, destitute and miserable, he turned and plodded down to the forest behind him. The bird watched on. At first, he twisted his head about with confusion and concern, but in his companion's body movement, he could tell that it hurt him to turn away and he followed in support of his decision. In some way, the wolf knew that this wasn't a resignation, but a hiatus. He felt he'd put a pin in his aspiration, but first he had his survival instincts to nurture. He was hungry and cold; that needed taking care of for a bit. The whistling wind continued to mock them and the specks of dead bone in the air continued to haunt them. It kept falling for many days and nights to come.

For a while, sustenance was tough to find. Playing games or exploring new worlds was put out of mind. At times, they were lucky enough to find an unsuspecting family of hibernating rodents tucked into a burrow that the wolf's muzzle could just about reach. Other than that, warmth was a priority. They remembered the emanating comfort of the lights inside the odd valley they had passed through, where they pressed their faces against the clear barriers of the lively dens and felt the heat of the gluttonous creatures inside. But there were no lights around them now, save for the mystified remnants of the sunlight that wheezed through the haze of winter's deathly dust. The cold snuffed out anything else. What was worse was that the emptiness of the land promoted a similar emptiness in the pair's disposition. There were no fresh creatures to encounter, no new landscapes to claim, no challenges to test or bolster their partnership, no sources of passion to enflame their sense of love and aspiration. Their days grew barren, void of intrigue. The fields where they might have danced were wiped away by a sterile force that seemed to bear hatred for expression and colour. Even so, they couldn't dance with stiff feet and empty stomachs anyway. So, they mostly sat, ate what they could, and sat again.

It was over weeks that the wolf's eyelids drooped into a consistent melancholy and the raven stopped tilting his head around so freely and inquisitively. They would spend many hours sitting out in the open and grew apparently numb to the frost's hardship, accepting it as a permanent fixture of their days. They had nothing to do but accept the emptiness and wait for change to come to them – the current forces were far too great for them to change things themselves, like trying to stop a thunderstorm.

A certain apathy grew over the slog of a long, *long* winter; a state of mind and mood that's seemingly not often heard about or noticed. It's the feeling of the agoraphobe that goes years without experiencing the simple social gatherings that come easily to the masses. It's the languish of the depressive individual that feels too hopeless to lift themselves out of bed, yet in staying there, drifts further away from the relationships and systems that might lift them out of their dismal position. It's the mood of the old homeless person who has spent decade after decade trying to pull themselves out of their sore penniless situation, yet try as they might, they fail at each attempt thanks to prejudice, preference, luck, and the dozens of other reasons outside of their control. It isn't brought about from large and fleeting traumatic events that somebody could reflect on, but is a naturally empty and consistently belittling state of life. It leaves somebody just as cynical and pessimistic as a broken heart or an invasion of security would, without any of the intermittent love or luck that would promote confidence and courage; something to set their mind back on a more hopeful track. Trauma and heartache are things that can be shown physically or conveyed audibly. But this was stagnancy, and the pain of stagnancy is hard to convey. It just happens.

Often, things seem to move slower when they're larger and mightier, and the large might of the static cold seemed to drag on forever. Every tree had lost its leaves, every lake was glassed over and every flowerhead had disappeared under the harsh monotony. Because they couldn't see a singular force coming down on them in an instant, like with lightning, they couldn't recognise it was happening and so they fell to it slowly and easily. Every other animal seemed to have gotten out in time and avoided it. They'd given into basic animal instinct and either moved on appropriately to somewhere they were better suited or hidden away in a long comforting hibernation with their kin. They'd resigned themselves to what they knew they were and followed their nature appropriately. But the unfortunate pair hadn't. They stayed awake through winter and felt its chill harder than most did. It changed them as much as any clash with a foe, awe-inspiring dream or turbulent storm. Its ability to shape their minds – not through turmoil but through weariness – would affect them even after the ice had melted and the flowers had bloomed again. Despite the change in their disposition, some link in the wolf's mind held onto *why* he was bearing through the long cold winter in the first place. In some way, this helped him justify his lethargic, lazy behaviour by convincing himself that he wasn't wasting his time, he was just biding it. The slow and pitiful routine that the pair fell into wasn't a resignation, it was just a hiatus. They were settling for scraps and saving their energy instead of playing and adventuring, just in case. Because when – if – they attempted to climb the mountain again, they would surely fall into the clutches of barbaric passages, step into ancient maws that tried to eat them up, and wander into roadblock after roadblock of drab granite that would deny them entry to the peak. At that point, they would need all the energy and strength they could muster. So, they would just keep simply surviving and biding their time.

Just in case.

PART 3
ADULTHOOD

12

SPRING

Months had passed. Months filled with inadequate tedium – sad examples of temporary homes and negligible quantities of nourishment. Weeks on top of weeks of trawling through the world, each day lacking any definition or individuality. But with each new day, the snow grew a little thinner and a little wetter. Blotches of greens and browns revealed themselves and white powder dropped off tree stems as it lost its power over the world. Eyes opened inside holes. Tweets and twitters grew in density, a sign that birds were returning. Winter had its time (as gruelling as it had been) but now it was spring's turn to rule.

Many animals woke, blissfully unaware of the torturous season they had slept through. Others had been touched by the sting of winter, but the refreshment of spring hit them suddenly and they left their recent tribulations in the past, focussing on the virile and fruitful period to come. The few animals that were winter favouring were well-suited to the cold season and would miss it; over the next month, they would feel the air turn against their favour before naturally giving into their own cycle and returning to climates that the world desired to keep them in. But none of this applied to the wolf and the raven. The black bird, in his deeply empathetic character, carried the shocks and stabs of their troubles along through his nerves. The grey dog, in his extremely active and anxious mind, was cursed to remember every fault and failure they'd endured. The sunshine wouldn't brighten the world for them as it had for the other beasts.

They woke one morning from under a dead tree overlooking a frozen lake. They didn't notice that the trim of ice on the surface had broken away to show the breathy promising water beneath. The weather was warming, but even as the ice melted away and the sun reheated the land, the wolf's eyes still squinted coldly, and the raven's neck still stayed stiff. The distant sky-bound mountains and deep northern lands were still topped with cold plumage. It was their expected arrangement; that was where the snow belonged. The wolf looked up to the summit of these mountains and recognised the snow, still as thick and blank as when they had tried to climb one of them. The frost up there never seemed to move. Meanwhile, he saw an entirely different picture when he looked back down to the earth. The immediate land around them echoed the beauty and colour of a glamorous woman, the kind that men fantasize about - the hills rolled tight in a curving dress of royal jade, overhung by newly bloomed flowers that formed waving locks of buttered gold. The face of the land was complimented with dabs of raunchy umber against the lips of the forest floor. Shimmering pools stared up at them, blue and deep, bright with affection for the coming life that would surround them. Mother Nature had made quite an entrance. But much like a young man who lacked the confidence to approach such a glamorous woman, the two felt disconnected from being able to mingle with the world in its beautiful state. They couldn't touch it – inside, they couldn't feel the joy and splendour that they saw outside. The world was out of their league.

They moved with a glaring lack of inquisition as the wolf reproduced mindless patrolling steps one after the other and the raven sat slothful on his back. Their thoughts had grown submissive to measly expectations, their union mechanical and expected. They'd both become used to a screen of frost blinding their way, unable to see light so that now, even in the glorious clarity of a new spring, they were blind to forward aspiration. A lone deer scampered beside them into a clearing of trees, clopping its hooves through the grass and shaking the bushes as it dove past. The wolf continued to walk on in the opposite direction. He felt he didn't have enough strength to hunt something so large right now. He'd been living off mice and winter flowers for a good while. His frame had gotten noticeably scrawnier; not that he was particularly muscular to begin with, but the bulk that was there had been cut away. Plus, he'd never attempted to hunt large prey with his limp before and the sensation of stiffness insinuated that he wouldn't be able to run forward with enough dexterity to reach his target. He predicted failure too much to even try.

The birth of spring continued into the weeks, and in that time the bugs and pests found their way back. Flies dotted the blue air like pepper grains on the gale. Iridescent beetles waddled from one place to another. Ants resourcefully marched en masse down tree barks and over fallen logs as they returned to their tiny volcanoes of refuge. All of these small, slow-moving snacks were easy pickings. It was from these crawling creatures that the raven found his own peculiar coping mechanism, to add a wash of comfort to their usually dull and dismal days. By lying among the anthills and letting the ants crawl all over him, the bird felt a particularly pleasurable and intoxicating sensation. The ants secreted acids for defence against predators that, at the very least, made them taste less pleasant. But many birds get around this unpleasantness by letting the ants rub their fragrant residue over them first; not to mention how the tingling sensation of the crawling ants can put birds into a state of ecstatic stimulation. The raven first succumbed to the aroma while gluttonously digging through an anthill, splashing the ants against his face. As they wriggled up his beak to escape being eaten, they crawled down his back and gave him a spine-tingling sensation, almost like a massage. Later he remembered the feeling, so he crashed into an anthill and let its residents swarm over his body before any eating had even taken place.

The raven explored this venture over the course of spring and as the weeks went by, the rapture of the ants' stimulation became just as much of a priority as eating them. At the very least, it made the ants themselves taste much better. Now his eyes tracked the ground at every moment for the possibility of an anthill. He looked over at the wolf far less, dissociating himself from what was right ahead of him. His beckoning croaks towards potential prey became non-existent. The wolf, in his pitiful state, had given up on catching prey and the raven, in his disconnection, had grown oblivious to noticing it. In the soft sunlight of a mellow day, at a dirt patch just outside the woods, the wolf sat sad-eyed and passive as the raven lay motionless on top of an anthill, waiting for his injection of joy to spill out. He'd provoked the colony by jabbing carelessly inside with his beak so that in a hectic eruption, the ants would spew out like smoke and wriggle across his limp outspread feathers. There came a tickling sensation all across his bones as they crawled across his face and spiralled around his thin legs. The plentiful patters of tiny ant feet made him feel as though he were lying on top of a rippling ocean made of undulating jelly. His body felt real, yet not real. He felt as if he were flying without having to flap his wings. It was a fantastic euphoria. Eventually the wolf couldn't see the bird for the smog of ants. This, to him, felt like a waste of time and wasn't beneficial for survival. They were consistently stopping at anthills to let the bird satisfy his wasteful habit. While he indulged, he never cawed. He sat uncommunicative in his own separate dimension. Yet the wolf still stopped and let his friend continue, knowing that the raven hadn't smiled all throughout winter. He sat beside the bird and kept his irks to himself; he let his friend smile for a while.

As the raven partook in his new past-time, the wolf looked around at the fields in bloom. He stared on at the galloping fawns that seemed akin to ones he'd taken down and devoured in his time. In moments during a hunt, they'd looked terrified and agonized, but these ones had survived to pass through a field on this bright spring day with an ignorant expression of happiness on their faces. He looked up at the zipping groups of bees and flies that littered the air. He hadn't seen these for quite some time as like many creatures, they'd hidden away from the cold. In hindsight, that seemed to have been the cleverest course of action instead of chasing mountains. He stared up at the trees. The death of winter had taken the lives of all their leaves and with it, their beauty. But with a little bit of squinting, he could see miniscule green baubles sprouting from the sad branches. The trees would bounce back, and their leaves would flourish once again, and again, and again. They would always recover from the turmoil. It seemed that the entire span of hardship and misery could have been cut from the earth's timeline and it would still look no different now to how it had looked before. Life appeared content in returning to a blissful unlearning balance. Animals had not been affected and the scenery didn't bear permanent marks, or at the very least it was strong enough to recover from them. The wolf looked down at his own paw, the one that now bore a limp. Its fur was a shade he didn't recognize, dark and blotchy. Then he looked over at his friend lying motionless on the ground, immobile due to a dazed sense of escapism. It was hard to recognise him as the energetic and high-flying bird he'd first met. He thought back to an earlier period in his life when he could run and bound freely, prime for hunting. He also thought back to when he knew his companion at the peak of expression and physicality, most probably his behaviour for most of his early life as well. For a brief window, their prime states collided, and things were perfect.

The raven continued to delight himself. At times, the wolf yearned for a distracting past-time like the anting that the raven took pleasure in. But for him, the ants were too small and his fur was too thick for them to make an impact. Considering that the raven treated his indulgence as a replacement for their games, any worry or annoyance that the wolf had with the activity was overshadowed by a sense of understanding for his friend's need to fog out the harshness of reality. The closest thing the wolf had to this was sleep. That came very easy, in fact he always seemed sleepy nowadays and it became second nature to simply lounge around. He had grown too apathetic and acquiescent to wonder whether this complacency was better than challenge or purpose. This is how they'd survived throughout the wintry season and continued to live through spring. As new life was breathed into the world and the babes of last year grew into the strong adults of today, the two friends remained stuck in time, as though the winter had frozen more than just the trees and the waters.

They commenced their mundane routine of wandering the nearby plains as they approached a lonely and unkempt pond. It was sprawled out in the middle of a mist-coated pasture that was scruffy with long grass. The wolf lay by the water for a spell, close enough that his neck could easily bend down and lap at the edge. The raven seemed somewhat out of sorts, standing an unsociable distance away and looking around at nothing in particular. Nowadays he was constantly on the lookout for the good feeling that ants provided and seemed desperate to spot any that may appear in the grass, in order to follow them to his new recreational activity. He carried on with his own dazed habits, pecking at crumbles of dirt and letting out curious croaks for no apparent reason. He barely ever seemed to fly any more, using the wolf to carry him around. In the same way that the sensation of anting made him feel as though he were flying, backpacking on the wolf fulfilled his requirements of getting around without having to put any effort in by himself. In turn, the wolf never enjoyed watching his fluttering friend's motions, now that he couldn't see his whimsical swooping. He simply had to carry him around, deciding where to go without getting any feedback from his companion on whether they were heading somewhere good. As dispirited as the wolf was from seeking new ventures, the raven's cries that he used to let out during moments of discovery might just about have reawakened a sense of inquisition in him, enough to explore an area of adventure or purpose. But he never got the response that he needed, now that the raven was always on his back. After their short rest at the pond, the wolf stood back up gently and turned. The raven was facing his way but not looking directly at him, standing some distance away. It was necessary at this point to alert the bird to his leaving, as he didn't seem to intuitively adjust to his guardian's movements anymore. Rather than call the bird over for his own convenience, he needed to walk over to where he was and bend down for him. The wolf took two steps forward and raised his paw to make a third step towards the bird. But he never made it to a third.

He was interrupted by something. A feeling of vein-shattering agony that seized him immediately and intensely. It was a thousand times greater than the moment his rib broke from his encounter with the moose. The power and impact of an entire antler was contained within one focussed and lightning-fast surge through the top of his neck. It felt so horribly visceral that his body decided to put him to sleep in a subconscious effort to manage the pain. 'It can't hurt if you're not conscious to feel it', his nerves seemed to say. The last image he saw was the raven standing far away, his neck jolting upwards and his eyes, after weeks of unfocussed wavering, finally fixing their gaze into his own once again. A familiarity of awareness and concern seemed to return to the bird in a swift moment. The nonchalance of their partnership had grown so common that they'd started to take their pairing for granted, but as the wolf collapsed to the floor, the panic that it might be taken away from them shot through both their minds and their eyes met in a fearful glare. Their eyeline connected only for a second before the bird saw him crash to the floor, as if the wolf had been pushed down by a violent and formidable ghost. As soon as he hit the ground, he fell completely to the abyss of unconsciousness.

In the aftermath of the darkness, he heard the demonic churning of something spiteful. The closest thing it could be likened to was the sound that a sentient fire might make when it roars in anger or cackles with malice. It was resonant, almost choking, defined by tin and cinder. It shuddered against his ears until its echo faded down to nothing. That was the last thing that touched his senses before he faded away.

13

HUMANS

Nature shook. The neutral instinct from all the nearby animals was to flee and hide, and every tree halved in density as flocks upon flocks of birds dispersed from them, cawing in fear as they did so. What had scared them was a monstrous ring that reverberated through the entire forest in the wake of the wolf's fall. The noise of the blast died down and with it, a morbid silence fell over the pasture in the absence of all the animals that had been scared off. After a grindingly long handful of seconds, any creatures that did remain were left to witness a strange and terrifying beast, unseen by any of them before, charging through the forest. They may have held fast against the loud boom, but the sight of this possible new predator – a gargantuan hard-shelled monstrosity – finally caused the last of them to bolt.

Only the raven stood still, because the raven *had* seen this creature before. Its kind had been sleeping in clusters on the flat grey plains of the strange glowing valley that they'd wandered through. Two shimmering clear eyes, a solid red shell and four round black paw pads that rolled about. He and the wolf had deduced that all the creatures had been sleeping due to the lack of noise or motion, but now the raven had the chance to see one awake. The difference between its dormant state and its waking state became immediately apparent. Much like the wolf's eyes, this beast's eyes had a golden flash to them, but the glimmer was much less natural as they shone intensely and ominously. In the way that some animals disguised their body parts for intimidation or concealment, this one had a false maw at the front filled with horizontal silver teeth. The raven knew this was a false mouth, as its real mouth was at the back, breathing. Its spewing breath was visible, blackened as if it were choking on heat. It seemed consistently angry, growling as it barrelled towards the wolf's limp body. Some feet away, its ravenous churning came to a halt.

The raven wasn't sitting still out of familiarity with the beast. He was as scared as any of the other animals but having been harshly snatched out of his mindless state, he was struggling to reorient to the terror of reality and his body had shut down, steady as stone. He looked on as the confusion and horror continued; without warning, the beast opened two previously unforeseen wings and seemed to give birth to three slender figures. They were the same species that had inhabited the odd valley, adorned with inconsistent coats of colour and shape yet with similar bodies and faces. The three upright creatures trampled over to his fallen friend. The bird observed them holding peculiar rods of intricate design which they pointed up into the air. Squeezing a jut on these rods caused them to release a gross cacophony that exploded out with uncomfortable volume – the same loud banging sound that had rung out after the wolf's collapse – all the while whooping and shouting in a joyful yet confusing celebration of dominance. The bird watched them extend their brutish limbs as they lifted the unmoving wolf, carried him to an inhospitable cube made of small grey trunks similar to those that the firefly balls had sat on, and shoved his flaccid helpless form inside without any care. He could do nothing but watch as they heaved the newly occupied cage up onto the back of their hardy red beast before climbing back into it and letting it carry them all away across the hill, with its spluttering growl echoing behind. In no time at all the event was over and in place of the wolf, there was only a sticky pool of crimson blood that dyed the ground into a morbid mosaic. Just like that, he was gone.

The abandoned bird snapped out of his shock-induced trance as the whipping motion returned to his neck. Small croaks emerged from his beak as though he were regaining the ability to talk. He hurriedly took flight, immediately cutting into the forest and fleeing through an entanglement of leaves as he chased after the waning sound of the beast's growl. Tightly bundled pillars of wood and a frantic pace made for a formidable obstacle course. The violent sunshine created an epileptic flash through the slits of the trees as the bird rushed past them. On top of his already panicked state, the flickering light confused his poor mind a little bit further. The intrusive sound of the brute that had stolen the wolf was so guttural, so unbelonging in the forest, that it had drowned out any trickles of water or singing of crickets. The further away it got, the more it echoed all around until its direction dispersed and it seemed just as all-encompassing as it seemed far away. The raven was surrounded by its spiteful hum as it bounced off every tree. The sun strokes rippled in his eyesight as he bolted forward, the reverberating snarl of the monster obscured his hearing, and the apprehension of powerlessness intruded on his flight. All his senses were clipped. As he became overwhelmed by the feeling of impotence, his wings slowed down and he grounded himself onto the floor.

The trees stopped whizzing by, and the sunlight fixed still. Softly, the final mocking murmur of the cruel kidnapper dropped into silence. The dismal bird stood alone, a failure. He could feel an empty space to his left, blatantly unfilled by familiarity. It was the feeling of losing a leg and expecting it to still be there when you step forward, noticing how hollow and exposed the space it used to occupy had become. You can feel it, because you can't feel it. The wolf's absence took a number of things from the raven as well: his sense of security, his confidence, his composure, and especially his sense of sociability, rewritten over their time together. He had grown to be more comfortable in the company of a wolf and presumed in that emotional moment that he couldn't go back to other birds after this. But he'd seen other wolves up on the mountain as well, dissimilar to the one he travelled and got along with. Seemingly, he didn't know other wolves very well either. He knew *this* wolf and *only* this wolf. Of course, his companion had felt the same way for a long time, unable to connect with the group that he was most alike yet disliked the most and unable to connect with the species that he liked the most but who he was unavoidably and detrimentally unalike. For the first time, the raven found a quiet and lonely moment to contemplate the effects of their pairing and what it had done to his own social behaviours, something that had been evident for a long while to the overthinking wolf but was newly and terrifyingly realised by the frightened raven. They had been alone, together. But now he was just alone, alone.

Elsewhere, a blackness was lifting.

A blur rolled into sight and assorted itself into shapes resembling glinted grey stripes. The stripes tightened into detail – grey bars sat straight ahead, like a miniature blockade of hard monotone trees from a strange valley. A slicing pain in the top of the wolf's neck became apparent before the rest of the world came into focus. While the pulse originated in his neck, it maliciously emanated through the rest of his body, causing a numbing fatigue. Constricting nerves made it insurmountably difficult to move as he could focus on nothing else. His mind tried desperately to integrate the pain so that it could feel like a normal part of living (as it had done with his limp) and he could continue moving. Soon enough, it worked. With quivering knees, he attempted to hoist himself out of the puddle of blood that he was stewing in. He couldn't help but let out a cracked whimper as he tried. It felt like his muscles were scrunching up like a ball of fragile paper, so he collapsed back down with a hard splash into his own blood. As he lay helpless, the red goo continued dripping out of the gape in his neck, down over his soggy fur and onto the icy metallic plate underneath him. Through the gaps in the bars, the wolf could make out normality beyond. It was somewhat hazed by his dizziness, but there was still the familiar trees and the wafting blades of grass standing respectfully in the quiet open. The slits in his confinement teased the idea of freedom – dangled the natural world in front of his face. But he was trapped inside a cold artificial box of tightly knit bars.

He heard an unfamiliar clatter coming from behind him. It was made up of a shrill ringing and multiple high-pitched cackles. He swung his head around to see a daunting structure; it was reminiscent of a tree, or at least had the rustic brown surface of one. However, it had been malformed into a large cube similar in design to the strange dens that he'd once discovered - the ones that had held comforting light and communal merriment. The curved boughs of many trees had been chopped, tamed and stacked up onto each other to make this one. Embedded into the sides were familiar clear panes of flickering gold light, where beckoning warmth dripped out and struck against the ground. The clear opening sat on the opposite side of a setting sun that inflamed the grassy nook he was in. The shade of the den stretched sideways, making it appear somewhat foreboding as from his perspective, it seemed to avoid the kindness of the sunlight. Muffled guffaws continued to come from within. He remembered the last time he heard something make those noises; the complicated creatures inside the artificial valley. But the sense of heartiness that defined their loving laughs back then had disappeared thanks to the nature of his current situation. The cube that he was sat in was closed into the back of the abstract beast that had carried him off. It was dormant, its eyes no longer glowing. The indented pattern of the creature's rolling paws had left streaks in the soft mud which disappeared into the gathering of pines where they'd seemingly come from. Beside the square den, a smaller dwelling stood conjoined onto the side of it with a gaping hole cut into the front that he could see into. Like many of the dark hovels he'd slept in before, the physical blackness of night was apparently stored inside, bundled in so tightly that the gloom pushed right up to the entryway. The only visible thing inside was a grimacing sharp tool that was propped against the opening. That was the entirety of any new and distrustful objects around him. The rest was familiar nature that he was separated from. His freedom to return to it had been stolen by these undesirable things, and he himself had been claimed by their powerful arrogance.

The raven plucked a worm out of the ground and chewed it. He was as hungry, as always, and now didn't know what else to do. As he partook in his measly meal, he noticed there was a grimy puddle nearby, so plodded over to it and peered down into the water. There was a common raven staring back with no more wit than the next member of its species and no gratuitous size that made it stand out in a crowd. No unique features except for that it was more dirtied and scuffed than most ravens tended to keep, but that was hardly a point in its favour. He didn't see anything on the reflection's appearance that excused it from being part of an average flock, and why it shouldn't just eat worms from the dirt. So, he continued to chew.

He finished his worm from head to tail and now wondered, with nothing else to do, if he should just look for more worms. Then, there was a movement in the corner of his eye; a shadow fled by. It was off in the distance between a bush and a thin birch tree and caught his attention immediately before a hopeful sight emerged; the head of a grey-furred beast with a long snout and glistening ember eyes. At first, seemingly in a moment of denial, he thought it might be his friend, having freed himself and found his way back home. But as the similar-looking body of a dog slithered out, the bird noticed that it was smaller with spikier cheek fur and a sly face that didn't recognise or respect the raven's presence. The thing was a coyote whose appearance sat in a torturous middle ground between the beloved missing wolf and the tricky fox that had once played with the raven's emotions. His hopes of a reunion were immediately shot down and his mood plummeted further when the newcomer dashed for the bird without hesitation. There was no pretence of a steady approach or feigned sense of likeability this time around. It was just another wild animal.

The raven instinctively arrowed into the air. He'd grown creaky at this – the thing he was born most suited to – but could always rely on flight as a way out to safety. Still, continuing his streak of terrible fortune, the canopy overhead was thick and low. Much like with the overgrown grass around the ponds, spring's bloom had pushed the foliage into a heavy and fertile explosion. He hadn't been grounded by the foliage, but his flight had been restricted to just above the forest floor; the air was no longer an immediate escape into the sky. The raven lacked his usual skillset and now felt more akin to the scampering mice and squirrels that he considered to be pointless ground-bound morsels. As the coyote leapt up to snap at the bird, he swooped in avoidance and then rapidly began to flap away from the danger. Just as the wolf had been caged in the tiny striped box, he too was now caged by the overhanging trees with a fleeting coyote hot on his tail. As he jetted as fast as he could in some random direction, he felt as though his fortune and safety were almost surely gone forever, until one tiny splinter of brightness seemed to emerge. This brightness came quite literally as a burning red beam of final sunlight in the distance, shooting down from some hole in the canopy like a beckoning rapture, where the bird could be pulled upwards into a hopeful light. He gave himself immediately to this spotlight – he needed to, for it was the only light he saw left ahead – and upturned abruptly like a stone on a bursting geyser. He passed into the wash of the sun's ray and the forceful light splashed against his black coating. From the ground, the lone coyote pointlessly pounced up. It was far from reaching its target but like many animals, it tried anyway out of desperation. The raven neared the pinpoint of light where the hole was big enough for him to escape through. He did so with such force that the leaves around him exploded out, like a fox bursting out of a snow mound.

His wings outstretched in the strength of the setting red sun, and he flung himself up and up, higher into the air than he'd ever gone before until the trees looked like grass, the deer looked like ants and the mountains looked like anthills. But with his new sweeping perspective, he saw the whole picture of the world. Ants in the grass weren't his current concern. He didn't belong alone; he wasn't bred to operate in such a way. Now he had only one thought in mind. As downtrodden as the wolf had become, he was still a wild animal with strong teeth and a set of legs that continued to always get back up. The bird needed that as his other half. He was no great hunter or tracker, but he hoped that during the time he'd spent with his more adept friend, he'd picked up some knowledge from him.

There was suddenly a swift knock of wood on wood, as the door of the den swung open. The wolf had drifted off again from inability to do anything else, but the slamming noise woke him in an instant. The voices within became clear now that they had a direct outlet. One of the creatures continued to vocalise as it exited the den. The wolf snapped to a prone position and bent around to see. A disastrously ruffled being with bony limbs swayed out with haphazard movement, lugging itself around without care or poise. The door automatically heaved closed behind it with another disturbing thud. It seemed indifferent to the wolf in its vicinity, almost like it didn't even care that he was there. It clutched a long macabre utensil as it sauntered over to the entrance of the attached mini-den, the one with the blade at the entrance and the darkness inside. In one swift tug on a slim vine, the creature flushed the darkness out, evaporated and replaced by a plenitude of light and detail – more menacing or meaningless components that seemed alien to the wolf. The human trudged inside beyond the doorway, deep enough so that the wolf's angle didn't allow him to see further. Some odd noises followed; clangs and squeaks that the wolf couldn't discern as anything familiar. After a short spell of anticipation, the thing stepped back out, pulled on its magic vine again and re-darkened the hut. It began walking back to the cabin's doorway with a confident swing, but now that it was semi-facing the wolf's cage, it noticed him. Saw him staring at it. Changing its direction, it wavered with a sinister dominance over to the back of the solid beast that the wolf was hoisted up on. It kept making permanent and unblinking eye contact with the hound, wearing a smirk on its sunken mouth the whole time, giving the impression that it had experience in staring down wild animals in cages. It exuded a sense of superiority, as though the act of flushing out and demoralizing difference in the world came as its inherent responsibility. It held the blunt mechanical rod with both of its dextrous paws. The tool was black, sleek and historically commanding. Just from the tool's menacing presence, the wolf could discern that whatever it was, it was the thing that'd hurt him.

Within the air of malevolence, the wolf's initial reaction was to defend himself. His neck sunk into his shoulder blades and his face creased with the intent to look intimidating. He let out a grizzle towards the creature in order to seem as scary as he usually did to prey that feared him in the forest, but the being responded in a way like no other animal facing the wolf had ever done before; it cackled, unafraid. After all, he was stuck in a small soulless box of its own design. In an instant, it changed from an open-mouthed guffaw to a gritted set of teeth as it smacked its harmful tool against the cage bars. They sung a metallic dirge that instantly discouraged the wolf as it reminded him of the powerful takedown he'd been delivered. His growling had been met with a stern physical lash; he'd never fallen so abruptly from a snarl to a whimper before; never felt the urge to stand his ground be so immediately replaced by the inability to do so, even against the moose. It had bashed the bars to both quell his resistance and to frighten him into behaving. Beyond that, it didn't try to reach him through eyesight or audible calls. For all the intricate tools and designs it carried and lived with, the creature didn't seem like it was much for communication. It angled its weapon longways and slowly edged it through a gap in the bars. The wolf attempted to back up, scared to even be touched by the heartless contraption, but he could only back up so far before the stifling bars blocked him from behind and he was at the mercy of the device. He pushed as far against the back as he could as the mechanism slid closer and closer. The end of the rod met with the wolf as the human pushed it against his skull.

He was already too pained and demeaned to snap back. The creature continued pressing down, below the ear and above his neck, as though trying to push him right through the bars or trying to puncture through his head with the blunt barrel. It pushed and pushed until the wolf squealed out, high-pitched and merciful, in agonising compliance. As soon as he did, the human whipped the tool away. It was as if that was all it wanted to hear. However, a look of apathy lay on the human's face - the sides of its mouth completely parallel with no hint of enjoyment. It wasn't done just for kicks but seemed as though the human felt sending a message to the wolf *must* be done – a necessary terrible action for setting an example or asserting dominance. It reminded the wolf of the black alpha in the mountains, who assumedly wouldn't have seemed as powerful and frightening to its peers if it hadn't taken the opportunity to scare and humiliate him in order to continue proving its own superiority. Gripping its painful accessory like it was irremovably fixated to its hands, the human strode away back towards the door of its lair and re-entered. The wolf felt it was undeserving of the warmth and company inside, while he was left shuddering and weeping against a backdrop of cold and unhomely metal.

The sun was disappearing and with summer a good while away, the nights were still chilly, washed over by a crushing blue. An arctic steam settled over the ground below the truck, creating an illusory musk. Now everything rose not from earth, but from a grave ethereal cloud. The tears on the wolf's face almost froze into crystalline droplets, as though his loneliness and lack of purpose could be preserved in ice forever. Void of every influence but the moonlight, his grey fur was tinted as blue as the rest of the world. He could have loosened himself from against the bars once the human had left but he'd stayed pushed against them in the corner and was now lay down against them. They were hard and loveless, but right there at the back of the cage was the furthest point from people he could get and the closest spot to freedom that he could reach. The metal floor seemed to bend subtly in the middle where his blood had pooled. His wound wasn't fatal and was now clotting – perhaps pushing it against the icy walls of his new room had helped. The audible cheers inside the hut had died down but the light inside still ebbed with a mocking sense of luxury. Met with the unfathomable fortitude of the sadistic construct he found himself in, the wolf felt no earthly way he could fight back or survive this. He couldn't seem to sleep from the torment of his dissatisfaction and felt like he would go rabid from the inability to do so. But he also couldn't take any action. He was stuck, mentally and physically, in the most horrid state between sleeping and living. Unable to do anything, he did nothing.

Even sleeping forever might have been preferable; what else would there be to do now without the chance to hunt, to explore, to learn or to experience, and with no proof or indication that he would ever get to do those things again? He seemed to constantly and exclusively face forces that further imposed on the little pleasures that he did try to claim for himself; forces that appeared incapable of being beaten or brought down, whether they were as small as a human or as large as a mountain. They constantly intruded on his freedom to play, to hunt, to dream. Now, his nature had been compromised so much that he'd been robbed of the freedom of his freedom. He couldn't even move. Despite the size of the cage offering room enough to select a particular corner to lie in, the fact of the matter was it was still a cage. A cage that imposed restrictions and limits to everything that he might do, besides lie down and do nothing. Any extra space was meaningless without the ability to be himself within it.

So, he just lay there, doing nothing.

He had given up hours ago.

The world was stooped in black and blue, so much so that any element of it was indistinguishable from the other, as both sinister apparitions and friendly images were muddled together. All the more surprising then, when a piece of the gloom separated itself from the rest, spearing towards him with intent. He didn't notice it at first among the rest of the blackness; his eyes were looking downwards and hung with dejection. But in contrast, the dark form fluttered towards him with ecstasy. It was simply black, but its presence could not have been brighter. As its dainty feet dove downwards, the steel stripes of his prison blocked them from fully reaching him but if they could, they would've planted softly down into his fur and hugged him tightly. The raven, having mustered his heart, had searched through the dusk and the nightfall over the blanket of trees for his forlorn friend. In the depth of night, the unnatural glow of the nearby den had been exaggerated and lit up within the forest for the bird to follow, like a star guiding a wise man on a holy mission. He pattered down on top of the cage, rattling it with his ebony talons. Underneath, his friend was trapped in the same box he'd been carried off in. The bars were strict enough that he couldn't just walk through their gaps to properly reunite with his companion, but at the very least, the raven had found him again.

The bird took a moment to settle himself from shaking; perhaps it was excitement of feeling whole again, or perhaps tremendous worry over how they would get out of here. The wolf still hadn't seen him, so he let out a squawk that caused the dog to raise his neck – however painful that was – at instant recognition of the sound. It was a throaty caw that generally belonged to ravens, but with the quiver of care and love that could only have belonged to one raven in the whole world. It was possible that, not content with cruel beings and the weathers of the world pushing him down, even his own mind was now trying to emotionally mock him with the imaginings of fictional hope. But the moonlight was merciful enough to highlight a distinct figure above, separated from the rest of the gloom and set against its shining silver orb. A small feathery figure looked down on him, darting its neck about. A group of stars bounced around inside a pair of reassuringly childish eyes. Again, he was almost too pessimistic to believe it could be real at all, but something inside him still wished that it wasn't just a torturous mirage. He also wished that the gaps in the bars were wide enough for him to stick his muzzle out and feel the closeness of his friend once again. Still, he used his snout to take one big sniff and he was comforted by the pungent smell of wet feathers. The image of the bird remained and stared back at him. The raven continued to squawk quietly with an inflection of pity and sadness. Then he stopped as they both realised that thankfully, if nothing else, they were both real and back together again. The bird fluttered down onto the lip of the trunk that boxed the cage in. Here, he was now eye level with his friend. The wolf stood up and moved from the back of the cage, stepping out into the middle of the space as he strode through the pool of his own blood and continued until he was up against the other side, the set of bars closest to the hut and the humans, but also to the raven. He pushed his forehead up slowly and affectionately against the front of the cage. The raven couldn't fit through the bars, but he could certainly wrap his talons around them. He flapped forward and grabbed as hard as he could around one of the icy bars. Now up against the bars, he too pressed the top of his head against the same one as the wolf. Despite the thick divisive form of the cage and its soulless temperature, they imitated closeness and imagined each other's warmth as they symbolically pushed their heads against each other. They felt, even in this horrible state, close again. They retracted their heads from against the cold pylons. In a flurry of thought, the raven whipped his eyes around in order to find a way out for the wolf and noticed an indomitable puzzle box clinging from one bar to another, sealing them closed. Being the intelligent creature that he was, he understood the mechanism immediately. He tried clacking his beak against the lock but all it did was create a resonant sound that implied fortification. He let out a shoulder-deep grumble to let the wolf know that force alone wouldn't be able to break it. The wolf's eyes didn't change, as if the idea of futility was already in them.

Suddenly, the moment was broken as more noise came from inside the hut. Another load of wooing and clattering. Then a secondary sound of patterned beats and symphonic tremors started up. It rumbled the walls and flickered the lights. Both had cared for a similar sound when they had first heard it, but this melody was harsh and indistinct; maybe it was due to the thickness of the walls and the violence of the beat, but it sounded heartless and repurposed. It lacked the strum that they had enjoyed when they'd first heard such a melody in the town. Not long after, its dubbed throbbing shifted to an intense screeching as the door swung open and one of the humans came out again. This wasn't the same one that had previously tormented the wolf – this one was incredibly rotund and had a mass of fur around its face. Its head was turned back as it walked out of the entryway, finishing an illegible conversation with its fellows inside and grinning. Strangely, the wolf thought it had a kind expression, although kindness and ignorance are both very hard to tell apart on the face. The open door broke the obstruction to the melody inside and the thump-thump-thumping flooded insensitively out into the open range before the door slammed back closed, dubbing the music once again. In an instinctual effort to hide from the emerging human, the raven fluttered backwards behind the cage. Holding another of the dangerous implements, the human waddled over towards the red-shelled beast that carried the wolf's cage, still letting out a dying chuckle. Both animals remained completely motionless. The wolf stood upright like stone. The raven stood on the flatness of the carriage's back, washed in the shadow of night and peeking from behind the wolf's confinement. The human didn't look up at the hound until it was close enough for any creature to be wary of a vicious predator, whether caged or not. It still wore a soft smile as it approached. When stood in front of the cage, it let out a connection of random noises.

"Ey thar, duggee!" it sounded out to the wolf, whatever that meant.

The wolf didn't react. He'd learnt not to after his last interaction. The human held its weapon up and the wolf expected it to use the thing as the previous monster had, but it held the weapon lengthways and propped it up at an angle against the back of the red beast. Although the human didn't mean to do so with any threatening intent, the nozzle was rested upwards so that it was pointed at the cage and the wolf – it'd put it down without much thought. Once its gangly paws were freed up, the human moved around to the front of the beast, opened its side wing and fidgeted around for something inside. The wolf was left with the hurtful rod that had caused him so much pain pointed right up at him, taunting him. Because he didn't understand the full nature of the thing, he thought for a moment that if he tried to make any movement at all, it might go off by itself and try to hurt him. The human hummed harmlessly as it searched around for something. Its nonchalant behaviour echoed behind the wolf's stress and fear, creating a jarring juxtaposition to his senses. Eventually, the being clambered back out.

"Nu yeh wur daan heer som waar!" it announced as it emerged.

It now held six stout silver cylinders compacted together that made a sloshing sound whenever they jostled. It'd also brought out a collection of flimsy white squares covered in black patterns and little images. It bundled all these items into the same paw so that it could use its other to close the beast's wing before it barrelled back to the entrance of the den and slammed it closed again as it re-entered. It had forgotten its weapon. What's more, it hadn't seen the raven spying from behind the bars. The two now sat with the monstrous weapon pointing towards the cage. It was apparent already, but its inanimate behaviour confirmed for them that the deadly nature of the thing came purely from the animals that held it. Without an intentional force it was just a lifeless rod, like how a sleeping tree could be struck by a thunderbolt and turned into a toppling renegade that threatened to crush anything beneath. That wasn't the tree's fault, it was the thunderbolt's. The wolf wondered, if the animal's intention was to inflict pain, why use the rod at all? Why not just use claws and teeth?

Nevertheless, his neck twinged a little with every movement, reminding him of what they were capable of. The raven wondered the same thing while staring at the lock. He wasn't capable of comprehending the concept of an intricately designed key that fit the mechanism, but he didn't need to. A tool was a tool, and ravens are very clever creatures when it comes to tools. The bird danced around to the front of the cage, to the back of the truck that the destructive device lay against. Only the last few inches of its barrel surpassed the edge of the carriage. If the thing were bumped, its nozzle could easily slide past the edge and fall onto the floor. The raven tiptoed up to the end of the barrel. The wolf tightened with worry, still unsure and terrified of the thing. He didn't want it to go off on the raven as it had against him; with a creature as small as the bird, its blast would be far more potent – even fatal.

The plucky raven locked the top of his beak around the hole at the end of the gun and carefully moved his little feet around, tilting the barrel slightly. The wolf wondered what he was up to; to him, this just seemed like madness. But the raven, in his daring and intelligence, had devised an idea. He lifted his beak off the barrel and turned his head back toward the cage, to eye up where the lock was, then went back to twisting the rod. It was made of a heavy material, already quite an effort for the little bird to control. Beyond the raven's intended motions, the weapon twisted sharply, and the end began rolling right across the edge of the carriage's back. The ridge of the barrel slid against the rim but slowly – thankfully – scraped to a stop. One more push and it would have fallen to the floor. As it teetered towards the edge, the raven saved its descent by jamming his beak down the dangerous opening. He then twisted it back ever so slightly to a point where it was safe, yet still pointed at a sharp angle. The bird looked up to check his progress. The end of the weapon was pointing directly towards the puzzle box on the edge of the cage. Though he was usually the methodical survivalist, the wolf never clocked on to what his ingenious friend was attempting, mostly because he would probably be apprehensive about using the weapon himself; if he had recognised the bird's behaviour, he would have been mightily proud of his ingenious friend. Even without knowing what was going on, the wolf sat docile at the fascinating process of the raven; he had come far from sitting slovenly in trees while the wolf took charge of situations. The raven had no way of alerting his ally to move back, so as he was known to do, he acted immediately and recklessly. He thought back to when the humans had walked up to his unconscious friend, pulling a hinge on the side of the rods to set their explosions off into the air. He re-enacted what he'd seen these beings do, hopping down and sticking out his talons as to aim for the protruding lever below. His little foot gripped between the gap and clutched down onto the small lever, clumsily falling backwards as he did and bringing the weapon down with him. But the mechanism was instantaneous and before it had time to fall out of place, it fired off. Some projectile travelled too quickly to see, but the end of the barrel lit up and the lock it was pointed towards had taken a hit, shattering apart in a flurry. The wolf rolled away in a frightful fit. While the lock split away from the set of bars, they were heavy enough to stay in place for now. The weapon toppled to the right; its calamitous end directed away from the raven as it hit the ground with a small tremor.

The instant reaction of both was to check back towards the door to see if they had alerted the monsters inside. The thumping inside continued - the shot had been no more resounding than the aggressive melody had been when the door was opened and more than likely, it had drowned out the blast. The raven picked himself up and let out a self-affirming chortle, then fled back up onto the lip of the carriage. The cage door now had a small gap where the bars had been parted. All the wolf needed to do was to push forward and swing the cage open, letting himself out and claiming his freedom. But he didn't. In fact, the wolf turned and went further into the back of the cage. The raven was confused. He hopped down closer to the foot of the cage and round the side next to the wolf again. He put his head close to the bars and looked up at his forlorn friend. Their eyes met. The blue hue of the deepening night truly did wash out everything, even the gold shimmer in the wolf's irises. The raven saw different eyes; eyes of pooling milky water and worn brass. Strangely, the redness of the veins that expressed his tiredness was still visible, as much as it contrasted against the world's indigo hue. Their sunny gold too should then still show through. But it didn't.

Despite the overpowering drumming of unwarranted noise behind them, their hearts and minds fell silent. For the first time, the raven questioned whether he should caw. He understood that something had changed. He was no longer the bird that stood back and did nothing except give encouragement, and his companion was no longer the wolf that would accept it. He'd been excited to release his friend and continue into the wild world as things had been. But he hadn't stopped to considered that the same excitement in his friend had disappeared – he hadn't thought he *needed* to consider it.

But the wolf had given up hours ago.

Once again, the moment was broken by the boisterous blimp of a human, absolutely incapable of exiting the den with grace. It seemed to notably waver with a lack of wit or focus and hiccupped violently. It breathed heavily as it approached with eyes darting around the floor.

"A sweer da gad, weir ees eet?" it seemed to half-anxiously announce. It bumbled over to the floor beneath the truck.

"Aha! Thir yuar!"

It bent down, almost falling forward as it did, and clasped its forgotten weapon with a swift lack of care for its power. When it tilted its body back up, the wolf was the first thing in its sights. Once again, this particular human seemed surprisingly cheery, with sleepy eyes and an optimistic grin.

It slurred out "Heeeee aggin, daggee! Yu gan beya gud boywinwegetyabacta-" its calls just became a string of abstract syllables to the wolf at some point. It finished with a high-pitched, almost innocent giggle.

"Hehyah!"

But then, in an audible tone shift, it bashed the metallic end of its rod against the top of the cage with a clang, as though it felt it was a harmless and affectionate thing to do; as if the underhanded reminder of its violent designs fell away under the joyful-sounding speech patterns. The human's disposition offended the wolf; the implication of nicety in the wake of his imprisonment and the casual approach to wielding such painful weaponry, like a dictator who believed their citizens were in full agreement with their oppressive restrictions and tyrannical actions. The wolf dipped his head with a growing discontent, a change in demeanour too subtle for the intoxicated lummox to recognise. The raven stood spectating all of this in the shadows, his eyes swapping focus from one subject to the other. He let out a concerned croak. As it was out of sorts, the human found it a curious sound for a wolf to make and half-reasoned that the source of the sound seemed to come from behind the cage. It tried looking around the back of the wolf to the source of the squeak. As if in sudden fright of the raven's discovery, the wolf tipped his head down in a swift enough movement to pull the human's focus, impulsively responding to his protective instincts over the raven. To him, it was bad enough that they'd sought to trap a vicious and steadfast creature like him in a cage; he feared they'd make short work of something as dainty as the bird. His sudden movement pulled the man's attention back towards him, keeping the raven still secretly blurred by the shadow behind the cell. The two held eye contact for a moment before the man remembered what it'd come back outside for. It turned with a newfound grip on its weapon, and tried wobbling left and right back towards the door of the den. Before it reached it though, its body tightened up as though a discomfort had gripped its loins and it let out a gassy "oof".

The human altered its stepping off to the left instead, towards the shack beside the den, clenching the space between its legs as it hobbled urgently away. Upon reaching the entryway, it pulled on the cryptic rope that made light appear and as the other human had done before, disappeared inside. The audacity of the human's nonchalant glee and oafish staggering spurred a boiling point within the wolf. Even if not through want for himself, but from his emotional response to these arrogant creatures, he stepped forward, and stepped again, and continued stepping forward until his paw collided with the gate of the cage, which he pushed out of the way in order to continue moving ahead. It wasn't aspiration or freedom or even survival that had urged him out of his confinement, but a fiery impulse that had built up and took control of his muscles. He dropped down from the back of the red beast. He'd intended to drop with a knowing landing, but when he hit the ground, he didn't anticipate that the abrupt impact would affect the clenching in his neck. While he didn't collapse to the floor, his body tensed up and he creased hard, dipping in agony and letting out a weak huff. If anything, it reminded him of what the men had done and made him even more resentful. The raven perched himself on the carriage's back edge to watch the wolf's recovery. The hound was too seething to let the pain stop him this time; his legs straightened, his back recurved, his head lifted, and he skulked maliciously towards the entrance of the small shed. On his way, he passed the entrance to the main den. Inside was the human who had stricken him and caused him excruciating pain, but it was hard for the wolf (who had been unconscious when the humans had picked him up) to know how many more were inside and how many of them had the advantage of their weapons. So, while he was denied vengeance against that certain monster, he settled for something similar.

He crept towards the open entrance of the attached shack, bathed in the sickly yellowed light that fell out of the opening. A hunter's spirit reignited inside the wolf and as silently as he had done many times before with his prey, he crawled prone and stealthily inside to avoid alerting them. Items of uncountable numbers and unimaginable intent lay upon the walls and ledges, all looking artificial and designed to hurt creatures or tear down nature. The man was nowhere to be seen but a loosely closed wooden door sat against the back wall. A sound emanated from the doorway, a high-pitched whistle. From the characteristics of its earlier calls, the wolf could tell the balloonish human was the one making the noise, but the only thing the wolf had to compare it to was the spiteful wail of the wind up on the mountain. Outside the door, he noticed a familiar sight beside him. The weapon of the human lay propped up against the side wall. The wolf passed it. He came to a halt as he knew the man was beyond the door. Knew that all he needed to do now was wait. The raven had flown onto the heightened windowsill of the main house not far from the open entryway. The light inside struck out and threw the magnificent flickering shadow of a giant angular bird against the ground in front of the building. He stood like a doorman at a private event, or like a deathly omen, waiting.

There was a gushing sound, like a small but tumultuous rapid of water swirling around. Not long after, the man emerged from the inner door. It opened the door by bumping into it with its back, still turned inside as it emerged – its paws were occupied, adjusting another puzzle box around its waist as it exited. It finished and eventually turned to see the wolf standing between itself and freedom. At the sight of the wolf, the man's face could have practically been mistaken for a still image. It didn't stutter, it didn't jump, it didn't double-take; its body became immediately statuesque with terror. Sweat had never formed so quickly on a brow. The only part of the man that could move any more were its eyes, the only sound its mouth could make was a stifled gulp. Its focus darted with fatal regret to the image of its troublesome tool, propped up against the entryway, out of reach behind the wolf. The animal's gaze was authoritative and devilish. After having been silenced by the initial retaliation of the first man, the wolf re-found his voice. Regardless of language, his resentful snarl told the man everything it needed to know about what the wolf was going to do.

"No... No!" the human stuttered out as its brain began to kick back into some sense of fight or flight. But just as the human was capable of moving again, it was robbed of its ability to do so. The great wolf leapt up high with a vile growl and plunged his claws into the man's chest, his fangs into its throat. They both toppled over until the wolf was on top of the human, whose attempts to scream were stifled after only a short moment as its mouth pooled with blood and its vocal cords were torn out. What the wolf did with him after that was pure catharsis, the lengths and details of which the raven didn't even care to look at. He stayed outside on the sill of the hut, which vibrated with the overpowered thumping melody coming from inside. The bird could only barely hear the man's faint gurgles and the wolf's ravenous grunts. These went on for a while until eventually, they died completely.

Moments later, the wolf emerged from the doorway. He was dyed crimson. The pool in the cage, the veins in his eyes, now the entirety of the wolf's body; it was apparent that passionate red seemed to stand out harshly in the saddened blue of the night. Despite having the desire to do so, the wolf didn't intend on storming the den and eviscerating the remaining occupants. They continued with their music and joy, ignorant to what had happened to their cohort. The wolf strode off towards the thankful freedom of the forest. The raven, appreciative to have his friend back, magnetised to his path. The killer's paws dripped with blood and left deep wet prints trailing across the hillside. Eventually the trail thinned, whatever blood remained on his fur dried up, and the stench of humans dissipated, along with the tracks that led back to them.

14

WOUNDED

When the sky-bound light of the following day eventually came, it was dampened and dispirited. The night's blue hue seeped into the waking air and had been muddied with a sickly thin grey that desaturated its colour like pouring bleach onto an azure blanket. The pair had sought to rest as soon as possible. While moving onwards, they'd managed to squeeze their bodies under a tangled wall of dead thistles that closed off a nook in the forest. In the shadow of such a cramped and forgotten hovel, they were removed from the outside world for the time being – safe, yet feeling like outcasts for having to escape to such an inhospitable hovel. The walk there had been tortuous. Though the blood had clotted, there was an unwanted nugget of lead tinkering around in the back of the wolf's neck that had found a home down in the shaft of his wound. It was a new piece of him that shouldn't be there, and it seemed to fidget around of its own accord, never letting the wolf feel comfortable and always keeping his irritation in constant flux. Each step came with a pause to let it settle and each time he began a new step, it writhed again. His limp had turned into a handicap. He didn't just waver to one side anymore; now his entire neck dipped, and his shoulder blades warped with each lope he slogged through. He sought now to sit down for as long as time would allow, and refrain from ever moving again as much as he possibly could.

The sun failed to strike through a set of dim clouds and before long, a dismal rain sunk from their dimness. The wolf's fur had stopped looking blue and started to look grey again, but the lack of any pure light kept his golden eyes dulled to copper. The water pelted down and did its work on the blood that was dabbled around his jaw and legs. His fur became sponged with rain which he took no measures to avoid, sitting under a thinly leaved tree that failed to keep out the downpour. The raven stood some feet away, shivering in his stance. He hobbled up to the wolf who sat curled with his back against a tree. Standing in the open, the rain had slipped against the raven's feathers, and he'd hoped to dry off in the snuggle of the wolf's fur, but the rain had gotten to him as well and the bedding of his tail felt as cold and soggy as standing alone. Still, he curved his head in slow pain and tried his very best to close the raven in a tight seal, placing his jaw over his friend to form a canopy in the usual way he did – as he had done up on the mountain – to keep out the cold. The bird croaked in thanks and relief. He didn't feel warm necessarily, but he felt cosy. He felt cared for.

Under the white noise of the pattering water, the raven's nerves had somewhat eased. His mind steadied. He thought back to the previous night, to the wolf in the cage, defeated by an inanimate object and devoid of motivation to carry on. The raven had always needed a tenacious and aggressive lead to follow, traits that the hound had once again shown as he took out his anger and revenge on the human once he'd been freed, but only when the human was defenceless and caught off-guard; it seemed that it was easy for him to act out when the odds were in his favour, but when backed into a cage he lost all confidence and strength. The raven thought of how many times they had been – and might still be – backed into a corner and how much more it mattered to continue fighting in these moments rather than just when victory was a certainty. Was that real strength?

He continued to think back to their turmoil in the winter, when despite physical shortcomings the wolf had risked himself to save the bird's life, still committed above all else to his friend even as the world was falling down around them. He assumed that the level of fear he'd felt during the avalanche was equally felt by the wolf and then accounted for how much empathy it must have taken him to overcome that fear in order to run right towards the source of it, for the sake of love. Would he always be willing to take those risks?

He thought on all the wolves they'd passed in their mighty domain, standing elegant and proud. They were definitely wolves of natural prowess and aggression. He remembered turning to the one he travelled with, comparing him with the others. There was more than just something different about him. The basic shape was there but every nuance was different – the walk, the lifestyle, the motivation. Was this even a wolf? Did *he* realise these differences too? Did *he* think he was a wolf?

He thought back even further, to the time when they faced the moose that had paralysed his ally. This was the moment when the raven had found out that the wolf was not all-powerful. He was stunned at the realisation that the wolf had flaws too and that he could fail. They'd been so confident in their union beforehand, yet had seemed to fail so many times since. That moment seemed so long ago, in the early days of their travels, before the winter. Had it really been so long? How many times had they had a win since then? How many losses? Had he really continued to follow the wolf after all of them? Why? Simply, because his nature relied on sociability – dependence on others. On him.

His mind drifted back further to the deceptive fox that had sought to trick him. She'd feigned interest and compassion, but only wished to fulfil her own needs. For all his shortcomings, the wolf at the very least seemed selflessly and genuinely concerned for another being. How many more animals out there had the compassion for the raven as he had? Were all other predators out there like a fox or a coyote, out for themselves, ravenous and mindless? Or were there others that might help the raven just as much while loving him just as fully? Was there another one of *him* out there – whatever he was?

He remembered the flock of birds that he'd flown with at the lake and how he'd felt a mild belonging for a brief moment. He swooped around and looked down at the wolf who had stared back up, incapable of joining in the flight. He'd had a forlorn wishfulness in his eyes, as thought he could join in. But unfortunately, this was the way it was; birds and beasts. The raven was a bird, but did he also want to be a bird? The raven didn't need another bird. He needed a beast. He needed to be beside an animal that, in heart as much as in body, was a wolf.

He flashed back to the thunderstorm they were caught in and how calmly and stoically the wolf had braved it – how he'd once again put the security of the raven ahead of his own with an astute approach to danger, shielding his friend from the deluge. The rain that hit them now was softly reminiscent, minus the crashing thunder and impending sense of doom. At the time, the wolf had prioritised finding safe respite. Now here, he accepted lying soaked in the downpour. Which was more commendable: steeling your nerves temporarily to escape from a horrible situation, or adapting in a way where you've accepted the horribleness as the norm? What made someone strong?

Then he went even further back in his mind, thinking to the day they met. How intriguing it was to see something so captivating yet alone, with eyes full of vigorous fire. As soon as he saw them, he felt the potential of a more prosperous and personal venture, desperate to separate itself from the rest of the flocks that flew through the forest every day. The elements of survival that the bird found difficult seemed to come so easily to the wolf in the moment of the hunt. While thinking back, the bird realised that the deer hunt was the last and only time he had seen the wolf hunt and live so easily; not since he had the bird following and aiding. In fact, he'd never seen the wolf indulge in a challenge where the raven wasn't cawing in a tree, distracting their prey and giving him an advantage. What had happened to the wolf that now lay beside him? Was it, maybe, that the raven had done this? He'd hoped that tailing the hound would help him become a stronger and more fruitful animal in himself, but instead it was the wolf who had devolved into becoming as small and fluttering a creature as an anxious bird picking at scraps. At what point had the wolf started following the raven?

He thought back one last time to before then, when he was just another small scraggly chick following a fast-moving unkindness, afraid of any living creature larger than himself. He functioned well enough, moving from group to group, area to area, season to season, with not much permanence or substance. There were other birds that looked like him and sat close by, but he remembered from an early age being prodded out of his nest to learn to fly and find his own path. Had he actually done that here? Was he capable of setting up his own nest – his own flock – and teaching them to fly? Could he fend for himself and, if not, was going back to a flock the kind of life he wanted to return to? If he did, would he have to accept settling back into a mechanical, uniformed community? Could the raven lead? Could he be strong and brave? Could he be a beast?

All these thoughts muddled the small bird's erratic mind. His senses knocked back into the real world and he took the time to look up at his guardian again. The fur of the wolf's chin curtained pleasantly over his newly dried skull. If nothing else, he at least still seemed capable of protecting the bird from the rain. He wasn't sure if the dog was a guardian at all anymore, but he was still most certainly a friend. The idea that late spring might stay relatively quiet seemed like a dead option, now that a sense of emergency had been awakened in them both. Though their unity had grown stagnant, the fear of that unity being destroyed had been held up to their faces and the thought of being separated again seemed much scarier and lonelier than any level of frustration or malnourishment or doubt.

They slept for almost a full day. They had, after all, been through an ordeal. The next morning, the wolf woke up to the lousy spindles of the dying rainfall plinking on top of his snout. The hidden nook was awash in the colour of wet dust as the morning sun bled in and stirred like paint into the milky shade. The rain felt strangely warm now. He raised his chin off his back leg to reveal the raven slumbering in the crevice underneath. Had it not been for the fraternity and dependence of his companion, he would have been content with staying asleep forever, just as he would have been content remaining in the cage. But the security of the raven had triggered his brutish instincts. He felt dependent upon the dependency of another. The discomfort of this dependency had grown too overbearing to ignore and he'd felt it necessary to escape the cage for the raven's sake, despite how tired and achy he felt whenever he moved. In order to keep his sidekick dry, he'd taken on a heavy rainfall over his own coat. It felt almost more like a burden than a purpose now, like having a marble or a pea lying under your back when you're trying to sleep; it seemed like such a small and shallow reason to stay awake but was irritating enough to make it so. However, as he looked down at the snoozing raven, he got that familiar feeling. It was the feeling he knew from bounding and chasing in fields together for no other reason than to enjoy the moment. It was the feeling of emerging from a soaking cave to see a black silhouette standing guard, repaying his care with companionship. It was the feeling that accompanied the visceral imaginings of being a winged amalgamation in his own luminous dreams. In his newly realistic state of mind, he looked down at the raven and reasoned that being side by side was the only way to have his own pair of wings. He took a moment to think back on all the sharp horrors they had endured and how much worse they would have been had he gone through them alone. How much quicker he would have given up. Yes, it seemed as far as things had gone now, this was the best way to be, clinging close to the little enjoyment left in the world while it remained. The alternatives – travelling by himself, enduring his wounds alone, joining another pack or starting his own family – were either worse, or impossible to achieve.

15

THE THRONE

Two little black eyes opened to see the world. By this point, the spiteful rain had diminished to a mere trickle. Once the sleep had crumbled from their eyes, the two stood up and continued making their way through the thickets. The wolf trod slowly as the raven hopped comfortably behind. He never fully took flight but made short thrusts into the air with his wings every so often. In the wolf's wounded state, it was rather easy for the raven to keep up on foot, in fact his stilted hops and the wolf's lumbering steps kept at very much the same speed. The grove they were in seemed unusually bitter and anything that did live there must have been hiding in the deepest recesses of thorns and roots, except for a few sturdy explorers. A bumbling beaver trudged its way across their path in the manner of a flustered businessman during a bad day. Overweight, ruffled and in a deep huff, it waddled through a hole in a tree before the two had any contemplations about hunting it. Further down the path they noticed a marmot sitting on a rock, which immediately hissed at them (not to defend its territory but seemingly out of an ingrained rudeness) and then flung itself over the back of the rock in a disappearing act, never to be seen again. What an unpleasant area of the woods, they thought, as even the smallest of animals seemed intent on standing their ground. Even though the promise of the coming summer should have brought warmth and liveliness, everything seemed cold in spirit. The woods were pressed by a glassy shade and the hostile behaviour of the creatures around them produced a glum atmosphere. The bushes felt more like overgrown weeds than fresh flora. The silence was equally chilling, as though everything was dead or as if time itself had been frozen by the cold hostility. At first, there appeared to be small flakes in the air. The flakes were reminiscent of the new-born snowflakes of a coming frost. The very thought of a premature winter was terrifying considering their past experience with that season, but instead these specks seemed much less lively and not nearly bright enough to be composed of ice. It almost seemed like dust hanging in the air. Dusty was exactly how this place felt; old and untouched and abandoned, like a derelict manor full of rotting beams and splintered bannisters and cobwebs wafting in a light breeze, haunted by spiteful sprites and eerily quiet thanks to the empty spaces of residents past. But the wolf felt that at the very least, it all seemed purposeful and was birthed from their natural kingdom of moss, stone and wood. That was, until a sight shocked and sickened him. He stopped dead in his tracks.

A trail of indents that disturbed the grass struck through the ground like surgical scars on an otherwise pristine body. It sickened him because he only knew one kind of thing that left tracks like this; the monster made of rolling round feet and gleaming eyes that had carried him off. They'd seen the tracks as they walked past the sleeping demon, after the wolf had made a meal of the human in the den. They could only guess at the power of the thing to be able to leave such deep crushing tracks through the earth. During their time with it, the lack of any scent or warmth of any heartbeat had led them to realise that it almost definitely wasn't a living breathing animal and was likely a moving construct, more like a rolling boulder or a tumbling avalanche than a striding moose or a trudging bear. But that made the thought of the things even more terrifying, as they still apparently seemed to have some kind of sentience – their eyes and their voices started up once they moved and then shut off again when they went back to their dormant state. Very odd. Too odd for them to comprehend, so they let the nature of the thing remain a frightening mystery and hopefully, they'd never have to see one again. Unfortunately, they had found its trail, but on the plus side it was nowhere to be seen and it seemed that the tracks led away from where they were, with the artificial monster now long gone.

Its streaks were strewn across the front of their path, not leading straight ahead but cutting across from their left and right. Some of the surrounding area had been cleared for the tracks as if they led somewhere important or frequently used. A rough board of wood had been skewered onto a pole some way down the trail with some of the humans' baffling shapes scorched into it. In his wisdom, the wolf applied the logic of a prey's tracks to that of the machine. If the ground beneath them had been deep brown and freshly upturned, then they would have been newly made. In that case, humans may be close by. The colour of the tracks matched the rest of the floor around them; it was all slightly sodden of course because of the rain, but it was all evenly set. Thankfully that meant the tracks were probably not new, but the wolf, being his newly untrustworthy self, didn't lower his guard so easily. They would make sure not to move in a direction that matched the trail. They crossed straight over and into the opposing forestry on the other side. Realising they had accidentally come close to another human artefact, the wolf hoped to get as far away from the path as he could. How prevalent in this area were they, he wondered? Would he constantly have to be on guard for the humans from now on?

Continuing on, his nerves began to settle from the hard sting of remembering his tormentors, but this wasn't the end of it. Not long afterwards, they happened upon an open grassless segment of ground among the trees. Here lay a small circle made of stones with a crumbling pit dug into it. At an earlier time, they may have found ashes mounded in the bottom of this earthen bowl, but they had long since been washed away and its creators packed up and gone. Though no remnants of fire were left to spook them, another artefact was left abandoned close by. It was a translucent cylinder laying carelessly off to their side, as if it had been tossed away without thought or concern. The wolf pushed his snout against it with caution at first, then when it seemed safely inanimate, pushed his teeth into it. It was crinkly and smooth, and the texture left a tacky feeling on his tongue. A tiny puddle of water sat trapped in the bottom, swishing about whenever the thing rolled. It seemed harmless but also just the sort of thing those awful humans would use, odd and seemingly pointless. Why trap water? Why not just lap it up from a puddle? Other unidentified objects of mystification were dotted around as they continued forward, like a spongy square that was seemingly made of rough hide. It seemed like some kind of container - a flap closed over its top and clung onto its front by the use of a small silvery disc, secretly concealing whatever oddities lay inside. The thing was manky and eroding from the multiple rainfalls and seasons it must have endured since being lost. By this point, it was coming noon and while the falling dabbles of water still pestered them, the grim morning sky began to reveal rays of the high sun. The rain slicked on rusted weeds, helping their colour to radiate even in the filtered sunlight. The hue of the world turned from a watercolour grey to a cider yellow with a forceful shift. Anything other than the dreary wash they'd endured that morning seemed like a revitalisation. The prickly and overgrown corner of the woods that they found themselves in became drowned in a nostalgic shade of sepia, as if the world were in mourning for memories of better, prettier areas of the wilderness. Fitting for the wolf, as although a hopeful and prosperous future now seemed like a callous pipe dream, the sense of silence and loneliness gave him plenty of opportunity to focus on memories of times and places that lifted his spirits, even if only by a fragment and even if it fuelled an unhealthy regression. But each artificial trinket they crossed seemed to intrude on his good mood again - each time they passed something of otherworldly form or convoluted purpose, it pulled him from his imaginings of fields and flowers and lakesides, things that felt comfortable and pure, into a world of engines and cages and false designs that formed a complicated and disagreeable reality. All these constructs were all relatively small, or at least smaller than he was. That was until the trees parted and revealed something preposterous, highlighted in the exposure of the overhanging sun.

Here the trees curved into a dome, as if they'd tried as hard as they could to conceal the grove from above but couldn't quite grow enough to cover the whole place. This left a circular opening of pure sky above, unspoilt by foliage, which focussed a twinkling sun-splashed beam down into the centre of the small grove. The grass was rich, fed by the unchallenged sunlight overhead and unkept from the lack of grazing animals that passed through this area. It had sprouted to an impressive length, where some clusters grew as high as wheat stems. An accompanying rushing sound and an unbalanced teetering motion relayed the wild and unmanaged density of the tall blades. Yet because of their length, a certain spot in the centre of the field was even more noticeable, where the grass had been flattened down by something large and heavy. Weeds and moss tried as they might to grow over it, but the stark vibrancy of its synthetic construction shined through the natural greens and golds. Whatever it was, it was abnormal enough to dominate the scene – too soft to be a boulder, too shapely to be a mound of dirt, too ornate to be a fallen tree. Due to its purposeful shape, even the two animals could tell that this was made to be a seat. It was a plush ledge constructed with comfort and leisure in mind. It was something dry, warm and soft. The raven literally flapped with excitement. Had they walked only a couple more miles, they could have slept here for the night on a soft relaxing bed. The raven immediately flew over for a closer look. The colours of the thing were mesmerizing, as it was made of so many at once. It was mostly a deep militant green separate of the moss that stippled it, but had streaks of red, cream and brown crisscrossing here and there. Wherever they crossed, they blended into dark amalgamous squares of all these colours. At spots, its covering was interrupted altogether by slashes and wounds, where stained white wool poked out from its tarnished openings. The small raven brushed the top of his head against one of these protruding tufts and felt awash with pleasure. It was cosy and reassuring, cosier than the wolf's soggy matted fur. He stroked his head against the nobble of fluff again. It was as if someone had wrapped a cloud up inside a heavy coat and it was trying to break itself out through cuts and holes so that it could escape back into the sky. The raven hopped up onto the seat a few feet above. The flooring beneath him wobbled, causing him to bounce up and down in a pleasing manner. They'd found something completely wonderful, comfortable and quiet and forgotten in a hovel. He turned to see the equally gratified look of inquisition on his partner's face. But instead, he saw a gaunt expression, and eyes that stuck hard with refusal to join in.

To the wolf, the sofa reeked of offensive synthetics. Not in smell (that had been washed out by rainwater long ago) but in appearance. It tainted his view with the painful reminder of humans. Everything else may have been low in tone and dampened by rain, but at least it was all recognisable and natural to him. However, the colours of this thing were controlled and unmeshed in the most obnoxious way. Much like the ropes of the poor aurora that had been arrogantly leashed to the sides of their dens, only humans would design something so needlessly controlled. All the objects they had passed so far had been small and dismissible, but this thing was even larger than the wolf. It obstructed his path, his view, and his new philosophy; a desire to avoid anything associated with the filth of people. He didn't want his friend to get comfortable on such a thing and he couldn't understand *why* the raven felt comfortable on such a thing, given their experiences. Perhaps the memory of a raven was just much shorter than that of a wolf, but he didn't think that was the case. He took a few intermittent steps forward, feeling more repulsed by the sofa the closer he moved towards it. The bird looked worriedly into his eyes as he moved closer. His face wore the expression of a stern mother trying to intimidate her young child into climbing down from some trembling unsecure place. The raven, similarly, looked back with infantile defiance. The look in his eyes portrayed his own philosophical stance. What did it matter what it was or where it came from? It was comfortable and interesting. His scavenger nature taught him that it was best to take whatever you could get, regardless of pride or morals or experiences. He had slept wet, slept cold, and slept dirty. These physical absolutes were much more real and afflicting than some sense of association or code. The events of hunters, avalanches and biting winters would eventually pass and dissolve into mere memories, the power of their impact only stretching as far as the mind allowed by dwelling on them. But whatever they slept on tonight, they would feel now. So, he refused to move, living in the moment and realising that the sofa was there and warm and comfortable and must be held onto for the fleeting moment of the present.

The wolf's mind, however, was a book of records that remembered everything the seat represented to him, as he did with everything else. The effects of hunters, avalanches and biting winters *didn't* stop once the events themselves had ended. They left limps in the leg and notches in the neck and a thinning of the stomach. He didn't want to carry these events with him, but the power of their impact exceeded far past the mind and even if he wanted to shake them, some events left wounds deeper than a conscious memory. Yet his care for the raven's well-being caused an impasse. His only instinct now was to stay by the bird and keep him happy and comfortable. He couldn't argue that whatever it represented, this was a soft and restful place to sit. While his body stuck in place some feet away from the seat, his face unfroze as the insistent scolding expression drooped into one of innocent begging. His brow raised and his neck, despite the niggling pain, tilted sweetly as if softly asking the bird to climb down. But the raven squawked, refusing to move. Before long, the wolf relinquished his stance to the bird's request.

He still couldn't bring himself to touch the thing. He skulked over to a nearby tree, made three pointless circles in a futile attempt to flatten the dirt into a more comfortable spot, then dropped with a sulking thud onto its roots. He looked outwards towards the raven, who'd realised the wolf had backed down and began revelling in the comfort of the seat by nuzzling his beak into the already shredded fabric. It pained the wolf to have something that he loved and something that he hated be not only within the same view but touching each other. The bird was honest and kind, almost too kind for the world. Meanwhile the seat, in ironic contrast to its soft texture, embodied the harshness of realism – in its invocation of the humans, it was a standing representation of his scars, a monolith to everything synthetic and confusing. Though he didn't know it at the time, the wolf had an unlikeable ultimatum to face; although his goal was to serve the raven, the raven would have his own goals. Goals that perhaps the wolf wouldn't enjoy. But in that turn of serving the raven, wouldn't his goals become the wolf's, no matter his own opinion on them? The realisation that he would ultimately be chasing things that he hated would have muddled his mind and sickened his stomach. But as a mercy of his nature, this contradiction was too much for a simple dog like him to comprehend.

The wolf paid the price of his own peace of mind for the raven's pleasure as he sat on the stiff roots of the tree. Enjoying his position, the bird bounced and nestled into the chair with a great deal of affection for it. The wolf lay alone in the corner, feeling as though his own affection and company had been undermined and cast aside for an inanimate object.

16

BEASTS

They languished in the grove for the entire afternoon and an entire night afterwards, with the raven practically comatose in a state of luxury. The entire time, the wolf wanted to keep his eyes down to the floor in order to ignore the reality of the seat, but his emotional senses compelled him to keep watch over the raven. Mostly, he tried to keep his eyes closed, so he wouldn't have to make the decision to turn away or not. At intervals, his eyelids would sway open, revealing once again the image of the bird snuggled on the sofa. The coat that covered the seat had seemed obviously synthetic and at first, he could notice the contrast between the green of its covering and the green of the moss that crept over its corners. But over time, the two shades seemed to muddle together and then blended even further with the surrounding grass and leaves. Its colourful boxes fell into the same palette as the blossoming buds, its streaks of brown looked identical to the standing trees around him. It became difficult to reason how the sofa should stand out differently from nature, his eyes tricking him by swirling the two worlds together; in a best case scenario, this might have resulted in the painful image of the seat disappearing into the normality of the forest around him, but in the wolf's pessimistic outlook, it instead created the illusion that everything else was becoming as unreal and unnatural as the seat, until even the trees that belonged to the earth - that had taken hundreds of years to sprout - seemed like a fake mockery that had been dreamt up as some perverse artificial construction on a whim. This infected view of the world came about more and more as he re-opened his eyes. In response, he kept closing them for longer and longer intervals, hoping that eventually he would fall completely asleep. By morning, the only thing in his view that still stood out as honest and alive was the unmatched blackness of the raven, whose coat still seemed so pure and void of confusion. The wolf wished that the raven's behaviour was as clear as his feathers. Yet with the world becoming ever more unrecognisable and undesirable by the day, the wolf had no choice but to dismally follow whatever erratic decision the raven led him to. The bird's familiar croaks and his admirable flutters were still the only unchanging reminder of better days gone by.

Mercifully, the raven only chose to stay with the sofa for a day, becoming bored in a very short space of time. The charm of its newness began to wear away like its flimsy cloth covering, until the raven let out a caw to his distant companion in a call to follow. With his defining limp of sadness, he rose to his paws and swayed over to the raven's path, uncomfortably passing the sofa as he did so. They exited the grove in a random direction – the circular lining was identical all around so choosing a specific route didn't seem to matter – and they passed back into the shaded blanket of the forest, away from the beaming light of the throne's altar.

The wolf drifted on like a shell on the ocean's surface, barely staying afloat but providing a hollow interior for any small creature (here, the raven) to sit safely inside him. He remembered having his own mind; remembered that this time last year he was on the prowl for fine feasts, exercising his confidence as a hunter and seeking to scamper through flower-ridden fields of emerald under clear skies. The only thing missing during these excursions was someone to do them with. This time last year, he was only a dozen weeks away from meeting the raven and finding that connection, unaware that any companionship would bring more changes to him than merely the addition of company. This time last year, at the turn of a new summer, he was simply a puppy who wanted – who needed – a friend to play with. Had his mind still been his own and not reliant on the will of the bird, he might have questioned whether that was a good thing; if it was better to live *by* yourself but also with the freedom to also live *for* yourself, even if it came with cold nights of stark solitude and fearful self-wondering. Or, was it better to act as a leaning post for another being and be the side character in another protagonist's show, where you act conveniently and mindlessly to the will of their script, but without the anxiety of having to write your own or carry the burden of twists and turns on your own shoulders?

The wolf had once been caught smack dab in the middle of this predicament. He couldn't seem to pinpoint when that transition had taken place, but thanks to the tumultuous travels with the raven twisting his body and mind, he now believed the latter. Because while sleeping twenty feet away from a friend hadn't been anywhere near as good as sleeping cuddled up next to one (as they had done on so many other nights before), it still seemed a lot better than sleeping in the hollowed-out hole of a tree, all alone. Every time his mind sparked the question of "is this better than nothing?", a fearful voice inside instantly answered back with a resounding "yes." His mind responded by reinforcing, confidently, that this was the choice almost all animals made when asking the same question. To be something singularly of one's own nature, or to conform into being the beast that one was expected to be – dog, bird, deer, fish, mouse? To be yourself and lonely, or to be complacent and together? The irony was that while he was trying his hardest to imitate a wolf in order to satisfy the raven, the bird no longer saw him quite like a wolf at all. But whatever he was, he was still a friend and still had usefulness to some degree, even if it was purely emotional. The bird hovered mystically through the steadily brightening grove, still never staying in the air for too long at a time, almost as if it couldn't - as though it were something else imitating a bird. The sun was now beginning to seep through the clouds more and more. Heading south, the essence of nature seemed to bolster as the bushes grew thicker and the bark appeared richer. The leaves glimmered lime as the foliage of the trees was spilled with the golden sunlight. Similarly, with the buttery sunshine against his muddied grey coat, the wolf appeared a sort of brass colour, befitting of the waning weighty footsteps that he took. Shortly ahead of him, the bird's to-ing and fro-ing was patternless and nonsensical. He looked like he was trying to choose a direction without the ability or confidence to commit to one. He flapped about as though he were excited to lead, but without the experience or decisive presence to do so. He whipped forward and then pulled back, then flew sideways, then perched on a branch, then hopped around in circles before shooting off to the left, then pulled up in a flutter, and kept up this erratic behaviour. If the wolf had his usual melodic stride, he would have had to keep stopping and starting to accommodate the indecisiveness, which would have been incredibly irritating. But as it was, his movement was so handicapped by fatigue, stiffness and pain, that his broken body matched the bird's unbalanced mind and they kept – in their disturbing new dynamic – relatively in speed with each other. The wolf couldn't help thinking that the raven seemed resilient to lead. And indeed, in his head, the bird thought that it would prefer the hound to be in front as he had been before, so that the raven could stand on his back again and the wolf could more actively protect him from any dangers. Still, the bird couldn't also help feeling like he was now the more powerful of the two, by having his companion follow *his* lead. He evidently liked being the admirable one of the pair; liked being the protagonist in his own story for a change. No-one could blame him for that, especially not the wolf.

In his head, the sense of strength and confidence swam around with the reservation and his usual immaturity. It was a new feeling that failed to mesh the instinctual nature of what he was with the forced behaviour of what he wanted to be. This conflict led to the imbalanced diving and reeling. The wolf sensed this conflict and pitied the bird somewhat but couldn't help feeling sorrier for himself. With so many previous failures resting on his shoulders, making decisions about where their journey would lead was a responsibility that he no longer wanted to bear. He was busy standing by, being the one that made the raven's journey as easy as possible. Despite the ache in his neck, the wolf swivelled his head around as they walked. He naturally paid attention to the raven through his highly sensitive ears and instead used his eyes to track anything around them that might lead to trouble or prosperity for the bird. His perception was still great enough that he could sense the raven's general placement without having to look directly at him, whether it was through a signifying sound or the subtle change of a peripheral shadow (he was able to do this with any animal, meaning he only had to make eye contact with those he conflicted with or was interested in). The wolf raised his head when at one point, he couldn't feel the bird's motion anymore. That's because, as he then saw, the raven had stopped for something.

He'd perched on an incredibly unusual bunching of stray wood and small logs that looked like it would make a solid nest for either a hundred birds or the world's largest bird. The clippings from the log pile trailed off towards the most inviting sight. Ahead of them was a warm-looking cave, dug into the side of some bunched earth and topped by a bank of drooping trees. It was quite similar the one they had taken refuge in during the thunderstorm, but it was at least twice as large and one-hundred times more inviting. The tuber of the trees on top ran through a fairly thin canopy of soil and dangled out over the cave mouth, almost certainly robbing the trees of actual nutrients but adding a bohemian curtain of roots to the entrance. It made for a perfect resting place, assuming the inside was large and well-elevated - maybe even a permanent home. The wooden stockpile outside was basically a luxury nest for the raven if it wanted. The wolf had heard scurrying and rustling on the walk here, meaning the area was likely plentifully dense with catchable critters. It seemed roomy enough to drag larger carcasses inside for extended feasting. The wolf listened hard for the one thing that was missing, and – yes! Far off to the left, not strong but definitely present, was a trickling sound. It didn't guarantee a plentiful river, but it guaranteed a local source of water.

It was perfect. Gloomy, solitary and seemingly pre-packed with quality-of-life additions. It was the idyllic home for an animal that preferred to sleep and live an easy life instead of one that sought travel and excitement. However, they weren't the only ones that had thought so. During their frantic plight in the rainstorm, they hadn't had the presence of mind to consider that the damp stony cave they took refuge in had already been taken by an animal, possibly a large and aggressive one. Here, they didn't have that excuse, and so it was their own bumbling fault that they'd stepped too close to the entrance of the cave and in doing so, had roused the interest of the creature that dwelled within. A carpet of coarse black fur rolled sideways with every earth-shifting step that the occupant took. At first it was barely seen in the gloom of the cave until the sun began to pick out the individual hairs of a wide and hulking body as it stepped out. The face (not unlike the wolf's) had a snout that topped a dangerous set of sharp teeth. On top of that were two black beady eyes stooped in red lines and a wild stare. They told the pair everything about the beast's personality - its temper, its impulsiveness, its arrogance, its lunacy. It had the powerful claws and dominating fangs of the wolf with the sleek midnight coat and glazed ebony eyes of the raven. If the wolf wanted to see his dream of the wolf-raven hybrid –

The Merger – come to life, this was as close as he was going to get. A bear.

He wasn't excited by it though. He disliked it.

At this point, he had resolved for his dream to stay as just that - a dream. He had given up on planning and hoping, tempering his expectations of anything that he couldn't see directly ahead. But he did see the cavern straight ahead, and he wanted it. He wanted the raven to have his enormous nest just outside the cave's mouth. The wolf's dreaming nature was dead, but he recognised that opportunity was staring him in the face. The bear had emerged already territorial, baring her teeth in a show of animosity on first sight. She ground her paws down into the soil as she stepped forward out of her home, her head bobbing unmanageably from the sheer weight of her body. Both the wolf and the bear's brows bunched up as they made eye contact, their gazes clashing as she raised herself up onto her back legs. Her move immediately shocked the wolf – she stood like the humans did.

Her jaw quavered as she bellowed out with a grinding and aggressive roar. Just from the scream, the wolf felt the echo through the ground at his feet. It was simultaneously incredibly deep and very shrill, shrill enough to make his snout wince from the volume. The wolf dropped his head beneath his shoulder blades as he would during a hunt and snarled with the most ominous noise that he could produce. By her very disposition, she was already wild enough to leap right into chaos; the wolf didn't have a choice in backing down away from the bear. He was incredibly tired and valued only two things in the world: good sleep for himself and everything else for the raven. He would share the cave if he had to, but he wouldn't leave. He asked for so little. Just one quiet dry cave to rest in. At one point, he may have tested an arrangement with the bear (similar to his arrangement with the bird) before diving right to contention. The bird, the bear and the dog; wouldn't that be quite a match-up? They'd be unstoppable. The might of the bear, the spirit of the raven and the loyalty of the hound to hold them all together. But the bear was far too erratic and antagonistic to co-operate with. She'd immediately jumped into conflict and the wolf had no other option than to meet it. She dropped back to her front paws with a thud and bared her teeth back at the wolf, who moved his left paw across his right one, taking a circular step. She shifted her entire body sideways apart from her head, which turned sternly towards wherever the wolf walked, until both beasts were circling each other with their eyes locked.

The dirt crunched beneath all eight of their paws. Twigs cracked under their steps, anticipating the break in tension when the two would snap and leap. Their snarls and growls encompassed the woods with an echo. There was no wind in the air to intrude on their voices. The raven's feathers caused an ill-fitting ruffle of softness as he flitted from the brambles onto a higher tree branch out of harm's way. He witnessed the familiar wolf eyeing up the bear who stood strong and terrifying by herself. Both beasts were in his sights as the raven had lined up for a full view of the show that was about to take place. His eyeline held the large nest of brambles in the centre as though this was the singular prize that each of them was competing for. It was selfish for the bird to think that was the priority, but in a way it was. The wolf, caring so much for him, hoped to claim the nest for his cohort's sake. The bear had presumably been collecting these wood trimmings together to then carry into her home and use them as bedding or blockage from the wind, for extra comfort. She seemed to have built quite a cloistered little den for herself, with a dampness and gloom that many creatures find perfectly relieving – comfort in the grim darkness away from the hectic sunlight. These were wonderful conditions to keep the bird safely in, the wolf thought. Two friends living undisturbed in the hidden shade of the countryside; unknown, snatching whatever token passed by and dragging it into their den. A decorated garden to lounge in during the days and a solid hovel that provided protection from the next cruel winter. Here, two misfits like them could hold out and need never be disturbed ever again. This is what the bear had, and the wolf wanted it. She was much larger and clearly stronger. With a wolf pack of only around three or four, the fight would have been made equal; on his own, he was disadvantaged. But at this point, drowned in savagery and with nothing to lose, the wolf was crazed enough to take on any animal. He eyed her up as he would with any prey or challenger, believing himself to be weighing the odds for tactic's sake. Her matted unwashed fur suggested a lack of self-care or personal standards. The scar that brimmed between her left eye and ear told one tale among many of anguishes thrown at her by the world's hurtful inhabitants. In her eyes, he saw a story of fervent rage built up from contentious experiences unknown to him. Thanks to her cruel and defensive lifestyle, rather than respond to events with wary independence, she would always approach them aggressively without leaving anything to chance. Seeing past the shell of the animal outside, the wolf recognised all this accumulative detail within himself - the scars, the lack of care, the pessimistic approach to other animals. He felt himself to be on equal ground with the animal he was facing, despite differences as a species. He attempted to intimidate her with short snaps here and there, where he would push a step inwards and bark menacingly. She continued to growl deep and circle around. Above, the bird watched them both. The reflection of their spherical movement glided around the edge of his great black globular eye. The glint of the sun hit it and reflected onto their confrontation. The wolf, as the intruder – as the one on the offensive – would be the first to attack and knowing his intimidation hadn't worked, he closed into the centre of the circle.

Then leapt.

The bear rolled sideways to avoid the wolf. His teeth were growling, and he swiped with his silvered claws as he fled through the air. Having missed, he landed on all fours beside her, dipping into his injured side as he touched down. The bear had stumbled impulsively to avoid the attack. Despite having to oafishly roll back onto her paws, she remained unfazed and still crazed. The wolf swept his tail around to face her again as she clambered back up and let out a decibel-breaking warble of frustration. She charged at him, her reckoning paws shaking the earth underneath. She was less agile at throwing her claws around than the wolf was, so instead she tilted her jaw open to reveal her piercing set of teeth as she neared him. They reminded him of the jagged rocky spires that tried to trap him into the collapsing maw atop the terrible mountain. She swayed her head in his direction, clenching her teeth back up in the process in an attempt to tear into him. The wolf, with all his dexterity and guile, knew to move *into* the attack to avoid getting snapped up. He swiftly lunged forward past the bear into the position she was charging away from. His tail followed, narrowly avoiding the bite.

Keep in mind what the wolf's body had been through at this point. The broken ribs. The bullet in his neck. The damp, heavy mud hanging off his whole fur. Malnourishment. Degradation. All pains that, in a moment of deep desire and adrenaline, he dragged around with him as an afterthought. Even after all the misfortunes that had birthed and strengthened these detriments, even after losing his aspiration and his character, these pains would never be as strong as the link between him and his willpower and tenacity. Perhaps that's why even after everything – the limp that made him look weak, the ragged muddied fur that made him look beaten and the undesirable frame that made him look small – all the other creatures and critters still fled when they saw him coming their way. On his trails, he was pulling along with him more weight than any average wolf and moving ahead just as well, no matter the reasoning for it. In that moment, he let go of the overthinking outcast that contemplated outcomes and wasted energy prancing through flowers. Instead, he embraced the beast that sprinted after deer and snarled at anyone that got too close. The bear, lumbering and imbalanced, still hadn't corrected to face the wolf after her charge. He swiftly whipped his tail around to face her back and then leapt at it, his claws like protracted daggers trying to grip onto her formidable coat and pierce through it. Her hide was thick and difficult to puncture, but he managed to find some way to hang on. She bellowed, her body vibrating from the echo that rung out. This caused the wolf to judder while he clung on to her backside. Her form was massive, and the wolf resembled a mosquito stuck onto the side of a boulder, but she was still too hefty to twist about and shake him off as an elk or moose would have easily done. He didn't thrash around but continued being a nuisance as he tried to sink his teeth into her rubbery flesh. She voiced her frustration with hammering cries as she writhed about in a lumbering attempt to detach the wolf. Her warbling was a mixture of discomfort and fury. As she failed to rid herself of his grip, the latter emotion grew stronger. Eventually she managed to wriggle free of the hound, whose claws slipped out of the grooves they'd latched into as he skidded back to his feet. She trudged around to face him. Her expression would have scared an insane person - she was frothing at the mouth with saliva and her pupils were contracted into nightmarishly focussed pinholes. She almost intimidated the wolf, but not quite.

The brawl persisted as both animals continuously charged and leapt at each other, connecting or not. The bear mostly used her giant hulking form to barrel at the wolf with her skull or shoulder, hitting hard but bluntly. The tenacious dog took these beats to the side with barely a shake. Despite being more handicapped now than when he'd once chased a fleeing elk, he still utilised his speed the same way, getting around at all her sides and taking hopeful slashes and gnashes against her fur as he tried to break through the skin again and again. Mostly they sought to intimidate each other and claim not just ownership of the grotto, but also claim the title of the forest's most vicious beast. Hunger and passion returned to the wolf, a confluence of his experiences – his falls and rises - exemplified and focussed into a pivotal challenge. An expert-level iteration of the elk chase. A second chance at the moose. A way to knock down any animals that would look down on him, whether they were a bear in a cave or wolves on a bluff. The depth of her bellows was resounding and earth-quaking like a thunderstorm, but he stood up to the giant beast that caused the enormous sound and sought to bring down her rule of the elements. As he leapt at her over and over, he was as much off the ground as he was on it, flying like a bird but just looking a little different, as many birds tend to do when compared against each other. A rush of adrenaline gave him the same feeling he'd had when he mauled the human in the shed. It felt something like tenacity without direction or hope. It was his rage.

Through it all, the raven sat on a flaky branch above, his neck swivelling from one contender to the other with an uncharacteristically concerned look in his eyes: his deep, dark, reflective eyes. He didn't caw in tribute to the wolf's assumed victory as he usually would. He stayed strangely silent. He glanced from the bear to the wolf, back and forth, as his cognitive processes worked in overdrive. Usually, the bird didn't appear to do much thinking and worked on impulse, but then usually the wolf did the thinking. Now the raven could see his guardian down below, throwing himself at the bear without concern or caution for each action. If he were still similar to the sensitive pup that he'd been when they first met or hadn't grown such a disregard for his own pain, then he doubtlessly wouldn't have been able to take half the blows the bear had already inflicted on him, pummelling her shoulder against his emaciated frame. The bird could tell he'd changed. No, this wasn't that young dog that danced in the field, or glanced up at colourful birds, or followed music to new ventures.

It was a strange time to start looking back through memories of those moments, but he did. A memory of their first hunt together appeared as a ghostly parallel over his stand-off with the bear. A vision of the elk flickered against the bear's fur, showing a dumb feeble animal that didn't stand a chance against an energetic and able-bodied hound. The elk's size barely held a candle to the bear's hulking frame that surely the wolf didn't stand a chance against, no matter how ravenous he was. The past memory of the wolf re-enacted the scene of a wily hunter with carefully chosen positions, mechanical limbs and darting eyes. It projected over the surface of a mindless invalid covered in dirt and without any idea of where he was going next. The bird wanted to see that old (or rather young) wolf again now; a smart, bright, hopeful wolf. Little did he know that the wolf had only the raven's best interests at heart, fighting just as much for the bird's sake as his own, with his only desire being to serve the bird who he loved so much and who had looked so happy and fitting upon the giant brambly nest. But something was wrong. Even as the wolf fought for the raven, a problem made it hard for the bird to notice his friend's true feelings.

In a metaphorical sense of the wolf's goals, it felt less like he was towing the raven along and more like he was pushing him forward with his snout. In the former example, the wolf would be putting himself first, but the raven would have been casually and safely brought along for the ride, whereas in the latter example, he put the raven first but with a forceful motion and a forfeit of his own responsibilities. The raven had admired the wolf as a species and envied their ability to command and lead, but once he was the one in front, he felt like an open nerve too small and fluster-headed to fend off any coming contenders. He admired wolves, but liked being a bird. Plus, with the wolf always behind, he didn't get the pleasure of admiring his friend as he walked ahead. The disadvantages of their new travelling arrangement felt fitting of their emotional dynamic as the bird was seeing less and less of the wolf and whatever he did see, he barely recognised. At some point – he didn't know when – the wolf had become the one who was doing the following.

The bird looked at the bear. He had previously thought that the wolf was a scary-looking and ferociously dependable creature, but this thing was a monument of animosity. She had three times as much fur as he had. Her teeth were three times as big. Her bark was three times as guttural. She looked thrice as warm to sleep next to and her home (which she already had ownership of) looked equally as warm and secure. It would have done a world of good to have been inside here when that nasty winter had hit, instead of freezing on the top of a mountain that he'd followed the wolf up. But, maybe for next winter...

The raven's eyes blinked as if to snap himself out of a train of thought. He looked at his dependable and loyal cohort, protecting and accompanying him even past the point of self-preservation or sanity. It occurred to him that the only reason those memories were there to remember was thanks to the wolf's acceptance of the bird throughout their travels. How could he draw lines between the good times and the bad when they seemed so intertwined with each other? When the tragedies of life had made them so much more appreciative of the comforts that they found in the world together? The soothing light of the aurora that quelled them to sleep after the wolf's injury. The confusion of the human valley that'd been made worthwhile by the delectable cuisine and soothing melody they'd found together. The exchanges of empathy, understanding and thanks that came in the wake of thunderstorms and avalanches. When the world gave them no reward for their exploration and bravery, they consistently rewarded each other's dedication and sacrifice with love and favour. They'd fed each other, protected each other, entertained each other, encouraged each other, saved each other and loved each other. Those days were not too long ago, but things seemed different now. Was the wolf risking his life purely for a friend? He wouldn't even put up with sleeping on a sofa for one. Was he going to run around and play if this open space were to become their new front yard? He always seemed so tired and worn down now. Although it may have sounded greedy on the raven's part, what good was the saving, protecting and feeding any more without the entertainment, the encouragement and the comfort? If, to the raven, what made the wolf more than just a wolf was fading away, then he would end up being just like any other wolf; always tired and hungry, never playing for fun, always acting on autopilot, fighting for no reason and settling for the cold lowlands of a grey world. In the midst of the fight, he had started to feel much more like a powerful old wolf and the raven started to see the same thing. But their differing viewpoints took them to different conclusions. The wolf, in the face of the world's hardships, felt like he should become more like a regular wolf. The raven, on the other hand, didn't want him to. Average animals didn't have a golden glint in their eyes. There were plenty of them out there: coyotes, otters, reindeer, sheep, raccoons, bears. Worryingly, the thought came that if he were to become just a regular beast, he wouldn't be much different in disposition or behaviour to the hot-headed bear. Except when it came to beasts, the bear was bigger and stronger.

Amid the wolf's assault, his teeth slid along the bear's arm and ground into her flesh. The fangs gripped in, taking even him by surprise.

His body swung up and then backwards before planting onto the dirt. She let out another wail. This time, it had a distinctly different echo of genuine pain and vulnerability as an anguished tone broke through the deep gurgling. The blood from her arm began to bubble out against his teeth. He dug his paws into the soil and yanked backwards, trying to pull her to the ground. His neck jerked and tugged similar to the way it would if he were eating a carcass. There was no way the wolf would ever physically be able to bring her down from pulling force alone, but he tugged at her arm anyway as his back straightened and his paws pushed forward. He wrangled and frothed as he fought against her natural weight, trying to throw her wounded limb around and tear it up as much as possible. Her rage grew – the more she bled the more desperate and wild she became. She threw the wolf loose as fast as possible, lobbing him to the side as he slid to the floor. Without gaining much momentum, he landed uninjured, rolling against the soft dirt and leaves. She was already prepared to return an attack as he stood back to his paws. She had raised her other arm and with claws already out, she clenched and pointed them downwards, hoping to dig into the wolf's side and drag him around in return of what he had done to her. Not that she hadn't been fighting for her life, but she immediately became more calculated as she realised the wolf was fighting with intense hunger and fury. With his natural intelligence having fallen to rabid recklessness and her impulsive wrath cooled by the terrifying pain in her arm, this decidedly brought them to a more equal playing field, mentally speaking. In his obnoxious courage, the wolf snarled to mock her, ignoring the fatality of the wide rigid knives on her paw. He had punched his back foot into the dirt already and prepared to leap sideways once she swiped at him in order to avoid her attack. Once her claw was down to his level, he could plunge his teeth into her other arm, wounding both her front paws and disabling her strongest weapons. He'd taken each bash from the bear with admirable resilience, but under the surface of his fur, the constant knocks were bruising his skin and weakening his muscles. Thankfully, due to her slow movement and burly frame, the limps and twinges from his past injuries caused very little handicap in his fight with her and he still had his greatest weapon - his bite. She growled back with intense hatred.

The raven, in his speculative position, saw the bear's mighty blow coming but had also seen the wolf's foot ready to push off. His leg looked shaky, and his breathing was heavy as he wasn't fighting with much conservation or efficiency. The bird wondered if he'd actually be able to dive out of the way in time or if he had a plan for what to do once he did. Either way, he knew something grim was coming. He squealed - uncharacteristically pitiful for any raven but certainly for this one in particular - then dove off his branch and fled forward towards the two contenders in a panic. The bear began to bring her lethal claw down with the force of a plummeting anvil. Swiftly, the raven dove through the air to race against it. The wolf dipped his body closer to the ground in order to bend his knee for a take-off. Their conflict was swiftly met by the interruption of a black bolt, intrepid and selfish and opportunistic. He unfurled his wings like a parachute pulling back on the wind, tilted backwards at the most precise moment, then pointed his needled talons out as he plunged downwards.

Down past the bear and into the wolf's right eye.

An immediate flash of agony and bewilderment struck the hound. His spine arced in reverse, causing him to stagger and fall backwards. His perception, where two eyelines crossed over to create one seamless understanding of the world, became flooded with a pool of red. His vision quickly split into a haze of confusion before one side dissolved into a permanent blackness. The bird still dug in, screeching and flapping his wings The two of them flailed about in the most frantic contortion, with the wolf yapping in grief and the raven screaming in panic, pulling himself from left to right. His talon had embedded deep into his friend's eye.

The bird rushed its wings about in the air as he tried to stay airborne, yanking the wolf's neck upwards as he writhed from one side to the other. The wolf was unable to comprehend how to even stand up as the simplest of understandings slipped from his mind. As their bodies stuck together, their hearts split instantly apart from each other. The wolf's last desire was to swipe at his friend but as the first few moments of chaos settled and he realised what was happening to him, he batted pathetically into the air. It was as though he was swiping past the raven, not with the intent to truly hit the bird but in a distressing attempt to ask him to stop, in the same way a person raises their hands when a gun is pointed at their head. Helpless, with the appeal of mercy being their last option.

"Please don't."

The raven wasn't hanging onto him on purpose. His talon had slipped into the pupil and its curved design caused it to stick in, their flailing making it more difficult to let go. The reservation in each of them and the lack of animosity only made things worse as they twisted and whimpered, dragging each other about in various directions without being able to let go. It was like the emotional detangling of two childhood friends trying to drag each other into each of their own life paths, sobbing away as they struggle to acknowledge that they must each now head their own separate ways. Or no, it wasn't *like* that. It was *exactly* that. An unwanted and gruelling event that ended with a whimper.

The awareness of what was happening returned to both the wolf and the raven. They oriented themselves to a better position, where the talon could follow its entry point back out of the wolf's eye and dislodge from him, albeit with some resilience. Bloodied, the raven's talon came out of the socket, leaving a gaping hole filled with mushed muscle and running tears. The bird flapped backwards and landed on the ground ten feet away from his wounded friend. The wolf re-climbed to his feet where his back bent forward, now hunched over in a cowering manner with his shoulder blades pushed to the ground and his head dipped downwards. His eye socket dripped onto the floor and a heartbroken murmur ebbed from his clenched mouth. He felt a sizzling pain in his emotions and a terrible mist in his head; those were worse than any broken rib, or pierced neck, or gouged eyeball. He wished he had the time to stop and understand what had happened, why it had happened, and where everything had gone. If only there wasn't still the hulking bear beside him, still on the attack.

The bear let out an egotistical growl of pre-emptive victory. The wolf, whose disposition had understandably changed in seconds, tried to step backwards. He'd felt backed into a corner, not from being out of energy to fight but from being out of reasons to do so. As he tried to move, the skewed disadvantage of his newly broken perspective took hold. His view betrayed the direction that he tried to step in. His bludgeoned eye made his vision lop-sided, and his feet failed to compensate, causing him to almost stumble over as he tried to move. His floundering made him seem even more foolish and meek. The raven's head whirred around but he stayed completely silent. Perhaps shock had taken hold. The wolf's vision shifted rapidly from the bird to the bear and back repeatedly. The bear began to advance forward to attack again. He didn't have time to stop and understand. Scarred and scared, the wolf stole a last look at the raven. His friend stayed entirely quiet, and it was only this unfamiliar silence that gave any indication that the raven was affected by what had just happened. Otherwise, he stood still, appearing completely fine. It's said that in an emotional situation, a second can last minutes, even longer. For the wolf's sake, it would have been kinder if that were true as his last look at the raven's face was far too fleeting and not nearly long enough to hold onto in the moment. As the bear moved forward, he had no choice. He wished he could stay, but he couldn't. He turned sharply in a flash and fought through his ruined vision in order to sprint away from harm. From heartache. From everything.

Feeling as though the danger had gone, the bear stood back down on all fours and relaxed her top lip over her vicious teeth. She sluggishly careened around to the right towards the raven's direction. She barely registered the bird and hadn't consider him a part of the threat. She threw him one glance, huffing in his direction without caring enough to drive him away too. Small and insignificant and without teeth or brains, he posed no threat to her or her shelter. He could stay. She trod back into the deceptively tranquil hole beyond the thick nesting of twigs, which the raven could have. For now. He still stood motionless, but eventually broke his deathly silence.

He cawed.

17

CONTRADICTION

The sun shone overhead, buttery and calm. But inside the wolf's head, a rainstorm brewed and bubbled and battered about. Far too often, it seemed the arrangement of the outside world mismatched and sometimes even mocked his own disposition, weathers and animals alike. The sun blazed golden whenever he felt blue. It highlighted synthetic human artefacts as though they were holy monoliths while he felt they were dreadful and hollow. Other creatures played vigorously in the open whenever he hid quietly away and rushed off whenever he came out. Other wolves strode through the land confident and tall while he limped and crawled his way over the simplest of hills, looking meek and scruffy when compared to their grace and might. His mind had pre-planned and overthought every encounter or fight or opportunity, only for a stroke of coincidence or a flash of misfortune to become the deciding factor.

Success that took him hours, days or months to achieve came to every other creature in seconds as they dove in, unthinking and (more infuriatingly) unfeeling. When he finally did give in to impulse and let his emotions carry him away, he was punished for it in a complete reversal to what the world was teaching him. Everything slowed down when he needed to go quickly and sped up when he needed time to breathe. Every animal who snuggled up in twos and fives looked on to him standing alone as though he were a force made to pull apart bonds or sicken hearts. Other creatures hid from his gangly unkempt sight, most times without him even getting the chance to see who was running away from him, when he only wanted another creature nearby for comfort. His own kind had unanimously viewed him as the runt of the pack that didn't quite fit inside a group of wolves, whether he believed the same or not. He was a grown animal, capable of hunting, thinking and travelling, but who had still not let go of the puppy inside, which didn't seem good enough for those in the wild – you must fully be either a baby or a beast, everything seemed to say. He felt out of sync, out of place and out of luck. He had thought the raven had been stuck in the same situation.

Slowly he trod on, with the blood in his eye drying up, yet with water unendingly cultivating and trickling out. There wasn't a twitter from birds nor a dribble of running rivers to be heard, nor the fleeting forms of game running through the distant trees to be seen. His senses were void of any prospects or stimulation. There were no colourful flocks in the trees, no wavering luminescent lights in the sky, no smells of delectable interest. The world had seemingly run dry of motion and sound, as silent and still as the raven in his last glimpse, with every part of his surroundings now reminding him of his absent 'friend'. The logic behind the raven's actions was not what confused him, in fact it was quite understandable. The bear was stronger, cleaner, had a nicer home, she was more aggressive and energetic, she had longer warmer fur that provided more comfort. Her capabilities were better suited to the raven's needs and so it was a natural choice between the two of them. But that's what caused the wolf so much confusion and heartbreak; that it was a logical decision, based purely off survival. Nature. Need, not want. That wasn't the emotional raven that he knew. He had solely worked towards helping the raven achieve or acquire whatever he'd wanted, not what he needed. The wolf wondered if the illogical – the emotional – had even crossed the bird's mind; if he'd thought about how much longer they had been friends, or if he thought about how much the wolf had done for him. How much they had done for each other. He had assumed when he had committed himself to the raven's side that the raven had come to the same commitment, to be each other's guide across any lake, hill or mountain. To stand united through any success, defeat, cripple or cage. He thought back to how he'd been when he had first met the raven. The wolf thought too much and acted too little and needed the right animal to make up for what he was missing - the correct shape to fit inside the empty space in himself, with him fitting perfectly inside the other's gap as well and together, making one correct working creature. He believed that animal was the raven, and thought they both needed each other to feel capable in the world. The wolf didn't expect the raven to turn out so... wild. Hadn't seen it become so wild. In his mind, the bird had become any regular beast just as much as he had.

It's important to remember that living beings aren't block

puzzles, where one shape goes into one hole. They're mailable, their shapes change over time and grow to no longer fit into the same gaps as they once did. But the wolf was in an emotional state, more pre-occupied now with the actions of the raven and his view of the world. It seemed now that that's how *everything* besides himself behaved. In the end, even the raven put basic survivalist fulfilment ahead of commitment and belonging. The world was telling him that what mattered was strength and brutality and mindlessness and selfishness. As he strode on, his teeth gritted, the blood from his wound clotted and the tears began to dry. If there was no corner of the world or living creature left that had heart, compassion or civility, then neither would he, even if he had to pretend at first. If love is fickle and affection is selfish, then it's better to bite the hand that feeds you before it has a chance to change its mind and stick its finger in your eye. If home is where the heart is, it's better to build a wall around your home before thieves rush in and steal everything out of it. Why extend your hand to others if it's only good to them with food in it?

Of course, not every corner of the world is truly so harsh. There are animals that flourish by avoiding conflict, that spend their time eating only fruits and sleeping in flowers. They exist only to be small and beautiful, then give birth to other animals who exist to be small and beautiful. Animals like butterflies and dormice and bumblebees, squirrels and bats and salmon. But the wolf hadn't seen these. He'd seen lucky old moose and deceptive foxes, judgemental wolves and crazed bears. This is what the wolf saw in the world - what the world showed to the wolf. Dormice fled from him, butterflies fluttered away, bats only came out at night and salmon were carried by shimmering crystal streams that would drown him if he tried to swim with them. We can only react and shape ourselves to the experiences and information that we're given. What else was he supposed to think?

Everyone was out for themselves.

Love was unsustainable.

He was a monster.

The wolf's wobbling stance began to straighten. He'd lived his whole life with a left and right eyeball converging into one perspective, but now that his vision was pushed all the way to one side, it took him a while to adjust. However, after a few hours of silent lonesome walking, he took to it with disturbing ease. Looking through a one-sided lens started to become more comfortable to the wolf and though the shifted perspective would never go away, he would grow more and more used to it, as he had grown used to the limp in his leg and the lead in his neck. At this point, he expected detriments to come along and stick around. Walking through the world with a tilted view would come easily.

He was a pack wolf trapped inside the body of a lone wolf. A puppy stuck inside the body of a beast. So, if it was the body that mattered – if everyone only cared about what was on the outside – then his outside would become his inside. He'd kill the puppy inside and behave like the scary, ugly, unlovable lone wolf they all saw him as. Even if he had to pretend. No more packs, alliances, companions, or friends. Maybe then he'd feel in sync. Maybe then he'd feel like all the other beasts. If the raven could go wild, then he could too. The wolf's steps straightened out perfectly. As the storm inside began to settle and his spirits brightened, a rain cloud rolled in overhead and a light drizzle started to fall.

18

FORGIVENESS

The raven awoke in the cocoon of his stately nest, with blades of light slashing through the cracks in the wood. It was a giant egg of snapped branches with a hole in the top that acted as the doorway. The nest was somewhat like a miniature scale model of the domed field that the bird had found the comfy human seat in, with the cosiest spots being similarly in the centre, this time constructed of fresh leaves plucked straight from the surrounding trees. Once the energy had returned to his muscles, he hopped up to his foyer of twigs and left through the shimmering sunroof above. It's a wonder what use the bear had for such a disjointed pile of sticks, whether she had gathered them at all or whether they had been around even before she moved into the cave next door. Regardless, if the bear had intended to use them at all, the raven had worked at the pile and made it his own in the weeks that he'd spent there. It was originally quite open and disjointed, but over time the bird had reformed it into a more secure and homely structure.

The raven perched on the rim of the wooden dome, awaking to the same sight he'd seen every morning during his time there; the bear lying lazily and obnoxiously in the morning sun, scooping blackberries into her mouth with a curl of her tongue. Plum-red remnants of the berries' juices stained her lips. Her oafish rolling sold her as an insatiable drunkard splattered with red wine. The rest of her day was spent trekking the local area, foraging from trees and rivers and rolling around in the grass. As she did this, a breathy mist was exhaled from the pores in the earth. It was the heat of the early summer sunrises; not a cold fog like in late autumn, but a heavy wet milkiness that made the air steamy. Her eating habits consisted of frequent and gluttonous portions, such as sucking a bush of berries completely dry or banqueting on an accumulated bouquet of dandelion heads. Bears love eating handfuls of ants which she dug out of anthills with her careless paws and scoffed down like chocolate drops. The crunchy, juicy texture gave her a fulfilling and euphoric sensation. The raven reminisced on a time when he also found some intoxicating escapism in anthills, bathing on top and feeling the ants wriggling around on him, releasing their pheromones all through his body. He felt there was no risk of anything happening to the bear if he were to indulge in one of these episodes now, but she treated the anthills so poorly that by the time she was done, any leftover residents lay crippled or deceased in small quantities around the mashed-up mound of dirt. Though the joyous possibility of an ant-bath was now out of the question, the raven could still claim the forgotten scraps as his own little nibbles. This persisted as a continuous theme in the bear's hunting habits; she ate often and in large variety but rarely left much for the raven to pick up afterwards and none of the leftovers maintained any of the original integrity that made them so sweet, be it fruit or flesh. She would decimate anthills, raze herb patches and scoop through beehives until they were bone dry. The bear didn't seem to pay much consideration to the raven as a presence in her daily operations, and rightly so. She hadn't asked for his company. The raven came in handy as a tool for extending her foraging efforts, used only to find potential food. But she didn't need him to act as a distraction when hunting for beehives or as a tracker to keep an eye out for movement when it came to finding dandelions. Her idea of fun consisted of long snoozing sessions and tree climbing, activities that the raven's wings weren't useful for. In fact, the raven rarely even got the chance to even extend his wings during this stint. She paid him very little mind in looking after his nutritional needs and barely showed any empathy towards his emotional wants, especially when stacked against her own. She kept him around (or rather allowed him to stay around) only for his limited usefulness to her. This went on for weeks. The raven was very, very undernourished.

For a while, the bird assumed that the lack of harm put against him by the bear was proof of some affection, however small. But as time went on, he came to recognise the bear's apathy towards him, the starvation of interaction slowly weighing him down until he began to wake up each morning drenched in angst and reluctant to leave his nest. The bear would go out scavenging regardless of the raven's presence, as he knew she would. While she was gone, he would peek out and hop around the open space. He picked at imaginary fortunes in the soil to trick himself into believing he was doing something useful, trying to steal a sense of individuality and capability. All the while, he suppressed any thoughts of the past (and with them, guilt over the wolf) as best he could. But his hunger and introversion festered, until one morning, as he lay curled up for another late morning in bed, he smelled something luxurious and transcendent and, more than that, reminiscent. Cooked meat.

He flung himself out of the large bowl of sticks and perched on top. Today had a gloomy overhang of grey clouds and the den was lit by a soft undersaturated tint of blue. Just by the cave's entrance, the raven saw that the bear had been out and returned with a large pink hunk of meat that exhaled a sweet-smelling waft. Its skin was blotched with crispy golden patches and as the bear sat ripping into it, juices ran out of the centre, staining the leaves below. The raven began to go mad with temptation. His mind was thrown back to a time where he'd tasted such a thing before – the details were difficult to remember since the weeks of lethargy had fogged up his mind, but the strong sensation of smell evoked the memory of tasting hot food at some point. Perhaps if he hadn't already known the taste, then the temptation may not have been so strong. However, the idea that 'it's better to have loved and lost than to have never loved at all' is only perpetuated by those who never have to go very long in between experiences of love, and just like how the raven had grown mad with loneliness in the wake of his lost friendship, he also felt the torture of a dry tongue and an empty stomach only because he knew how much he loved the taste of good food in his belly. It felt especially unfair that he would be denied such a sense of happiness when it was so very close. The raven timidly bounced down to the ground, landing with a soft shuffle. The bear couldn't hear him over the sounds of smacking and chewing as he plodded closer to her, pausing cautiously between each few steps and cawing as if to discreetly ask for a sliver or two. The bear ignored him. The raven stopped six feet away, cautious not to push his luck but desperate to try. He tilted his head and cawed with a louder, more pleading tone. Without looking up she rumbled back at him, dismissive and warning - this was *her* meat. No doubt it wasn't hers and she'd swiped it from somewhere in the vicinity. Although judging by the drips of blood on her paws, it was evident the owners had either received fair warning to let her have it or were no longer around to argue. Regardless, she now sat tearing into the joint of meat with her teeth and as the raven looked on, his hopes to relive some luxury in life disappeared down her throat.

Luckily his hopes weren't fully squandered. The bear let go of the bone with one of her hands, causing it to dip towards the ground. It was decimated, but strands of sinew and one adequately sized lump still sat on the end. It was barely a bite for the massive bear but would rejuvenate the raven for the first time in a long, long time. His eyes flicked upwards to the bear who had paused to steadily scratch the back of her neck. Glancing back down to the bone, he could now peck at it. He hopped confidently towards it, assuming that what was left would go unnoticed by the bear and that she wouldn't mind much. He stood under the wedge of meat – it wasn't hot enough to be smoking anymore, but its heat was still emanating unlike any regular nourishment. A flood of long-lost satisfaction came back to the bird as his beak neared the meat. He opened wide, an inch away from clasping his succulent prize.

But then a growl was heard, stern and unfriendly. The bone rose as the bear angrily noticed what the raven was doing. Not even the leftovers. She wouldn't even let him have ten percent of her things, as she grumbled in a dominating manner. Then, drunk on the prospect of the meat, the raven flapped its wings and hovered up to the bone anyway, clamping on for just one small bite. Now overwhelmed by selfishness and feeling disrespected, the bear's signature rage emerged. She lurched up quickly to her feet, swinging the bone around with her right hand like a neanderthal with a club and throwing the bird off. He tumbled down onto his feet, croaking in shock. Her foreboding grunts evolved into a deep growl that called for retribution. Immediately, this arrangement – their cohabitation that the raven had forfeited home and heart for – had ended.

In a last effort to gain some kind of profit from the time he'd invested and the sacrifices he'd made, the raven pushed off the floor and forward into a flight. Not towards the bear (he wasn't stupid enough to attack her even if he went for the eye again), but towards the remaining meat. He just wanted one, good, last taste before death. He flew fast, managing to needle his beak into the chunk of food that was left, seizing the exposed bone with his talons like a convenient perch. His mind set aside the situation as he stuck his tongue out the edge of his beak and felt the remaining meat juices flow through the gap of his mouth.

He could almost, very briefly, just about, taste-

THUMP

The raven was battered by the bear's paw. His talons scraped against the bone perch; it almost shattered as he was yanked away. His beak was torn out with such force that it could have snapped off inside the meat. The raven, usually not the one taking hits, let out the shrillest squeal that he had ever done before. He was flung nearly ten feet away before crashing down into the warm soil. Because the bird was light, he didn't stop with a single thud. He rolled limply with his wings flailing about before juddering to a halt against the soil. However, the bear had struck at an angle so that only the soft furry side of her paw had hit him. Although the impact was still strong and the bird still hurt, she had missed him with her claws. He quickly lifted himself to his feet. Events were moving quickly, and he only just about registered the bear storming towards him. She was still roaring like a child in a tantrum but with seven hundred pounds of flesh and two rows of teeth to back her up. Panicking, his body responded before his mind did. He immediately did what his instincts always told him to do - fly. He escaped behind the cave and back into the forest. There was no way she could keep up with him and in only a matter of seconds the bear and the grotto shrunk into the distance as he left her behind (unfortunately far later that he should have). The bird was still out of mind, naturally aiming to get as high and far as possible. He sped so fast that a rushing noise filled his little skull, almost like the sound of a tempestuous gale in a storm. Yet the air was completely still, and it was only the bird that fled like the wind. He ducked around and fought through limbs and branches that stuck out in the low air of the forest. The trees here were uneven – some taller or thicker or more branched out than others – and speeding through them was like an obstacle course. The raven's heart raced. His wings, which had been barely used for a while now, became sore and hot at their sudden burst of use. He panted and huffed, feeling scared and panicked and infantile. His mind was a rushing blur, unable to focus. He simply aimed to get up and out of this twisted foolish forest. He turned his gaze to take a quick glance back at the cave. Too far gone to see now – a distant memory, thank goodness. He spun his head back around, but it was just a moment too late as he bashed full force into a fairly thick branch. The raven spindled around and plummeted down like a maple seed falling from its foliage and spiralling towards the ground. He whirled like a yo-yo and hit branches all the way down before he collapsed head-first with an unwelcome thump into the dirt below.

The whirring sound of wind in his head stopped as all motion came to a sudden halt. He lay limp for a while, submitting to the throbbing sensation with his face stuck down in the mud. Eventually he found the energy to roll backwards and flip over, his legs quivering as he tried to stand up on them. Dirt stained his face and wings and though he didn't seem to have broken or cut anything besides the tree branches, he was quite bruised and felt too weary to fly again now.

He looked around. The forest here was still. Some distant chirps gave a sense of normality that helped his mind calm down from the anxiety of his escape. The territory ahead was unexplored by the raven; it was somewhere new to travel through, like in the old days of last year, and a familiar feeling of prospect washed over him. In a moment, the hot mist that the bear's aggressive presence had created seemed to lift away. The raven had been searching so long for somewhere safe, away from the cold winter and the aggression of other animals, that he'd forgotten what it felt like to throw caution to the wind and move ahead into the unknown. Still, with his mind now clear, he felt saddened by the reminder that the last time he travelled through any new or stimulating places, it was with a dear friend. Now he was all alone here. It had been a long time since he operated alone and he didn't know how to live as such anymore. Conflicted by the excitement of new opportunity and the fear of his own vulnerability, the raven stood motionless, hoping for something to show the way. The forest was spread all around and stretched out forever as far as the raven knew. Beyond the valley of trees, the sun seemed to be coming out. The light shifted from a grey day to a flood of sunshine that obscured the distance – though it was harder to see what lay ahead, the brightness was a far nicer future to look ahead to. Further ahead, the trees were engulfed by this screen of platinum light, making the forest seem more spaced out and breathable now. At the sound of a high-pitched tweeting, he jumped to look to his right. Amid the wall of light that lay beyond, a collection of ten or so dots seem to scurry by in the air, flitting about and making pleasant midday chirps as they passed. It seemed to be a family; a collection of birds swinging through the tree trunks and dancing around each other while heading off to somewhere unknown. Maybe for a drink of water at a nearby lake, maybe to their home in a thick and hollow evergreen not far from here. Maybe they had heard a commotion nearby, where a predator was making its move on a prey and they were going to pay witness to it, perhaps even benefit off what could come from it if they were scavenger birds too. From this distance, it was impossible to know who they were or where they were going. The raven just watched as they happily let out their songs and passed by, off to whatever destination they were aiming for. The sight of them conjured up the same image of the wolf and the raven, slinking and treading through lands far away during days long gone. The regret that he'd been suppressing finally rose inside. The raven had made mistakes and he hoped those mistakes didn't condemn him to a life of seclusion; after all, the bear, the wolf, or any other animal he may come across also had flaws. Hopefully, he would get another chance to do right next time. As he watched the family of birds disappear towards the east, the raven had the chance to fly off and be among them.

But those particular birds were leaving, and the raven's wings were too sore and tired to follow them right now. That was okay. Another flock would certainly pass by at some point. When he was feeling more up to it, maybe he would try to group with them and see where they led. Or maybe he'd fly in a completely different direction and see what came from that. He would see what creatures came by and if he felt he could belong with any of them. He hoped that they would be as interesting and loving and accepting as the wolf. He would have to see where life took him. He just knew that whether it was in a grouping or alongside a special individual, he absolutely needed to find another place to belong. Because there is no anxiety in the world more harmful and harrowing to endure than the anxiety of feeling alone. The call to a connection was an automatic necessity that ran through his bones. The irony was that he wasn't alone in this feeling; it was an impulse shared by every living creature around him, as separate as they were in space or species. This included the wolf, whose bond with the raven had at one point been so strong that it would forever tether them together through memory and fondness, no matter how far away from each other they now were.

19

LONE WOLF

It was the awkward time between seasons. Awkward yet beautiful, where the cold of night hung around a little while longer in the morning, evident by the dew that glittered on the grass. Summer was trying hard to keep the leaves green and full, while the coming autumn attempted to dry them up and pry them from their limbs. It was the perfect time of year for change, for new life and a new view of the world. Rainbows could have blushed at the palette on display; the waters were crystal blue, the fields were tranquil and verdant, and the kingly glow of the maple tree's golden crown was being usurped by all the other trees as they too flaunted shades of red apple and flushing lemon. All this colour was emphasised by the daybreak that pierced the treeline from the adjacent plains. The edge of the woods was now close enough for the wolf to see the open land outside of it, to his relief. He had been wandering in there for some time without any bearings or inclination of how to get out. The chalk white colouring of the standing birch trees cast slatted bar-like shadows over him that began to release him as he stepped to the forest's edge. In a similar sense of release, there was the feeling that a clean slate lay ahead, and he was coming out to a new part of the world as a tougher, more cautious, more steel-hearted being. His paw scrunched on top of some newly fallen leaves as he moved toward the opening in the trees. The view above the trunks began to shift from predominantly leafy canopies to open skylights. The trail of leaves became scarce until he began to once again feel billowy grass underneath his feet. Despite the white intensity of the daylight, the field was chilling to the touch, with the grass still ice stiff from the night's coldness. It was solid enough to make crunching noises under his paws as he crept deeper into the field. Time had sealed up the wound in his eye socket. He'd had a whole summer to adjust to a new single-sighted outlook and solitary lifestyle. The blood had clotted and dried, leaving a deep recess - even with the sunlight trying to pick out its crimson hue, it mostly appeared only as a bottomless cavity. The rest of his body, on the other hand, had never fitted more with the title of a grey wolf. At one time, he had been so void of stains or cuts or anything that showed off the weariness of experience that he appeared as a pure unspoilt silver, practically without shade. At later times, he had taken his experiences far too hard on the surface, where his lustrous coat had been tainted with blackened blood and gritty dirt. But now, with regular washes and a naturally dwindling brightness, his colour struck an appropriate hue between the pure naivety of white and the harsh gloom created by stains – an average grey.

In front of the wolf lay an expanse where the floor was intertwined with sections of grass, snow and soil, somewhat like a mosaic of crossed seasons. The snow was thin, a result of the growing cold temperatures and the natural height of the terrain. It wasn't dense enough to hide the saplings that protruded from it. They were infant trees, still far away from having any effect or value on the landscape in the way a mature trunk might. They were young and without character; twigs so small that the only thing stopping the wolf from snapping them under his paws was the awareness he had for his surroundings. More impulsive animals may not have been as observant or careful towards something as inconsequential as a meek sapling. The forest hadn't ended abruptly, rather the birches thinned out then dotted around and eventually became loners that stood here and there, while some young misfits like pines and spruces broke up the monotony of white trunks. The wolf sought to avoid the trees. They were spaced out yet still plentiful, even when walking out in the open. He treated them as though they were watchtowers, where stepping too close would put him into their field of view. Instead, he kept a good few feet of distance away from the trunks, twisting through the open spaces between them. Ironically, he felt more comfortable out in the open areas of the field where there were no structures for an animal to sneak out from, no blockages or barriers for him to get obstructed by and no branches above for birds to be looking down watchfully at him. He'd had bad experiences in many forests, but it was impossible for anything to take him by surprise in an open field. In these vast clearings, there was nothing. It was quiet, it was empty, it was solitary. That's where he felt safe. Rightly so, as far as his logic was concerned. Terrified by anything bigger and irritated by anything smaller, the entirety of the field was thankfully restful; no scuttling of squirrels, no hacking call of crows, no thwomping hooves of oafish moose trying to lumber their way from one place to another. Even the morning crickets had ceased their chirping as there were no bushes to hide in and sing out from. No, the only noise was of water nearby. It wasn't the blatant spilling of a river or the abrasive gush of a waterfall, just the subtle sound of a still pool lapping against the stones on its bank. The wolf was drawn towards it for a spot of rehydration and perhaps an extended moment of tranquillity.

He travelled through a vast plain in the centre of which was a watering hole, whose surface ebbed thanks to a slight persuasion from the wind waving across the top. There were no trees around the water's edge, dissuaded by the natural pebbles and rock shards that formed its bank. The immediate space around the water was monotone in shade as the white frost of autumn crept onto the granite outcrops that rose beside the pool. It would melt by the time noon came around, but would grow ever thicker as the days became colder, until the water was frozen over and the whole place was entrenched in frigid colourless snow. The wolf was on the shallow side of the lake where he could step down to the water easily. The opposite edge rose into a cliff side where the sparse forest he'd emerged from wrapped around the water's edge and rose over the precipice. He'd travel in the opposite direction of this, away from the trees, away from their leaves and all the shades of flame and copper that had begun to emerge. The slated flooring around the bank was layered on top of itself forming podiums, almost like areas for guests to sit at while waiting for a drink. It was quite eerie to see such a lack of density or diversity of animals at the pool, as this place seemed so well-suited to major social gatherings. But as the wolf trod closer towards the cluster of rocks and water, he saw why there were no other creatures about. A conglomerate of wolves – a family – had set up near the water. He didn't know if this was their home or they were just passing through, but all other wildlife had been driven away by their presence and would stay away as long as they were here. Very few animals act as a match for wolves, especially a pack of them, and there isn't much an entire family of wolves couldn't turn into prey. There were eight of them in total. Of note, three of the adolescent wolves were aggressively rolling around in a friendly fight, nipping at each other and falling over themselves in a bumbling, almost drunken way. One wolf, seemingly a lazy elderly slob, sat some distance away from the others on one of the outcrops that rose and hung over the water. It draped its paw over the edge of the rock as it groomed its shoulder with its tongue, taking great care of its silvery suit. It gave off an air of privilege and reputation. The remaining wolves were slumped in a group, resting on their bellies upon a platter-shaped pedestal of grey stone that had the pool's water spattered over its surface, giving the floor a titanium shimmer. Safe, confident, lazy and proud, their eyes fluttered in the direction of the lone grey wolf, but they felt secure and ignorant enough to pay him no mind at his current distance. They saw him as just another wolf like any one of them, and not much of one at that. One of the wolves was clearly the mother of the pack, sitting with its head held high in an elegant manner. It was on a rock that sat higher than the others yet was tucked into the groove of an even higher stone plinth – practically a throne – upon which sat the pack leader. It was an adult male wolf with an earthy tint of brunette on its body and white fur over its legs that fused in the middle to form a fuzzy strip of dulled amber. The changing tone in its fur seemed to foreshadow the changing season, much like how the cold white snow would soon creep up on the dark soil. It was roughly the same size as the lone wolf but brawnier, more well-groomed, more accurately proportioned, more attractive and healthier.

The grey wolf kept marching. It was the pack leader to first notice the loner's unwavering path towards its family. Confident, it raised its head, lapped its tongue across its top lip, then barked in a way that was non-threatening but clearly aimed at the wolf. It was as if it were alerting him to their presence in some arrogant assumption that he merely hadn't seen them, or like it was calling out that he had accidentally wandered into a place that he didn't belong, using the least amount of effort and recognition it could spare for the ugly loner. The wolf strode forward without a change in his pace or shake in his resolve. He didn't care what the king wolf thought, wanted, or did to him in retaliation. He wanted a drink, plain and simple. The wolf's silent continuous marching was designed with hard steps and a deadpan focus and could only be interpreted as one cold, blunt dismissal of the pack. He showed no signs of slowing or moving away from them. Still, the other wolves remained ignorant to his wants as he walked silently towards the water. The pack leader though, feeling disrespected by the runt, stood on all fours and slunk down the steps that led from its podium. Only at the movement of their great leader did the other wolves twist their full focus towards the intruder.

They watched as the two walked towards each other. The aristocratic wolf that lay on the outcrop pried its jaw up from the moss that it was resting on. Its glance was sinister, hoping for drama and spectacle. It didn't care who was on top – a pristine patriarch or an uncommon underdog – so long as it had a supplier that it could siphon home, security and food from, like a parasite. The three boisterous adolescents that had been playing together came to a sudden stop, now standing and wavering restlessly back and forth, wagging their tails, panting with their tongues flopped out and occasionally yapping excitedly. They of course rooted for their leader; their teammate in the competition of life and its violent throws. They prioritised strength, confidence and aggression, something they'd found in their current king. While all other parties remained tense and silent, the three young wolves betrayed their immaturity with their ruffing and stomping, lacking any sense of subtlety. They were more akin to hyenas than wolves. The rest looked on as the head wolf and the lone wolf grew ever closer to each other. The leader stopped in place before it got too close. But the lone wolf still didn't stop marching. The patriarch had held very little opinion of the loner on first sight, judging him foremost on his wounded and undernourished appearance, and thought the slightest of intimidation would have been enough to send a message; to convince him that he wasn't wanted here and should turn around. Now, as he kept walking towards the patriarch, it started to view him as more of a threat, like an intruder with purpose and intent. As its alpha predator sensibilities kicked in, its ego took over. It ground its paws into the earth, pushed its head down into an aggressive stance and began to growl. It assessed the grey wolf as he approached. One-eyed, limp-legged and tatty-haired, he didn't give off a strong impression and if he dared to get any closer, the pack leader would take him down easily. It snapped, displaying its sharp teeth as it did. Its neck lunged forward as it barked as if to continuously try and intimidate the intruder and push him back. But the lone wolf didn't stop marching.

He didn't snap back or lurch over defensively as he walked, nor did he stand as if ready to fight. He just kept walking silently. He wasn't intimidated, he didn't care to fight, he wasn't here to join the pack or take over. But he wasn't going to leave. This spontaneous change in how wolves worked put the pack leader in a state of unease. The grey wolf emanated an aura of unfamiliarity, displaying the awkward behaviour that caused him to travel alone in the first place. The alpha wolf's opponent acted as oddly as he looked. Oddness was unpredictable. Unpredictable was dangerous. His lack of intimidation was, in itself, intimidating. For every sharp jolt forward that the pack leader took in order to discourage the oncoming wolf, it took two subtle steps backwards. On and on the wolf marched, closer to the opposing alpha as its barking and lunging continued. The grey wolf closed into the stand-off. Just as they came into clawing distance of each other, the head wolf came to notice that the loner wasn't staring it down at all. Hard as it was to tell with his one gaunt darkened eye, he was staring *towards* the head wolf but not *at* it, as though looking right through to the pool behind. He just wanted one small taste of fresh luxurious water, without all the needlessly disproportionate challenge that stood in the way. He'd had enough of fighting for the littlest things and wasn't going to play the game that way anymore. The pack may have ignored him on his arrival, but it was *he* who wasn't paying any notice to *them*.

The two came as close as they could to each other, with the patriarch wolf still tense and ready to lash out, snarling and choking at the outcast. However, he simply veered around the side of it and walked past towards the waterfront. He didn't flinch once. The other wolves panned their heads as they watched him walk on without ever acknowledging them or their leader, whose barking had wound down to a stop as it stood up from its lurched stance. Within seconds, the head hound was glancing around, returning to a state of docile awkwardness as if perplexed and a little ashamed of being ignored. It followed behind the young scrawny wolf while remaining at a distance, like a watchful member of mall security tailing a suspicious youth with no real power to really detain the potential threat. As the invader stepped towards the water line, the patriarch remained at a distance, ready to escort him out with its imaginary sense of authority.

The grey wolf stood at the edge of the rippling crystal surface and looked down into its mirror. He saw a wolf. But also, not a wolf. His one eye stared softly and blinked slowly, eyelid hanging in a tired, serious manner. His brow clenched together in the middle, causing an extreme overhang that put a veil of shadow over and around his eye sockets. Sentiments of constant unhappiness and confusion over the world made little things happen across his facial muscles, like the tightening of his cheeks and the way his rigid dried teeth were clenched. He saw one yellowish-milky eye that bore loathing and impatience, always shifting his view to a single perspective. The shadow of his brow kept his remaining eye well-darkened most of the time, but when he lifted his head a certain way and the sun hit it from a specific direction, there seemed to be some kind of golden fleck that still glinted through. His other eye was replaced with a hollow painful void, sitting as a constant reminder of something important gone missing. He felt the cold wind blow through the cavity of his eye socket. He saw a coarse unkept fluster of drab grey fur that covered his body, neither audaciously bright nor weighted with black mud. His size was shorter than a regular wolf, his stomach was bloated since he'd started foregoing any restraint or quality in what he put inside of it. He took his eye away from the water and looked back. The head wolf stood at a distance from him, but still held its family in the back: its wife, its children, its brothers, its friends.

The wolf looked back down into the water at himself. His head made a quaint tilt and the wolf under the water mimicked this movement. He recognised that it wasn't a real animal in the water, just something that tried to reflect one. It wasn't somebody else, but it still wasn't him either. He felt an element still kept him from recognising this reflection as himself. He felt like he was a wolf, but he didn't see much of a wolf in the water. He turned to his side to see an empty spot next to his reflection. He had only his own reflection to look at, with no comparison or second party to help him come to an agreeable reasoning. He tipped his paw forward and plunged it into the cold shallows in front of him. Step followed step until his body was mid-height in the water. He picked up his paws and wagged them furiously, throwing his body into the deeper parts of the crisp pool. On the land, the family watched as he splashed about, dunking his whole body and face under the crystalline lake. The water hydrated and cleansed him, filling the gaps between his teeth. It was so refreshingly chilly that he felt an almost minty sensation as he blew air bubbles out of his nostrils. Some minutes later, he made his way back to the shore. Droplets aggressively trickled onto the stones as he exited the water. His fur was saturated with a cold damp which he vigorously shook off once his four paws were back on solid ground. He washed himself at every opportunity he got now, with each pool and pond he came across being a chance at rejuvenation, washing away any creeping crust that his wounds might grow or unwanted blemishes that rougher experiences might bring.

After rinsing his fur dry as much as he cared to, he stepped back across the rock slabs that comprised the floor in front of the watering hole, back towards the wolf pack. He now sought to head off past them into the direction he would have continued walking had he not detoured to the pool of water. Once again, he didn't care to interact with or acknowledge the happy family, and certainly didn't want to indulge in their hierarchy's displays of pointless reputation. He cut his sight towards a path that curved past their leader and stared dead ahead towards it as he trod. The lead dog still seemed confused, cautious and irritated, dipping its head and stepping back and forth as it struggled to decide whether to grow aggressive again or not. Apparently, it was trying to think of every other outcome for the situation besides the one that the lone wolf was after; to just let him pass. While the chief wolf was still contemplating, the lonely wanderer walked past. As he did, for whatever reason, he allowed his eye to drift towards its face. For one slow drawn-out heartbeat, the two met each other's gaze. Maybe he made eye contact out of some tiny unwanted residue of respect left over from his meeker days, as though he were at least trying to acknowledge the leader, its domain and its patience as he utilised their pool. If so, this gesture went misinterpreted. The alpha's teeth flashed. With an immediate sense of hostility, it instantaneously shifted into a wild state and snarled with a gurgling resonance that showed its intent and desire to fight. The chief pushed itself forward as if to take its first swipe. There was still a noticeable restraint, as if desperate to give some show of authority but only for a surface-level reason, like a show of ego.

This ego was immediately squelched.

The lonely wolf replied with an awful, despicable tone; so morbid that it would be unimaginable to hear from a creature outside of fiction, let alone nature. The chief wolf's bark was that of an animal. The grey wolf's snarl was that of a monster. He'd nurtured these vocals to match the monstrous face he saw in the lake. As he retched, his head bore down over the supposed top dog, pushing it to the ground in shock and fright. The noise was alien to the leader and its fellow wolves, who had jolted in surprise at the sound of the loner's snap. The chief whimpered at his feet, trying to back away in apology. Then, adding to his confusing and unnatural behaviour, the wanderer refused to take the fight any further.

Unlike these wolves with their clan built on ideas of strength and reputations, he didn't care to prove his might or claim retribution. He instead retracted his shoulder blades, brought his head back up, straightened his brow, lowered his tone, turned back away, and continued walking. The family watched on as the wolf returned to his eerily silent state and his chillingly lonesome venturing. He wandered away from them into the open meadow and towards a thin slither of forest on the other side. The wolf didn't *want* blood. He didn't *want* to fight for anything. He barely wanted the luxuries that warranted a fight. But the intent for blood that everyone and everything around him seemed to have now brought him to an immeasurable level of rage. He just wanted to live in peace and then die, and if the heartache of either kindness or callousness were anything to consider, he'd prefer to live and die as plainly and unseen and unspoken to as possible. He found any show of kindness – the kind that might lead to love – to be too untrustworthy and turned himself away from the paths of good things; the risk of losing his last eye was too great to even try. As for the callousness of other beasts - ones that would demand attention or respect, or stand in his way despite him trying to tread the most insignificant path – he would return the behaviour that they seemed so adamant in perpetrating. The passionless beastly aggression that seemed to serve them so well, he would return on them threefold and see how they liked it. He'd hold up a reflection of what they looked like to him, to show how hurtful and meaningless it was to disturb his peace. He'd return an egotistical bark with a repulsive snarl. An eye for an eye.

The thin line of trees ahead of him acted as a veil to the next field, an area that turned down the side of a hill which dipped steep into a valley. Beyond that it rose again, even higher than the hill that it descended from. Past that lay a series of bluffs that rolled into the distance, concurrently tinted with a deeper shade of frost blue as the chill in the air draped thicker over each one. They were curtailed at the horizon by a series of sharp mountains. Dusted with the early snow of the high norths, they resembled a white picket fence that boxed in a giant garden - its thickets, its waters, its residents and visitors. Beyond that, anything could lie in the next garden. Maybe better things, maybe worse things. Maybe along the way, he'd come across something – an event or an animal – to reshape him in the way the raven did. To change him as drastically as he had changed from when he had first met the raven. He was still nowhere near an old wolf despite his scars, and though he was much more hostile and defensive now than he was during his days before the raven's company, there was still plenty of time for more change. Still, he was incapable of hoping for this. All he could do was walk and see what happened.

Some cruel animals grow even more cruel. Some lonely creatures stay lonely. Some beasts suffer misery after misery and never get a break from it. This is the sad truth, as much as optimists might tell you otherwise; the world is chaotically unpredictable and often harsh. There are no rules or magical governing forces, just the unknowable diversity of the world where anything and everything can happen. Winter can be warm, summer can be cold, light can be terrifying, and darkness can be comforting. It's contradiction after contradiction. In short, it's wild. But this also means that there's no vindictive force of evil or predetermined misfortune that guarantees one to suffer or lose. No prison of fate decreeing that those who are down should stay down forever. Other animals manage to shed the coats they wear, change their shade or even (such as in the case of the caterpillar) grow a set of wings after spending what seems like a lifetime stuck on the ground, slowly trudging along. They join in at watering holes filled with an abundance of species all coming together and enjoying themselves. Others dare to take on a pack leader and make themselves the alpha, or mate for life and build their own pack. Some animals try and try again to climb a mountain and after many failures, eventually, they make it to the top.

Maybe the wolf would get crueller. Maybe he'd stay lonely. Maybe he'd stay miserable. Or just maybe, instead, he'd visit somewhere new with whole different animals, or rediscover his ambition for being a leader, or meet a creature worth trusting again, to give his heart to and bond with. A creature who, whether they had wings themselves or not, could make him feel like he was able to fly. Maybe he'd wander close to the mountains again, remember something inside that compelled him to reach the summit, and try again to make it to the top. But we can only react and shape ourselves to the experiences and information we're given. He would have to wait and see what the wild world offered him. Right now, the wolf wandered alone over a silent open valley at the turn of a crisp new season. Winter would return in just a few short months.

The wolf was young, and he was getting cold.

Take flight at every chance you get.
Be a contradiction, if it's in your nature.
And whatever you do,
don't become an average beast.